Even Trade

TJ Arant

Contents

Suspicion always haunts the guilty mind.

William Shakespeare, *3 Henry VI* (5.6.11)

Chapter One

1978

Tippy Taylor always looked the part.

If he was in front of a classroom, he could rock the dashiki like a new age radical, pick the Afro out and put the peace medallion around his neck, nestling just below his sternum, its fake gold finish making a riot in the sunlight. Give him a minute and he could look like Sly Stone with a master's degree, preaching to everyday people about letting you be yourself again.

If he was in a Metro council meeting, he would shift to the double knits, the wide lapels, the loud tie and the shoes that stopped short of pimping, short of platform, but still raise him a few inches above his five feet, ten inches. It was an outfit that looked good on Channel 4, especially when he was standing next to a white man, with drab features and no fashion sense.

Tippy Taylor could look that part.

He looked the part for sure in Nam. He was the one with a headband and the fatigues unbuttoned, with the M-16 slung on his back. If CBS had a camera nearby, he'd have been ready to look like the GI who was done with it all, the one doing his drafted duty, the one determined to do it his way, on his terms. Give him an order, and he'd see about it. That was the part he looked.

Except that was only the part Tippy Taylor was playing. The one with the script. The one that was just for show.

Tippy Taylor was playing a part and he looked the part. But Tippy Taylor had a whole different gig in mind. A whole new bag.

He had found himself about to sink into the mire, and he had found a way out. All the letters to the editors couldn't change his life. All the lectures to rapturous students couldn't make it better. TV appearances and sweet clothes couldn't make him a different person than he was.

And who was he? A black man. In Nashville. In 1978. With all that meant.

There wasn't much he could do.

And he'd already done so much. He'd secured a place as a limited term faculty member at Vanderbilt. He'd filled courses so full that they'd had to move him to the big lecture venue in Furman Hall. He'd been interviewed right in front of Kirkland Hall, just as the Chancellor had left for the day, a distinguished figure reduced to background on a television newscast. What the hell couldn't he do?

He couldn't change the arc of history. That was the goal, wasn't it? Dr. King had said the arc of history is long, but it bends toward justice. Tippy Taylor wanted to bend it now. He didn't want to wait. He wanted everyone to get what they deserved. Right now. He wanted to snap that arc in two.

He wanted everyone to get their just desserts. And that included the ones who had it all. And the ones who didn't deserve it. Especially when those groups intersected. And they always did.

There were the people who faked their way and got away with it because they looked right and knew somebody. There were the ones who thought they were moral, who knew they were not. There were the ones who had done wrong and pretended that what they did was right. They all knew. They all hid beneath the patina of respectability, of superiority, of virtue.

They always looked the part.

And Tippy Taylor wanted no part of it.

"I should have been an investigator." That was the thought he had. "I should be both investigator and judge." He had walked in the streets of Baltimore as a youth, making his way along dangerous places, finding his voice, thinking of himself as a righteous man.

Then he had been drafted, and had gone to war, too young, seen too many things a young man should not see, things even a mature man should not see. He walked the jungle and stayed alive. Too alive. Too alert. Ready to see everything an instant before it happened, ready to see the things that would kill him before they arrived.

He had read a story once by a white woman, Flannery O'Connor. The Violent Bear It Away. The title struck him. The story was about a boy who didn't want to be a prophet. That spoke to Tippy. He was a prophet. He didn't necessarily want to be. But he knew he had to be.

And the title could be his theme song. The Violent Bear It Away. Such motion. Such intent. Bear it away to where? And how violent? Sounds like something Curtis Mayfield should have had on the Superfly album.

Tippy believed he knew. He believed that the knowledge he had, the prophecy he could deliver, would bear away the sinful, the iniquitous, the liars, the pretenders. He could write about it, to be sure. He had a manuscript that would lay it bare. He could write about it in The Tennessean and The Banner, whose pages welcomed him. He could preach it in the classrooms. He could preach it in the streets.

But in the end, those would not enrich him. Those would only serve to start the opening of a necessary discussion, put it in a public place. They would only advance the cause.

Who would advance Tippy Taylor, who always looked the part?

That was the beauty, of course. Tippy Taylor, the peace warrior. Tippy Taylor, the justice maker. Tippy Taylor, the public intellectual. All these were acceptable, even if they were uncomfortable to some.

But Tippy knew who he was, and even though he was all those things he was something else. He was a man. And that man had his own version of justice, one that would not preclude a little bit of dirt, a smidgen of revenge, and a soupcon of spite. Just a little to get even, to get right.

He'd thought all this as he walked from the bus stop to his place. He knew who he was, and he was satisfied with it. Things might not be quite right, but they damn sure were ok. Right up to the space between the o and the k.

Tippy unlocked his door. It had been a long day, but a good day. He had locked away his treasure where no one could find it. If they came for him, he had taken care of that. If they wanted to shut him up, he had outfoxed them.

There would be no shutting up Tippy Taylor.

As he entered his apartment, he thought he could sense something a little different. He looked to his table, where the typewriter sat. Nothing appeared to be disturbed. In the area of the room with the sofa and the flea-bitten blanket, there was nothing. It was every bit as rumpled as he'd left it that morning.

He looked to the bedroom, turned on the light, half expecting to startle an intruder. But there was no one there. There had been no one there, as nearly as he could tell. Only the tick-tocking of his alarm clock. Everything was quiet. Everything was undisturbed.

Tippy reached into the drawer of his side table, extracted the eyeglass case. He took out the spoon and reached into his pants pocket, taking out a folded paper. Walking in the bathroom, he pulled two cotton balls from the little case they were in and took a length of rubber hose.

He sat on the bed, put the contents of the paper in the spoon, and began to cook it with a match. Slowly the brown powder liquefied, and Tippy took the syringe from the eyeglass case and pulled the liquid into it. Then he pulled the rubber hose tight around his bicep, pulling hard enough that, with his balled fist, he got the vein to protrude.

With the practiced air of a man performing a ritual, he put the needle into the vein, and emptied the contents into it.

Then he breathed. For what seemed like the first time all day, he breathed deeply.

Ten seconds later he felt it, the feeling of bliss, of release. It was as if a thousand angels sang briefly, and then after their glorious fanfare, a low hum took hold. He could feel it like a complex chord throughout his body, the kind of music that must be heaven-made. It felt like a thunderclap that had its edges filed completely down, as if it was far away and inside him, all at once.

He thought of it as a motor that had hooked into the energy of the earth, its RPM tuned to the exact frequency of his heartbeat. One, two. One, two. It was binary. It counted only as far as he needed to count. One breath in. One breath out. Every part of Tippy Taylor was in harmony with the universe.

He was at peace.

Tippy thought to himself how lucky he was. He only had to use the drug in a maintenance way. He was not hooked. He was no addict. He had this completely under control.

He was able to stop.

One day in six or seven. No more. There was no need. Not when he knew this kind of bliss was available. He could wait for it. He did not need the gratification every day. He could deprive himself as long as he needed to, since he knew how to get here, and how it felt once he got here.

Tippy closed his eyes. He thought of his mother, the woman who had raised him after his father left. The woman who would point out the men in the street who were addicts. "Don't you ever be like that trash, Thomas." No, ma'am. Not me, he'd said. And he meant it. He would not be like them.

He conjured in his mind men in his unit in Vietnam, men who found that heavy horse in the jungle, so cheap and so clean, and they blew their minds with it, blissed out ten days a week. Hell, how any of them stayed alive was a series of miracles. They were addicts.

But not Tippy Taylor. Tippy was the master of his fate, and he was the master of himself. No one else was his master, and no one would be, either.

He felt the fingers of the drug encircle his neck, a combination of cool and warm, the sort of mystical juxtaposition that was impossible in the physical world, but entirely logical in the fixed rumble of the universe. Cold and hot existed together, he thought, just as two ends of one thing. The drug made it easier to let go, to feel the truth. It was blissful. It was easy to relax in the cradle of the cosmos.

The cold/hot of the universe tightened, making him aware of the slow thump of his pulse in his throat, the thump as it harmonized with the cold/hot, as it made itself one with the heartbeat of the universe.

The fingers tightened now, less comfortably, the universe making its harmony more heated, the thump of Tippy's pulse quickened. This was not the way things went.

The thought occurred that the drug was cut with something, that the harmony had been disrupted.

He felt himself heaved onto his back, a force landed in his midsection, and he forced his eyes open.

"I thought you'd left us for a while, Tippy." He had his hands fully around Tippy's throat and his legs pinned Tippy's arms. "I'm glad you're still here. Be a shame if you didn't know what was happening to you."

"I don't know you." Tippy croaked this sentence. He was having trouble getting his breath.

"Sure, you do, Tipster. Think hard enough. It'll come to you."

Tippy felt weak. His heart had stopped pounding. He absorbed the weight of his assailant, giving in to it.

And then he felt himself letting go. The drug was helping. It was allowing him to feel the universe again. The low rumble of thunder, the language of the cosmos, began to splash like the waves of the ocean, letting him accept.

He was returning. Falling into the arms of whatever god was in the drug. He fell asleep softly, peacefully.

Chapter Two

THERE ARE MEN WHO will go out of their way to make the world mad. And sure, I've been mad at the world at times, but I never thought it was a good idea for it to be mad at me. Not that it ever stopped the world. The world had a mind of its own.

The man in front of me seemed to be mad and to have a mind of his own. Wardell A. Robinson, Attorney at Law, his business card said. It also said his office was on Jefferson Street in Nashville, Tennessee.

The card could not possibly have communicated his presence. Skin the color of obsidian, sleek and black but not without hues of other colors, notably a dark navy and a swirling darkest green. The neon beer light played off his skin, making his brown eyes notable for their incision, the contrast of dark inset with darkest.

His powerful chest strained against the well-made suit, a charcoal pin stripe that seemed light on his skin. He kept his hair cropped close but had acceded to the times, and wore a mustache and goatee, tightly trimmed and edged. Everything about him spoke elegance, power, and presence.

What he was doing in Hannigan's on a rainy Wednesday in March was what he was about to tell me.

"You don't look like much, Trade," he said.

I look like what I am. A twenty-seven-year-old Vietnam vet who lives rent-free in a garage apartment. A guy who doesn't have a real job. From the outside, a long-haired hippie bum who probably drinks more than he should. I stubbed out my cigarette.

"I imagine you were already in your office on Jefferson Street by the time you were my age, right?" It wasn't hard to believe. I put him in his mid-forties. He'd have missed World War II, might have been too young for Korea. "You didn't have to spend a formative year dodging Charlie in the jungle."

His mouth closed, and his nose flared a bit. "I suppose that is a fair enough statement, if you mean to imply that I took everything seriously and made my way in the world as best I could. As a black man, it pays to be disciplined and precise. If you are not, you have no chance."

Katie came by the table. She's older than she looks, and people sometimes treat her like a kid. But she's no kid. And she's waitressed enough across the street from a college that she can size up a situation quickly. "What can I get for you, sir?" she asked Robinson.

"What would you suggest? I don't know this restaurant."

She smiled. "Anything you want is fine. I wouldn't follow the example of Jackson here, though." She gave a look that generally qualifies as "her eyes twinkled."

Yeah, she could do that. It was annoying.

He smiled back. "Then I will avoid what I assume is bourbon and opt for lemonade. If it is freshly squeezed and not too sweet, that is."

"I will see to it personally," she answered back, smiling.

"And if you can manage it while you're working this man for a tip, another bourbon." I held up my empty glass.

She stuck her tongue out at me. "You could learn from listening to civilized people talk," she said, turned on a heel and left.

"One never knows, Mr. Trade," he said when she had left, "whether he'll be welcomed in an establishment in this part of town."

"It's 1978, Mr. Robinson. Aren't we past that?"

He shook his head. "When you were in Vietnam, did you feel in your heart that we were, as you say, past it?"

I couldn't say that. Too many units were divided along racial lines. Too much of what was wrong back home came over with the young men who were fighting. You would think that you'd have to drop that, with the necessity of trusting each other with our lives. But it was never far from the surface, and sometimes, maybe many times, it came out.

"Why don't you tell me why you came to see me?"

"You know Tippy Taylor?" He turned his face, his right eye peering at me, as if to gauge the reaction.

Everyone knew Tippy Taylor, at least at Vanderbilt. A Vietnam vet with a huge Afro, dashiki-clad most days of the week, Taylor had returned from the war, got a master's degree in History, and managed to get an impossible-to-get gig as a Lecturer in Vanderbilt's History department. I say "impossible" because Ivy League Ph.D.'s had trouble getting an interview for a faculty position. Tippy, whose given name was Thomas, was a celebrity of sorts, a Pied Piper for the small but growing African-American population of Vanderbilt students, and a near-constant on the editorial page of The Tennessean. He was universally regarded as one angry dude by the university and the city. I figured him at least as a guy on the make, though what he was made for was anyone's guess.

I knew him because, before I got fired as Assistant Dean of Students, I had worked with him to get a young man out of a jam.

I also knew he had been found in a dumpster two days earlier, behind the apartment he lived in, in the section of town known as The Gardens. The Gardens could be a dangerous part of town.

I knew the community was devastated. I also knew that the police said they had no leads and no suspects.

"Yeah," I said. "I'm sorry to hear he's dead." Nobody deserved a dumpster for a coffin.

The lawyer sighed. "We're all sorry." He looked up as Katie brought a lemonade, and she smiled her winningest smile. She dropped off a bourbon for me too. "I tell you, Trade, this feels like something that's going to set off North Nashville. You know what I mean?"

"Last thing it needs," I said. "You got this. And you got the Davis Cup. Of course, you got the usual, too." The Gardens was on the north side of town. If Nashville had a wrong side of the tracks, it was the north side.

He agreed. "It's a mess."

The Davis Cup was a new flashpoint in the city's race relations. Vanderbilt had agreed to host the Davis Cup zone finals at some point. But then it happened that South Africa was in the zone finals. With apartheid, the South Africa team became problematic. And so, the protests had come.

Vanderbilt claimed that their open forum policy meant that anyone, no matter their politics, was welcome. Others disagreed.

Tippy certainly disagreed.

"Tippy left an envelope with me," said Robinson. "It's addressed to you."

I raised my eyebrows. "Why me?"

"You did him, or somebody, a good turn. He trusted you." He leveled his eyes at me. "I would like to trust you too. But you don't look like a good bet."

I didn't look like a good bet to make the week without a fight. Or a bender. I knew that. "Look. Tippy asked me to help a young man who got himself in a jam. I did. I didn't ask for credit. I didn't ask for compensation. I did the right thing." I leveled my own gaze at Robinson. "If he trusted me, it's because I trusted him." I leaned back in the booth. "You don't have to."

He wasn't looking at me. If you asked me, I'd say he was looking inside himself, but I would say for sure he was thinking. After a moment, he said, "Ok, Trade. Tippy said to give you this. I'm going to comply. God knows, trust between folks who look like the two of us is rare enough."

He reached inside his suit jacket and produced a business sized envelope. On the outside, in a gentle, almost feminine cursive was written, "Jackson Trade." Underneath was printed, "Not You, Wardell!" I laughed. Tippy Taylor had opinions all the way to the end. He spoke from the grave.

"You haven't looked at this?" I knew the answer, but it was worth it to hear, to know for sure.

"Tippy said it was for you. Not my place to disagree."

"You have any idea what it says? From something Tippy told you, maybe?"

He leaned in over the table. I don't think I'd want to be cross-examined by him. "Anything he told me would have been shrouded in privilege."

"While he's alive, that's true." I pulled out my Case pocketknife and slit the envelope open. "Tell you what. I'll waive privilege on this letter. If I let you read it, will you waive yours?"

He leaned back against the red vinyl of the booth. And without smiling, he became a bit friendlier. "Yes" was all he said.

I opened the letter. It had been typed, which was not unexpected. Tippy was a writer, if not exactly a scholar. His pieces tended to show up in popular journals, not the peer-reviewed kind that got you tenure. But Tippy wasn't aiming for tenure. Vanderbilt was a convenient perch to build his reputation as a public intellectual. What was coming next was anybody's guess, but Vanderbilt's history department didn't mind having an outspoken activist on its faculty. As long as it didn't have to tenure him.

Jackson,

If you're reading this, then I'm gone. One way or another. You remember that feeling, back in 'Nam, in the morning? Like that day might be your last one? Hell, man, I know you do.

Not a one of us that came back didn't spend our last month all seized up with worry. Got this close, I got to get out now. Whatever it takes.

Well, my brother, that's the way it feels now. I have done pissed off too many people, and I'm in a bad way.

See, I've been writing a book about my experiences since I got back. Nashville's in it. Vanderbilt's in it. This is a piece of contemporary history. Not gonna be a lot of footnotes, you know what I mean? But it's real, and it's true, and it's about capturing the character of this place.

This place is changing, man. But it's not changing fast enough. Same damn things that have been going on are still going on. That's in the book. People got secrets. That's in the book. People tell lies. That's there too.

I know you catch my drift.

It's all good until last night. I'm walking down Jefferson, coming back from a thing over at Fisk, and I hear a car gun its engine. Jackson, I ran my ass a full block and cut down an alleyway, and damn if the son of a bitch doesn't squeeze off two that barely miss me.

Some cat wants me cold on a slab.

So I wrote this, just in case. I'm giving it to Wardell Robinson to give to you. Wardell's good people, just a little stiff. But you can trust him. If I'm gone, man, I want you to find out who. It might be the book. It might be something else. You know me, Jackson. I got a big mouth. I know a lot.

I mean, who hates me enough to put a slug in me? But then again, maybe you'll see things I don't.

I can't leave the book out where you can find it in my apartment. But if you find a key to a locker in my pad, you'll be able to find the book. The book will give you another key, where you will find more. I can't tell you that part. You'll have to be smart, pay attention. I'm not putting everything in this letter. Just the start. The rest I'm leaving for you, but you'll have to find it.

If it sounds like I'm being too complicated, maybe I am. But it could be more than one person, and I don't want the wrong person paying for this.

Hell, man, maybe we're reading this over a drink. Maybe this isn't the last day before this boonie rat buys it.

But if somebody did me, Jackson, find out who it was. Fuck them up bad. And leave the others alone. I'm serious. I don't want harm on innocent people, no matter what they might have done before. I just want the one that did me in.

And he signed it, with that delicate signature, so unlike who he was in public.

I handed the letter over to Wardell and he took it, looking at me for a long moment before putting on a pair of glasses and getting to the task.

I lit a cigarette and inhaled. There was a time, long ago, when the first breath of tobacco gave some kind of pleasure. Now it only marked time. I took a sip of bourbon. Another marker.

A lot of people I knew in the Army had died. Markers. But once we got back to the world, the markers were supposed to stop happening, at least the way they had happened. We were supposed to be solid for a while. We did our service. Time to come home. Make our way. Live a life.

And now Tippy was a marker, a moment in time ended. I pushed another drag out through my nose, took another sip, and waited for Wardell to finish.

When he did, he put the papers down on the table. He removed the glasses and rubbed at his eyes. He wasn't crying. But he could have been misting up. The strong hands reached into his suit jacket and brought out a handkerchief. I thought he might dab at his eyes, but he had recovered, and merely began cleaning the lenses. I waited for him to speak.

"Well, what do you make of it, Mr. Trade?"

"Don't be a stiff. Call me Jackson." I half-smiled, and, after a second, so did he.

"Wardell," he said, offering his hand, which I took, first in the regular handshake, then, after a brief hesitation, in the friendlier, thumb lock grasp. "All right, Jackson, what's next?"

"I need to see Tippy's place. That's for openers. For that, I'll need a key."

He was making a note. "I can get that. What else?"

"You're his lawyer, Wardell. You know his business better than anyone else. Contracts. Maybe for this book? Rumblings of lawsuits? You know. The confidential stuff."

He nodded quickly. "Let me put a brief together for you. There's some, but not as much as you'd think." He kept writing. When he finished, he asked, "When was the last time you saw Tippy?"

I could answer easily. It was etched in my mind because it was the first day I'd spent watching the daily protests around Kirkland Hall.

For the first time, Wardell registered surprise, his eyes opening wide. "What are you doing that for? It's an unusual way to spend your lunch hour."

I'd worked at Vanderbilt as an Assistant Dean of Students for a time. That's why I was able to help Tippy's student out. I was fired for breaking several bones of my wife's lover. Art Blake, the Dean of Students, needed someone not on his staff to keep an eye on the growing protests. He was paying me as a contractor, and my job was, for the duration until the Davis Cup, to keep an eye on the faculty and student protests.

All that would have taken more time than it was worth to explain to Wardell. "I'm trying to keep everybody on the right side of the law."

"Mighty white of you," he said, with just a hint of sarcasm. "Who are you working for?"

"Art Blake, the Dean of Students."

He relaxed a little. "Blake's all right. I have had a conversation or two about young people who got sideways. He's honest."

"Yes, he is. Honest enough to fire me when he couldn't keep me, and honest enough to tell me that he would try to resurrect me. So far, I've failed to rise."

"What did you make of Tippy when you saw him?"

"He looked tired. He had a cold." It had been a cold and rainy March, and nobody felt very much like spring. "The protesters that day were almost all white faculty and students. He told me that it was the History Department's turn that day, and he pointed out a couple of faculty. Two graduate students. He just laughed. 'I don't even know why they're here,' he'd said. 'There's a good one in that department, maybe two, but the rest,' and his voice had trailed off. Just tired of the bullshit, I thought.

"I felt that weariness from him as well." Wardell put the notepad and pen in his pocket. "When he brought this letter to me, now that I know what was in it, I believe I saw weariness. It wasn't fear. It wasn't anger, and you know Tippy had a lot of that going on."

"Got that right." We all have anger, those of us who came back from the war. Black guys have that, and they have the anger that comes from being Black in America in 1978. Tippy had the double dose. "But he didn't seem angered even by his department colleagues the other day."

"What do we do next?" Wardell didn't seem ready to leave, but he had finished his lemonade and we were about at the end of what we could do with what we had.

"Let me know when you have a key." I really didn't know what else to say. Until I got into Tippy's place, I couldn't do much.

We stood up and shook hands again. This time, the thumb lock ending with fingers grasped. He surprised me by bumping his fist against mine at the end. When I smiled, he nodded approvingly. I'd passed the first test. "You'll figure this out, Jackson? For Tippy?"

"For Tippy."

He put his left hand on my shoulder and looked me in the eye. "Good. Brother needs his friends now more than ever."

He turned and walked toward the front of the restaurant, then stopped and looked back. "Tell Dean Blake I said hello. He'll remember me." He took another step and turned again. "Maybe this will be the work that resurrects you."

I waved goodbye. There was no resurrection here. Just a chance to help a guy who couldn't help himself anymore. And that guy wasn't me.

Chapter Three

DEAN ARTHUR BLAKE LIVED on campus, in one of the two-story cottages known as West Side Row. The gabled set of houses had filled various functions at Vanderbilt over the years, and the bottom story of the middle one had housed Blake and his wife, then Blake alone after her untimely death, for many years. A kitchen and bedroom occupied the back half, while a living room, which Art insisted on calling a parlor, and his study formed the part facing Memorial Lawn. In all the years I'd known him, I had stood in the kitchen and sat in the study. I can't recall ever being in the parlor, since it and the study each had their own front doors, and I don't even imagine what his bedroom looked like.

Besides that, the bourbon was in the kitchen behind a glass pantry door, and there was a decanter of bourbon in his study. Why would you go into the other rooms?

We were in our usual positions. The Dean was seated behind his desk, leaning back in his high-backed banker's chair, and I was sitting in the captain's chair, the one with the University seal on the top piece, the chair the University had given him on the occasion of his twenty-fifth anniversary. He had his bourbon in a highball glass, mixed with water, and I had mine in a rocks glass, diluted only by the ice that had melted.

"So, how is the protest business?" He said this and his red handlebar mustache twitched on one side. As long as I've known him, that twitch has never augured well.

"To be honest, I thought I'd see more of the activists from outside VU. It's been pretty tame. The Divinity School faculty and students are leading the charge, such as it is, but other departments take a shift here and there." I sipped a little Maker's Mark. Dean Blake had a higher class of bourbon in stock than I could usually afford.

He shifted in his seat and leaned with both elbows on the desk. "I don't know how I feel about all this, Jackson. It would certainly be easier all the way around if the University just said it was bowing out of hosting the Davis Cup."

"Sure." I left it at that. Art was going to give me the other side. I didn't need to.

"On the other hand, the Chancellor is adamant that this deserves the same support as the Grand Wizard of the KKK got when he came a couple of years ago. Open Forum. Part of an education. We don't approve of apartheid, but South Africa can come."

"To play tennis," I said. "Far as anybody can see, they're not talking. They're just hitting little yellow balls."

"That the side you're on?"

"I'm not taking a side. I'm just relaying what the protesters are saying."

Blake set his mouth like a clothesline. "I don't really mind the professors and the students. I don't really mind the whole thing, as an exercise in intellectual pretense."

I had to admit there was something mildly silly about Ph.D.'s carrying signs and chanting politely. "So why am I watching them?"

"In about twenty days, Vanderbilt will see the largest demonstration it has ever seen. Perhaps the largest Nashville has ever seen. There will be people from out of town and out of state. The merry band of professors and students will be joined by thousands of others who will shut down 24th Avenue in front of the gym, and probably for blocks around. All while we have thousands of our own students on campus.

Right on Fraternity Row." He looked down at his glass. "It has the potential to be a godawful mess, even if it goes well. If it goes badly," he looked back up, "well, it can't go badly."

We drank in silence for a moment. Art got up, picked some ice from the bucket and made another. "You?"

I shook my head no. "What's the next piece of this, boss? You said you didn't want me just watching faculty walk in a circle."

He stood looking through the venetian blinds. He was a big man, tall and normally in control. His shoulders sagged a little, and he brushed the blind as if to wipe dust away. "There is a meeting at St. Mark's CME, over in north Nashville, tomorrow night. It's a council of war, I gather. The activist groups and their leadership will be there. Metro Police will be there. It's supposed to be a coordination meeting, so that everyone will be on the same page."

"Seems unlikely. Who's representing campus?"

"We were not invited." I started to say something, but he raised his hand. "I know. It would appear to be an oversight. Or just plain dumb. I mean, where do they think the protest will be happening?"

"Exactly."

"Well, our Campus Police reached out to Metro Police, and they have consented for us to send a representative."

"Mercer?" Don Mercer was a lieutenant in the Campus Police. And he was black. That might help.

"No. Don is a policeman, even when he's in civvies."

"Who, then?"

"You." He waited for my reaction and didn't get one. I was beginning to sense a set-up, even though I'm sure Art wouldn't have considered it such. "I can't have any of my people in this. Campus Police can't be in it." He sat back down again, holding the glass between his palms. "Metro trusts you. You've been right twice when they were wrong. I trust you. And I believe you can get everyone else to trust you."

"Because?"

"Because Tippy Taylor made it known you're a right guy. At least, that's what everyone has heard"

Had they heard it because Wardell's letter leaked out? Had they heard it from Tippy himself? And if they had heard it, did they believe it? "Tippy's dead," I said. "What the hell's his opinion go for?"

"Wardell Robinson called me this afternoon." Art's eyes never left mine.

"Yeah?"

"I know you're working for Tippy. Working for a dead man won't pay the bills."

I didn't like the way this was shaping up. Watching PhD's wander around pretending to protest was one thing. Putting myself in between Metro, VU, and all the organizing groups in north Nashville? While I was looking for Tippy's killer? "I don't see this, Art," I said. "It's loading a full plate with a shovel."

"Think of it this way. I'm going to pay you to do what you are already doing for free. You can wander around doing Tippy's work while you keep an eye on things for me."

"Not the same thing."

"What if it is? What if the person who killed Tippy Taylor is someone we all need to keep an eye on? What if finding his killer depends on watching the protest? Or its reaction?"

It was a stretch and Art knew it. But it wasn't like anyone was paying me to do Tippy's bidding. Tippy sure couldn't.

"Ok. It's one thing to watch the faculty. It's another altogether to sit with outside groups. What are you calling me so that the Internal Audit people don't get huffy?"

He grinned. "You are a Consultant for Community Involvement." He raised an eyebrow and twisted one side of his mustache. "Given the way you exited my staff, pretty rich, eh?" And then he laughed, a sharp hoot followed by a wave.

It was hard not to join in. It was pretty rich, after all.

"Yes," I said, "somehow it's all appropriate."

Now the task was to see if I could manage all the involvement I was about to have.

Chapter Four

Go to the north side of town. That's where Tippy's place was. The Gardens. A place where white folk don't usually go.

Nashville's always been divided down a seam. White folks on one side. Black folks on the other. North side had its own restaurants. Its own barber shops. Its own groceries. Its own high schools. It even had its own universities, public and private, and its own medical school. Segregation might be gone but segregated never left.

It was also the sort of place where people were angry. Disappointed. Maybe even ready to start a fight.

And on the other side of town, a university was ready to host a country that practiced apartheid. On the other side of town where folks from The Gardens never really felt at home. And now the university over there was about to demonstrate why you didn't feel comfortable. All over again.

Nice, right?

I had the key from Wardell and found Tippy's apartment. It was on a side street off Hyde Street, a nondescript brick building that housed maybe four apartments.

"Hey, motherfucker," said a voice behind me. "What's a white sonofabitch doing up this way?"

There's not a good answer to a question like that. I put my hands up and turned slowly. "Ain't nothing going on here, man."

He was tall, a couple inches above my six two, and he looked like he could take on a fight if you brought it. He wore aviator glasses, but you got the feeling it was more for style than function. "Asking again, man. What are you here for?"

"You know Tippy?" I asked. Best to be honest.

"Everybody knows Tippy," he said. "Everybody is reading about him in the papers too."

"I'm a friend," I said. "He left me a key to his place. I'm just here to do something he asked me to do."

He moved toward me, and I didn't move. Did he have a gun? Did he have a knife? I didn't know, and I didn't want to find out.

"How are you a friend of Tippy?" he asked. He stopped. He didn't move closer.

I turned to face him full on. He wore a loose-fitting coat and a sock cap. His hair spilled out underneath the cap. He was light skinned, and his eyes were light. Not blue, but not brown. "I knew Tippy at Vanderbilt. We were friends." I didn't know if that would pass muster, but it had the advantage of being true.

"Tippy lit up those fuckers," he said. "I don't know nothing about you, though. Don't know if he had any friends that look like you."

I considered my options. Either I could try to make this conversation half what it should have been, or I could really leverage what I'd done with Tippy. "You know Rodney Glenn?"

He looked confused at first, then looked at me clearly. "Rodney was at Vanderbilt."

"That's right," I said, "and did he finish?"

"Word is," he said. "But there was trouble. White girl said he got out of line."

"That's right. But how'd it end up? Did he graduate?"

"Rodney graduated." He cocked his head. "What are we talking about this for?"

We were talking about Tippy coming to me with the problem. We were talking about me sticking my neck out about a kid who got caught in a long-playing race game, the one where some white man didn't like a black man even looking at a white woman. He didn't deserve what he was getting, and I put a stop to it. That was when I was an Assistant Dean of Students, back when I had some authority. Unlike now.

All I said was, "I helped out Rodney Glenn. I helped out Tippy. You can't ask Tippy anymore, but you could ask Rodney. I'm a friend. I have a key that Tippy gave me. And he gave me a job to do." All the while I kept my hands where he could see them. "I'm just here for that, and then I'm gone."

His eyes, unusual in color but sharp, regarded me. I couldn't call the look suspicion. It was more like the look you give a puzzle when the pieces don't fit. And it pisses you off.

"How about I go in with you, watch you do what you say Tippy told you to do?"

I considered the options. I didn't know this guy, and he could still pull a weapon out, outside or inside, and do some damage. Or he could get inside and take whatever of Tippy's stuff he wanted. Or he could be legit.

"How about you tell me why I should?" His jaw clenched. "You could be a friend of Tippy's. You could be a friend to the neighborhood, just wanting to make sure I'm doing what I'm saying. Or you could be wanting to go inside and fuck me up."

"Fuck you up out on the street, white ass, if you mess with me." He didn't sound friendly, and I didn't think he meant it to be friendly.

I put both hands up. "Ok. You made your point. I'm going to leave now. I don't need trouble from you. That's not what I came here for." He looked like he might make a step toward me. "All right?"

The look he gave me made me glad I could see his hands. "You don't belong up here, man. Get back wherever you came from." He took a step then, and I stepped sideways, putting myself where I could run down the sidewalk but keeping my eyes on him. I backed away, scanning behind me and still watching him. "Go on. Stay outta here, white ass."

I didn't say anything. I just kept backing toward my car. All the time he stood in front of Tippy's building, glaring. He pounded a fist into his other hand. It was impossible to tell if it was done for effect, or if it was unconscious anger. It didn't matter. I got in my car and drove off.

I ended up at Hannigan's and had a cup of coffee. Katie had already brought a bourbon and when I waved it off, she looked surprised, but changed the order. "You ok?" she said, standing beside the table.

"Yeah. Just got something to work out later tonight."

"Ah," she said. "You got woman trouble."

"The only woman giving me trouble right now is you." I smiled what I imagined was a beatific smile.

She smacked me with the dishrag she had. It was wetter than it should have been.

"Thanks, Katie. That takes care of today's bath."

I saw the problem. I was completely out of place in north Nashville. But my options were limited. I couldn't be other than what I was. I couldn't not go into Tippy's apartment, not if I wanted to do the job Tippy wanted me to do. And maybe his place was being watched, or maybe not, but a large black man had been Johnny on the spot and found me there.

I decided I needed to just stake it out. See what opportunities presented themselves.

I got back in the Impala, drove north, and parked down the street from Tippy's place. It was 10 p.m. on a Wednesday night. There shouldn't be much happening.

There was the usual sidewalk traffic. A few people hustling from job to home. Some teens who probably should already have been home. More than one old person, walking painfully from some place to another. It wasn't so much that the neighborhood was blighted. It was more that the neighborhood was sad, desperate to find something, some thing, that would advance it.

There was nothing going on in front of Tippy's door. Nobody seemed to be watching it. Nobody even seemed aware of it. A single naked bulb burned above the door.

At 10:45 I eased myself up from my semi-crouch in the car, opened my car door, and shut it quietly. I looked up and down Hyde and, seeing nothing, crossed the street. No one was in sight.

I strode to the front door and let myself in, locking the deadbolt behind me. I felt along the wall and located a light switch which, when flipped, illuminated a bulb over what should have been a dining table. Instead, there was a working desk with a Remington typewriter. There were sheets splayed around the typewriter.

I walked toward the couch in what passed for a living room and flipped the switch on a bargain basement floor lamp. Tippy hadn't spent big on lights and furniture.

I looked around the open space. It had the feel of something that had served as a crash pad, some place for a weary soul to come and sleep before setting off again. It wasn't that hard to believe about Tippy Taylor. Activist professor, writer of letters to the editor, and all-around gadfly. What else would he have needed but a crash pad? There was a dusty smell to the place, as if he hadn't crashed for a while.

The typewriter, though, he had spent money on, as if that was the one thing he cared about. It spoke to the book's importance to him. He must have been writing it here. I looked at the papers arrayed around the typewriter. There was nothing interesting there.

I gave the place a gentle toss. There's something about being in the home of a dead person that makes you want to take it easy. I wanted to find his manuscript, and to do that I had to find the locker key. I had a feeling that the key might be in plain sight, and that a more thorough search might cover it up rather than unearth it.

I made my way through the kitchen, where I mostly found unused and outdated food. A box of macaroni shells that bore a date four years old told me that, while he may have thought about cooking, he rarely did. The garbage can was filled with discarded mail, most of it addressed to occupant. His sink reminded me of mine. Except his was cleaner. We were both disorganized housekeepers and didn't much care.

I walked into the darkness of his bedroom, the one other room in the apartment. I had to feel for the switch but when I did, I saw an unmade bed and an alarm clock on a tiny side table. Next to the clock was an eyeglass case.

I didn't remember Tippy ever wearing glasses.

The closet was small and populated sparingly. Tippy had usually been in jeans and sandals, fatigues or a dashiki on his torso. It was his oversized Afro and his beard that were his distinguishing features, not his clothing. The dresser was a small piece of furniture with cardboard bottomed drawers. There wasn't enough there to notice.

I felt around the edges of the drawers, then behind the mirror, looking for a key, perhaps taped to the surface. When I came to the small nightstand, I examined the lamp and shade, and the clock. There was nothing.

I picked up the eyeglass case and opened it. A small locker key was there. So was a burnt spoon and two syringes.

I knew the signs. In Vietnam, some guys found themselves using in order to stay sane. Heroin there was cheap and pure. By the time I was there, we got tested on the way back to the world and, if a guy was using, they held him there in country until he detoxed. Tippy had been there before that program. Did he come back with the habit? Or did he develop it here?

Those were questions I couldn't answer. I pocketed the key and shut off the light, making my way back through the small apartment, putting things back as I'd found them. I turned off the last living room light, and exited, locking the front door behind me.

The street was quiet, and the early March breeze was both wet and cold. Tippy's place was on a darkened part of Hyde, the only lights coming from a couple of porch lights here and there on the street. It was not a place I wanted to tarry long.

I got to my Impala and started to put my hand on the door handle. But something wasn't right. Maybe the shadows it cast were just a little wrong. Or maybe there was an imperceptible noise, something that should not have been there. I felt the hairs on the back of my neck rise. I backed away into the middle of the street.

As I did, I saw two figures, one the front seat and one in the back jump quickly forward and push open the doors. Two black guys, neither as tall as I was, stood by the car. "Hey, brother," said the one wearing a UT sweatshirt. "What you doing tonight?"

I heard a click, and the second one, a shorter version of his companion, brandished a switchblade. "You ain't from this neighborhood. What you doing in that house?"

The UT sweatshirt angled closer. "That there is a fine question, Maurice. Can you answer Maurice's question, my man?"

I stayed loose. The switchblade wouldn't do any damage unless he got close enough to stick me. I angled back, canceling Mr. Sweatshirt's advantage.

"Just helping a friend," I said. It hadn't really worked earlier in the day, but it was true.

"Breaking into folk's houses, that makes me think you are helping yourself." The switchblade carrier, Maurice, moved in a straight line, while the sweatshirt continued to angle, cutting off my escape.

Then the sweatshirt reached behind his back and pulled out a little 25 caliber, the kind of nickel-plated Saturday night special that might not be much good but could still mess you up if the shooter was close enough. And Mr. Sweatshirt was close enough.

I shifted my sight from one to the other. I would take my chances and just hightail it, had I been thirty feet away. The blade was no danger and the .25, depending on the sturdiness of the gun, would be at best 50-50 to wing me. Of course, a lucky shot could make all that irrelevant. But it was a moot point. We were no further than ten feet apart.

I saw a flicker in Maurice's eyes, and I instinctively moved to my right, further out into the street so that I could see what he saw behind me.

There, with what looked like a short barrel .44 magnum, was my interrogator from earlier in the evening. He had the revolver pointed at Mr. Sweatshirt.

"Having fun, Lester?" His delivery was dry. He didn't expect an answer.

Lester, the sweatshirt, answered anyway. "Come on, man. This white boy ain't supposed to be here. He was in that house for a good half hour."

"That's right," Maurice chimed in. "He broke in. He's a thief."

"And y'all the neighborhood watch, right?" The big man smiled. "Put your toys away and go home."

"But," Lester began to say.

"But nothing. I got this. You go home." He lowered the revolver. "And Lester, put that damn peashooter back in your pants."

They showed their displeasure by mumbling. Maurice spit on the Impala. But they walked east toward the more brightly lit part of The Gardens. Lester looked over his shoulder once, then stuffed his hands in his pockets and shook his head.

"Thanks," I said. "Did you do that because you want me all to yourself?"

"Don't be a smartass, Trade." I guess my surprise showed. "I talked to Rodney Glenn. I got the story."

I didn't relax, but I felt a little better. "Then we're cool?"

"I'm not crazy that you came back, but I guess you had to, if you are really doing something for Tippy. But yeah. We're cool." He holstered the revolver and walked up, hand outstretched. We shook in a customary, but halting way. "Stump Collins," he said.

"Call me Jackson," I said. "I appreciate just now."

"You need to come back up in here, you let me know. Belle's Dinette. They'll know how to get me."

Belle's was over on Jefferson and was an institution. "I will."

"I'm serious, Trade. This whole town's on edge right now. Don't come here unless you let me know."

I was willing to make that deal.

Besides I had a locker key. And the next morning I needed to get downtown to the bus station.

Chapter Five

The Greyhound bus station occupied the entire block of Commerce Street between Fifth and Sixth Avenues. For decades, the city had tried to find some way to clean up the area around it. From Commerce to Broadway and from Fourth to Eighth, a constant torrent of runaways, hustlers, transients, would-be musicians, aspiring songwriters, and Fort Campbell soldiers arrived, some with dreams and some with only a past, but all with desires. The area around the bus station catered to the basest of those desires and the most basic of their needs.

In other words, there were flophouses, brothels, gambling dens, and bars for almost every type of bus traveler. Straight or gay, old or young, or just weird and damaged, there was something for you when you disembarked.

And disembark they did. People from the coal country of eastern Kentucky to the rolling hills of north Alabama found their way to the city where the country music was made. Few found what they were looking for. But in the maelstrom of downtown, they found something.

The bus station itself was a brightly lit rectangle that smelled of cigarette smoke and stale sweat. I'm sure that the black and white tile floors were mopped at least once a day, but the smell told me that the mops were sour, and the water didn't stay clean long. There was too much traffic, and too much of the flotsam and jetsam of life, for it to be otherwise.

I arrived about eight in the morning, just as the runs from Knoxville and Memphis were arriving. I was struck by the number of people, mostly men, carrying an instrument case. I was surprised that there were so many young people. With two full buses arriving at once, the terminal had the feel of a much larger city's terminal. Hell, I guess if they all stayed, Nashville would in fact be a larger city instead of the overgrown town it really was.

The lockers were on the side of the terminal opposite the ticket windows. They were metal, with three hooded vents cut into the top of each locker. Stacked four high, they looked to be about eighteen inches square, with two feet or so of depth. Enough for personal items but not enough for real luggage. The luggage lockers were on the outside of the terminal, under the overhang.

The key had the number 36 stamped on it, and it was a cinch to find its matching locker. The key turned a lever and the locker popped open. Inside were two yellow manila envelopes, one large and one smaller. Inside the larger one was a sheaf of papers. A quick inspection showed that it was a manuscript, and the number of pages suggested it was a book. Good enough.

The second envelope contained a plastic bag with a brown powder in it. I knew what it was, and it wasn't what I came for. I guess Tippy kept it here because he didn't want to keep heroin at home. Anyway, not my problem.

I kept the envelope with the manuscript, replaced the packet of heroin, and turned the key. I had three hours before I had to be "on watch" at Kirkland Hall, observing faculty march in a circle, so I took the book, cut across to Broadway and walked the mile or so to the Arby's at West End and 18th. I ordered a roast beef and potato cake, then sat down to have a late breakfast and a short read.

Tippy was a good writer. I already knew that from his letters to the editor. But his manuscript, which began with his birth in Spartanburg, South Carolina, was written with the kind of urgency that made you keep turning the page, wondering what would happen next. His childhood in Baltimore had been hard, his whole community segregated from any form of equality. It wasn't an unfamiliar story to anyone raised in the South. Or probably even in the North. But in Tippy's telling it took on the cast of a personal journey, from somewhere bad to somewhere, he might hope, better.

Except he didn't get "better." Instead, he got Vietnam.

We were always out in the field, operating out of forward base camps. Each man usually carried an M-16 and ten magazines with 200 rounds, but I carried fifteen to twenty magazines, plus water, food, and all the rest of the things I needed. In addition, the mortar squad I was in had to carry an .81 mortar, plus tube, tripod, and mortar rounds. When you got it all on my back that meant my 150-pound body was carrying about 120 pounds of stuff.

Ain't no thing, all the brothers in the unit said. We've been carrying more shit than we should for generations.

I had been there. I knew what he said was true. And while you could have said that the white guys were carrying that much too, that would have missed Tippy's point. It was new for us. It was war. The black guys had been grunts since their ancestors were taken to America.

I don't think anyone who wasn't there can begin to comprehend the filth we lived in. In monsoon season we got soaked to the bone and we would be covered with mud. Then the sun would come out and we'd be so caked with dried mud that you couldn't tell one of us from the other. Since we didn't have spare uniforms, after about six weeks in the field we would be walking in tatters. Our feet had been in wet boots so long that we all had jungle rot.

And while we did that we were ferried in and out every day, usually on a Huey, with some of us in the chopper and the others, with all their gear, hanging on outside. They'd drop us, and we'd hump it through the jungle, looking for NVA or VC, breaking about 3 to set up camp. Set trip flares and Claymores, dig holes and fill sandbags.

It was bad. And here's what I learned. The black guys and the country boys didn't complain. The white boys from the city complained like hell.

That's when I realized I might have some white allies. At least potentially.

I had long finished my sandwich and potato cake when I realized I'd been reading for two hours. I had fallen into the web of a writer who knew how to paint his picture. But I'd stopped looking for his murderer and that was the whole reason for the manuscript. And it was getting close to 11:00. I needed to get to Vanderbilt.

I went by Branscomb Quadrangle and dropped the manuscript off with Blake's secretary. Dot was a quietly efficient woman who had surprised us all, back when I worked for Blake, by showing up at a Christmas party with a previously unknown, but movie-star quality man who turned out to be her husband. They also had movie-star quality children who were all straight A students.

Wendy Williamson, who was Assistant Dean with me at the time, said what we were all thinking. "Dot? This is your family?" When Dot nodded, Wendy said, "We had no idea."

"Well, you never asked, so I never said anything."

That's why I wasn't worried about dropping the envelope off with her.

She looked at me with the same cool, measuring gaze she always did. "Do you want the Dean to see this?"

"I don't care if Art sees it, but he won't know what it means." I met her gaze with my own measuring one. "And I trust you implicitly, Dot, to know what to do with confidential documents."

She unlocked the lower right drawer of her desk and placed the envelope in the hanging file furthest in the back. "It will be locked here until you return, Jackson." She locked it back, put the key in her center drawer, locked it, and put that key in her purse. "Now, what else can I do for you?"

I took her hand and kissed it. "You're a peach, Dot."

She shook her head, disapprovingly, while smiling. "And you're a mess."

I wandered over to Kirkland, walking down Rand Terrace. It was not the most direct way to go, but it was the best way to get a gauge on what was happening on campus. If there was going to be anything interesting, it would be happening in front of Rand. But today was warm, the March sun was shining, and people had better things to do. Performance art or protest, there was nothing today.

There wasn't much more happening at the Davis Cup picket in front of Kirkland. I recognized a couple of my professors from undergraduate days. If custom held, this would be the History department's turn again. They walked in a tight circle, white hands holding white placards, chanting, "The people, united, will never be defeated." Over and over.

As historians, they might have known that wasn't true, or at least that it hadn't worked that way most of the time. They probably taught, at least half of them this morning, that the people, united, had wilted under superior firepower.

I didn't see any reason to correct them, though. I sat on a bench under a magnolia, lit a cigarette, and watched them.

They had brought a number of students with them. Some I could identify, by their age, as likely graduate students. Some of them might truly have been there for the protest, but some might have been there because it wouldn't have been a good idea to piss off their thesis advisors. Still others were undergraduates. The crowd was overwhelmingly white. Just one black female, who looked to be about nineteen, was in the group of thirty.

I ground out the butt I was smoking and leaned back against the bench. The peace of the moment combined with the quiet of the protest, and I felt almost sleepy. I sensed, though, that I was being watched, so I didn't shut my eyes. I just let myself lapse off into that thousand-yard stare that I've seen other vets do, except I was staying alert, just in case.

I saw two figures break off from the group and approach me. The female was about five-ten, blonde, and wore wire rimmed glasses. She had the air of someone who was used to being obeyed, and a woman who liked to be obeyed too. She was good-looking enough that she was, in fact, obeyed. Her heels clacked on the brick walkway. The male was younger, an undergraduate most likely, but her acolyte certainly. He wore Duck Head khakis and a blue cotton pullover sweater. His feet were clad in Topsiders. It wasn't the quintessential preppie uniform, but it was a version of it. He was a big guy, the sort whose brain hasn't caught up with his body. As they approached, he looked from me to her several times, his eyes narrowing each time he looked at me.

All he wanted was a signal from her, and he would do anything she said.

They stood in front of me, the woman with her hands on her hips. "Yes?" I tried to put my voice in neutral.

"Why are you watching us?" she demanded.

"Do I look like I'm watching you?" I asked. "I think I look like I'm sitting here, enjoying a lovely March day."

"You are out here every day. Watching. Are you with the police?"

I pretended to survey my looks. "Let's see. Ponytail. Beard. Bell-bottomed jeans, flannel shirt. So far I'm not getting the policeman vibe, lady. What you got?"

"You could be some kind of undercover cop," the male said. "It's the sort of thing cops would do. That might even be a wig." He moved in front of her, in a wary posture, as if to protect her.

"And you watch too much Hawaii Five-O." I leaned back and put both arms out over the back of the bench. "Our paths just happen to cross, that's all."

The woman peered at me. She had striking ice blue eyes. You could get lost in them, or you could fall through them to your death. She was beautiful in a Valkyrie kind of way, but thinner.

"You look familiar," she said. "Do you work here?"

A voice over her shoulder said, "He used to. But he's just too damn sorry to keep a job."

They turned and I could see my friend, Don Mercer, lieutenant and second in command of the VU Campus Police.

"There you have it, ma'am. I am declared a worthless derelict, which would seem to rule me out as an undercover cop. And this would make perfect sense if I'm just enjoying a warm place in the sun before slinking back to Skid Row."

"Jesus, Jackson, you are really a piece of work," he said. "Dr. Winter, you don't have anything to worry about from Jackson. He's only a threat to himself." He gave me a hard look.

"If I had a cap, I'd tip it. What was it? Dr. Winter?"

"Dr. Willa Winter," she said. "Enlightenment History."

"She's just published a book on the social contract and John Locke," said the male. He said it as if he'd never known anyone who'd written a book. It's possible he hadn't known anyone who'd read one before he got to Vanderbilt. "The New York Times reviewed it." He was breathless. His teeth almost gleamed as he smiled at her.

I don't believe I've ever looked at anyone quite that way. But then, I'm harder to impress.

"Ah," I said. "The social contract. Then I would assume you surrender to the will of the University in exchange for its protections of your other rights. Tenure, for instance."

She blinked. "I apologize. Clearly you aren't exactly what you seem."

"Why's that. Because I know something about John Locke? That almost seems insulting, Dr. Winter."

"Really?" She had come for a confrontation, had been let down, and now was gearing up again. "How is a compliment insulting?"

"It's a little insulting that, whether I'm a policeman or a vagrant, you believe that my knowing a little Locke is about the same as a bullfrog who speaks French."

She stared at me. Her acolyte wasn't sure what the insult was, but he balled his hands into fists just the same.

"All right, folks, let's just everybody get back to what they were doing," said Mercer, motioning Willa Winter and the male back toward their protest group. "Go back to what you were doing. I'll just sit here and have a word with Jackson."

She continued to stare for a moment, but she and the student finally made their way back, picked up their placards, and chanted, not without a couple of last, parting looks. The undergrad made sure I saw his lengthy glare at me.

Whatever.

Mercer sat next to me on the bench. I offered a cigarette, which he took, and we both smoked in silence for a minute.

"Why do you have to get into it with people?" he asked. "Are you just naturally provocative, or do you turn it on and off, depending on your mood?" It was still March, and even though the temperature was just in the 60s, Don wore the summer short sleeve uniform. If you saw him in the winter issue, you'd assume he had gone a little to seed. His paunch stretched the shirt a little. But in the summer short sleeves, you could see his powerful, dark arms. You'd think twice about tangling with him, paunch or no paunch.

"I don't provoke people, Don. If I say something and they get mad, that's on them, not me. I'm a peaceful person. Besides, I shot my wad on Locke there. That's all I know about him."

"I don't think there's anything peaceful about you, Jackson. It'd be nice if you found some."

"You're just saying that because you can't keep up with me in the bars."

"Nobody keeps up with you. And that's not something to brag about."

"Forget all that. Who's Dr. Winter? I don't remember her from my time here."

He adjusted his belt. "She supposed to be hot stuff. At least her picture is in the university magazine. The impression I got is that Vandy's lucky to have her."

We smoked in silence. "Was Vandy lucky to have Tippy Taylor?"

"Doesn't matter now, does it?" he said, and rose to go. He adjusted his gun belt again. "The Dean told me he hired you to shadow some of this. Be careful, Jackson. Call me if you need anything."

I stood too. "Thanks, Donnie. I don't know what I'm doing, and I'm running full speed in the dark."

"Don't run drunk in the dark, brother." He field-stripped the cigarette with his fingers. "I've seen you do that, and it ain't pretty."

"That's the truth. Ain't nothing pretty about it."

Chapter Six

THERE IS NOTHING THAT focuses the mind of an academic like the arrival of someone he considers inferior. The academic game is ruthless enough among those with the same credentials, the same backgrounds, and the same color skin. But let in someone with lesser credentials, a different background, nay even a Black man? Let me just observe that hell hath no fury like an academic injured by the very existence of someone like me.

Would these august personages be interested to know that, among their number, they have initiated four women, like credentialed and like in background, like to them in every way except their gender, about which these males have agreed to foreswear discussion? I do not judge if they do so because they want to or because they must. It is no matter. They have admitted them. What they say when they're alone is not my business.

But who would they choose to speak out, to complain bitterly, do you think, if they knew that one of the four made her way through graduate school as a lingerie model and dancer? It would be bad enough if she were on Broadway. But in a Chicago dive? With a pole on the stage? Would they choose a decorated Vietnam veteran or her? Would they choose neither? And what if both were superior to many of their number?

You know the answer, and I do too. But there is nothing that focuses the rage of an academic like inferiority. And I have been the target of that rage. If they knew her secret, she would too.

She feels enough of it because she is a woman.

I finished the highball glass of bourbon and considered pouring another. Rain was beating the windows, but it was supposed to be over in an hour or two. Since I had to be out later, I decided against it.

Tippy Taylor said he had something on several people and one of them would kill him. Would it have made sense that a woman with a past, a past she really needed to hide, would commit a murder? I guess it depended on how true the secret was, and how much it would damage her prospects. I could find out tomorrow how many females, besides the stunning Willa Winter, were in the History department.

I flipped forward a chapter or two, and found:

I live in a bad place. It's not bad because of the people who live there. All of them look like me. All of them are viewed by the world in the same way. A lecturer in History at a private university. A neighborhood thug. A political activist or a drug entrepreneur. Get south of Jefferson and you're all just black folk.

The badness of the place is not that we're all victims of the same prejudice. The badness comes when we forget who the allies are and who they are not. The badness is when we start tripping, and treat each other the way that we are treated, when we turn on each other. When we do that, we do the work of our enemies for them.

There are good men and there are bad men. And all of them are armed. When the work of reason and persuasion is done with guns, there is no gentle persuasion nor sweet reason. What does that poem say? The best lack all conviction, while the worst are full of passionate intensity.

Before I finished, I found a passage near the end.

Back in the war, soldiers found ways to distract themselves from the constant toll of war. Some drank. Some smoked weed.

Some found heroin and fell in love with it. Others did bennies. I didn't do any of that, not because I was virtuous, but because I was afraid. My fear was that, if I ever let myself lose contact with reality, I'd never find my way back. If where it took them was so good that people wanted to go there all the time, I was afraid that I'd just want to stay.

Thus, I never did any of that. The man who loses himself loses everything.

Unfortunately for me, Tippy didn't name any of the folks whose secrets he knew. One clearly was a female professor, and one was a person in the north Nashville community who maybe had a grudge against Tippy. Or maybe not.

Tippy took the third secret with him. What was a man who declared himself permanently clean doing with a bag of horse, two syringes, and a burnt spoon? Unless he wasn't telling the truth.

And if he wasn't telling the truth about that, was he telling the truth about anything?

I packed the questions into the back of my head and headed out in the rain to St Mark's CME. It was a small church, neighbor to a convenience store on one side and a barbershop on the other. Its red bricks were chipped in places and the masonry was tired.

The gaunt black man who stood at the door gave me an equally tired look. "Help you?"

"I'm here for the meeting." I hoped that would establish enough of a reason that I wouldn't have to try to explain my purpose in being there.

He looked me over. I suppose it felt as much like a visual frisk as anything. "Stairs are on the right side, front, up by the altar rail."

Inside, the weary little church was dimly lit. The pews bore the marks of years of care. They were worn smooth, but they were polished and inviting. The walls were newly white-washed. Everything bore the mark of simplicity, something well-used and serviceable.

I could hear the murmur of voices before I entered the short stairwell. Four steps to a landing, then four more. It was a cellar that had a wet chill to it, probably even in warmer months. But in early March it was cold enough that no one had taken a jacket off.

In the center of the crowd was a white Metro police captain and a black man with his back to me. The captain was gesturing and speaking quietly. The black man was stone still.

"If you don't have anything to hide," the captain was saying, "then why are you holding out on us?"

"If you trust us like you say you do, why do you have to know everything we are doing?" The black man's words were followed by a chorus, agreeing.

Just then the captain's eyes saw me and, as he looked, so did everyone else. The black man turned.

"Mr. Trade." The black man's face was hard and surprised. "I certainly didn't expect you here." He gave a tight smile. "And I didn't hear that you were interested in coming."

I touched the bill of my cap in a kind of salute. "Mr. Collins. I didn't know you'd be here tonight either."

"You two know each other?" The Metro captain looked from Stump Collins back to me.

"Mr. Trade and I have had a couple of conversations. Just casual."

"That's it," I said. "Casual."

A regular uniform Metro guy approached the captain and whispered at length. He nodded. "Please come up to the table with us."

"What?" Stump Collins leaned against the table with both hands. "Trade works for you?"

"Not at all. Mr. Trade is representing Vanderbilt's interests in this."

When I got to the table, Collins reached across to bar me with his arm. "You work for Vanderbilt?"

"I'm here to carry information back to the University," I said. "They don't want me to represent them. They just want my ears."

"Why can't they do that for themselves," asked Collins. "Why are they sending you?"

"It would appear," the captain said, "they don't want to seem to be involved in coordinating." He looked to me for confirmation. "They prefer to be invisible. Is that it, Mr. Trade?"

"Like I said, I can't speak for them. I know they want me to listen, and to report."

Collins exhaled loudly. He sat down and looked around. "Ok, then, let's give him something to hear."

The captain, whose name turned out to be Leo Borelli, and Collins began their conversation in public, although the public was mostly Collins's. It had the feel of a poker game, with everyone watching the raises and the calls.

"We are bringing a demonstration from the Capitol all the way down Broadway and West End to Memorial Gym," Collins began. "We demand a security escort the entire way."

"Do you expect problems?" Borelli raised his eyebrows in surprise. "It's going to be protesters all the way down."

"If there's a group of protesters, and they are mostly white, and they want to march down Jefferson to protest at Fisk, don't you think they'd want police protection?"

"It's not the same thing, Collins."

"The hell it's not." He looked at me. "You don't think you'd want police protection, Trade?"

"Probably not. But then, I have friends there." I winked. "Maurice and Lester, for two."

He pulled his aviators down and looked over them. "Right."

"At any rate, the route you're describing is entirely commercial. It's not as if you're marching through a residential area."

"A residential area where the white folk might be scared that we're coming to steal their things? No sir, you march through a residential area, and police better be everywhere."

"That's not what I mean."

"It doesn't matter what you mean. It matters what you say. You're saying black people can't have police protection when they stage the biggest march Nashville's ever seen."

Borelli was talking more quickly. "You're deliberately twisting my words." He looked at me. "I am trying to plan a peaceful demonstration with him." He pointed at me. He wanted reassurance.

It seemed to me that it would be more peaceful if he just did what Stump Collins was demanding. "I don't have a dog in this fight."

The men around us were egging Collins on. "Tell it, Stump." "Don't let him push you around, Stump." "Amen, brother."

"Not only that, but we also want a permit to construct a stage with sound amplifiers on the Capitol grounds, and another one constructed outside Memorial Gym, and we want the one at Memorial to be left up overnight to be used the second day. That means we'll need security at that site 24/7 until we're done with it."

"I can't negotiate that. One's state government, the other is Vanderbilt."

"What the hell, man? You set this up as a negotiation, then you tell me you can't negotiate?"

"Seriously, Mr. Collins. You know I can't bind the state government to anything. Or Vanderbilt either. That's private property."

"Police come on private property all the time and bind all kinds of things," Collins said, to more shouts of agreement. "You do anything you want on our side of town. How come you can't do the same thing on the west end?" He pounded the table. "I'll tell you why. Because it's black people asking. That's the only thing I see."

Borelli looked at the three uniforms he'd brought with him, as if he expected one of them might step forward and give him a magic sentence to say. They just stood there, one black officer and two white ones, staring straight ahead.

"Let me try this, Mr. Collins. I will contact the department of the state government that issues permits like you're talking about. I'll see if they will grant that activity." Collins began to interrupt, but Borelli raised his hand. "I wonder if Mr. Trade will communicate your request to Vanderbilt."

"I told you. I'm here to tell them what I hear. I'm not here to speak for them. I guess if they want to do it, they'll call you."

"Fair enough." Borelli looked into Collins's eyes. "I'll relay the request for a police escort. I'll tell you, though, because of the high-profile nature of this, the decision will probably have to come from the mayor's office. It's not something I can grant on my own."

Collins was nodding the whole time, although the way his shoulders were implicated, it might have been fairer to say that he was rocking, a little, back and forth. "All right, Captain. If that's the best you can do, then it's all you can do. Maybe next time we need the mayor here if you aren't the man who can get things done. Because there are going to be more demands. And they are not going to get easier."

Borelli rose. "Just work with me, Collins. I'm trying to do right by you people."

"You people? You mean the citizens assembled in this room?"

Borelli sighed. "I'll be in touch, Collins." And with that he motioned to his officers, and they left.

The men in the basement waited until the last feet had left their view, and then they began whooping and hollering.

"You showed him, Stump."

"Attaboy, Stump."

Collins rose and stood on his chair. "Fellas, this is just the beginning. We are going to be heard on this. We are going to express our doubts about South Africa. But the doubts are really going to be about the United States, and about Tennessee, and about Nashville, and about Vanderbilt."

It was revivalist in fervor and righteous in temper. The crowd of men cheered in the damp church basement. I sat dead still in the center of it. They had forgotten I was there.

After a while, the cheering subsided and the men left, in twos and threes, to go about their business. Stump Collins crooked a finger and me and then pointed to the seat next to him.

"I thought you were going to tell me when you needed to come up to this part of town."

"If I'd have been going over to The Gardens, I would have. This isn't The Gardens."

"This is still not your part of town. This is my part of town. You know that."

"Are you saying that I can't come to a part of town where black people live if I don't get your permission?" I could feel my heat rising a little.

"You can go anywhere you want. You maybe can't go anywhere you want and be safe."

I didn't know if it sounded like a threat or not. "Ok."

"Why are you mixed up in this stuff here?"

He knew I had worked at Vanderbilt. "They trust me."

"Why not send somebody else? You don't work there anymore."

I couldn't tell him that Blake didn't want his fingerprints on it. I couldn't tell him that Blake was trying to resurrect me. All I could tell him was, "I don't know. But I need the work."

"What are they paying you? I can beat it. You can be my man working with the Metro boy."

"It's not about that."

"What's it about, Trade? Why are you in this mess that don't belong to you? I kind of understand Tippy. That's a personal request. But this shit? I don't get it, man."

I wasn't sure why I hadn't just told Art to get somebody else. But I was sure that it was too late to get into it with a man I hardly knew. "I'll see you later, Stump." I got up and walked away.

"Wait." Stump scribbled something on a scrap of paper. He handed it to me. "That's an address. Meet me there tomorrow. 2:00."

"What is this?"

"Tomorrow at 2. You'll see."

Chapter Seven

THE NEXT DAY FOUND me back on the north side, in a small store that bore the address Stump Collins had given me.

There was a red Coca-Cola dispenser in the middle of the store. It was the chest style, the kind you used to see everywhere before the tall Coke machines appeared, the kind where you put your nickel in, opened the lid, and snaked the bottle you wanted along a little track, gripping the bottle by its top, until you reached the opening where the latch gave way when you pulled the bottle upward. It was a simple piece of machinery, designed to do one thing and one thing only. Deliver a cold bottle of Coke, 7-up, or Mountain Dew to a thirsty patron.

To the left of the Coke dispenser was a table. On the wall side, there was a vinyl banquette whose covering had long ago split, and which now showed a foam cushion that had been victim to one too many pinches. On the other sides were decrepit cane chairs, in a similar state of wear. Old black men occupied all save one of the chairs, each with a soft drink bottle, and each pondering the set of dominoes being placed by the two rivals in the center.

Smoke rose and hung in the air, as cigarettes were forgotten, or dangled in mouths, or were lit and then inhaled. Seven old men, passing the time, comfortable here as they might not be in other parts of the city, each one absorbed in the present moment. A couple of them wore overalls, and the rest wore clean work clothes, the sort you could wear doing anything from grease monkey work to appliance repair. Some of the ensembles were green, others a dark blue, but each one bore the mark of having been worn in the service of making a living. These were their work clothes, though they were working men no longer. But these were the clothes they had, and they continued to wear them.

They took no note of me or, if they did, they didn't betray it. No sidelong glance. No turn and stare. Though they might have stared, given that a strange white man had entered their sanctuary. I kept my distance and leaned against a tall cooler that contained beer and malt liquor. But as my friend, Don Mercer, said to me once, he always knew the location of every white man in a space. I figured they did too, and I could at least be polite and stay quiet.

Until Stump arrived, that is.

Stump let himself in and the screen door slapped shut. One wizened old man looked up and grunted. Nobody else took their eyes off the dominoes.

Stump walked over to me and elbowed my side. "You reckon you'll do that when you get old? Sit all day with other geezers and waste time?"

"Except for the geezer part, that's about what I do now. Why think it'll be any different?"

"I don't know, Trade. I don't see you making it to that age."

"You know something I don't?"

"Just a feeling." He jerked his head in the opposite direction, toward a closed door. "Wanted you to meet somebody." He turned and walked to the door. I followed.

He knocked and without waiting turned the doorknob. We entered a smallish space with the window on the back of the building, positioned high so that light got in, but you couldn't see out. The light made a small spear as the dust in the air contacted the light. The room was darker than it should have been, and the spear of light, combined with the goose-neck lamp on the table, caused the darkness to stand in relief.

At the table sat a dark-skinned man, older even than the men playing dominoes. His sleeves were rolled to his elbows, which were placed on the table. He was bent over a newspaper, the light from the lamp causing the newspaper to show yellow under the incandescent bulb.

He paused to look up, first straight ahead, then turning to look at us. "Stump?" He then rose and grasped the back of the chair with one hand. His clothes hung on him like they'd once fit, and so knew his body, but only gave him the slightest shape now. The rest of the cloth surrounded him without form.

"How's it going, Mr. Pennypacker?" Stump moved toward the old man and extended his arm, supporting him and easing him back into the chair.

"Who's your friend?" He said it without inflection, as if he didn't know if I were a friend or not, or even if he wanted to know.

"This is Jackson. I wanted him to meet you."

I approached Pennypacker slowly, waiting for him to make the first move.

"Why? This fellow don't want nothing to do with me. I'm pretty sure of that."

"How can you be sure?" Stump had slipped down into a crouch in front of the old man and was at eye level with him.

"Because you said you wanted him to meet me. Didn't say he wanted anything of the sort."

"I don't know you, sir." The three of us now made a tightly constructed group, all of us close enough to whisper and be understood, if we wanted to. "I don't know why Stump set up this meeting."

"That's right. Mr. Pennypacker don't know he needs to talk to Jackson. And Jackson don't know he needs to hear what Mr. Pennypacker's got to say. Only Stump Collins knows that."

The old man continued to stare at Stump, but he said to me, "Better come around on this side and sit down, Mister. Maybe our friend Stump will tell us what he means."

I did as he said and sat lightly on an old cane chair. It squeaked as I sat, and I could feel it give a little. As I did, Stump rose and crossed the room to get a stool. He sat and towered over us. I had a feeling he liked that. "Tell Jackson about the steering committee, Mr. Pennypacker."

"That's old news. He don't want to hear none of that."

"I think it'll be all right. I think Jackson here needs to understand about how things are. He spends too much time at Vanderbilt."

The old man pawed at an imaginary spirit, keeping it away from him. "Damn Vanderbilt."

"I hear you, Mr. Pennypacker. Tell him about the committee."

The old man finally looked at me. "Tell me, sir, and I'll listen. Listening is what I do best."

He exhaled, sort of a "giving up" expelling of breath. "It all started in '57, at least that's when we found out. The year before, Ike had signed the bill to make the Interstate highways. Three of them were going to come through Nashville, and the first was I-40." He looked at Stump, lifted both palms upward. "You sure?"

"Just tell it, Mr. P."

"So, the city has a gang of experts come in and tell them how they should route it through town. Turns out these experts said to run it off US 70 and come through by Vanderbilt, Centennial Park, and down Charlotte Street by Baptist Hospital. But you know that's not going to work, right?" He turned to me, making sure my reaction was what he wanted. "That's close to Belle Meade, where the rich folk are. Vandy and Centennial, them's two bright jewels in the city's crown."

Plus, I already knew where the highway had gone. "So that's not where it ended up."

"You got that right. City made themselves a new plan. Instead of Vandy, they sent it right between A&I and Fisk. Instead of Baptist, they ran it by Meharry Medical School. And instead of Belle Meade, they tore up Jefferson Street."

Stump made sure I saw his head nodding affirmatively. "They couldn't have made what they intended more obvious."

Pennypacker waved away the invisible spirit again. "Except they didn't make it obvious at all. For nine years they denied they even had a plan. But they did. They had already had a so-called public meeting they kept secret, approved the plan, and then waited. The community didn't even know there was anything going on until they started tearing up 18th Avenue North in '67, saying they had to widen it for the interstate and had to tear down all these houses."

He turned to face me, his whole body turned now, and essentially turned his back to Stump. "I'm listening, Mr. Pennypacker."

"Before it was all over with, North Nashville lost one hundred square blocks, and sixteen blocks of them were small business. Sixteen square blocks of black-owned businesses. Over six hundred houses. Twenty-seven apartment houses. Six black churches. All demolished. Eighteen city streets dead-ended, so you can't get from one place to another." There wasn't much light, so I couldn't really see his eyes clearly. But where there was not light, there was heat, and it radiated from him, like a banked fire that hadn't gone out. "Can you imagine what that kind of destruction does to a community? They might as well have dropped a bomb on Jefferson Street. It wouldn't have had a different effect."

I now faced both the old man and Stump. I looked from one to the other. One was old and tired but still able to say his truth. The other was young and strong and ready to make some noise.

"Tell him about the Committee."

Pennypacker rearranged himself in the chair so that he no longer faced me directly. "A couple of professors from Fisk and A&I formed a committee. We researched how all this had happened. We went into the city archives, and we found how they'd publicized the required meeting by putting the wrong date on it. We found the original recommendation that sent the highway through Vanderbilt. We found enough that we got lawyers to try to stop it all. It was corrupt from the beginning."

"How did that turn out?" I knew how it must have turned out.

"The judge said that there was no doubt the plan would wreck the black community. He also said no law was broken."

Stump stood and leaned, put his hands on the table. "You see, Jackson? You see why we have to say 'no' to this mess at Vanderbilt? You have to say 'no' every time. Because Nashville just doesn't get it."

Pennypacker turned to face Stump, at the same time holding a hand up. "I told my story, Stump. Now tell me what you brought this man down here for. The real reason."

"I think I know, sir." When I spoke he turned back toward me. "Stump wants to make a believer out of me. He wants me to see what he sees when Vanderbilt hosts South Africa for a tennis tournament."

Stump snorted. "Better be clear, Jackson. Ain't no way you ever will see what I see. But I do want you to understand a little better. It's not just that North Nashville is hurting. It's that Nashville took the black community and tore it up." He was leaning on the stool, calm and collected. "If you understand that, you can do your job, whatever it really is, better."

Pennypacker jerked his head toward me. "Job? What's his job?"

"Beats me, Mr. P."

"I am a kind of go-between."

"Go between who?"

My hand unconsciously felt for the beeper. It was there still. "Vanderbilt and Metro. Vanderbilt and Stump's group. One time, even between Metro and Stump's group."

Pennypacker seemed to consider what to say next, probably wondering what advantage it was for me to know the history of the I-40 displacement. After a few moments, he seemed to decide.

"All right. Seems to me Stump must trust you enough to bring you here for the truth, so maybe I will trust you with some more truth. You up for that?"

"Like I said, listening is what I do."

"This business we are in now? This protesting about letting South Africa play tennis? It's important. It's symbolic, but it's important. Like Stump says, every time you see something like this, you have to say no."

Stump nodded his head. "That's right, Mr. P."

"But it ain't enough. It ain't ever going to be enough just to say no to the symbols. You have to say no to the real things. Once you know what happened to North Nashville, you have to say no to unfair things, like black people not getting loans. Like a black man's house being worth less than a white man's house, even if they are exactly the same damn house. Like young men like Stump getting followed around every time they go in a store. You hearing me?"

"Yes, sir. I hear you."

He dropped his voice. "Then hear this. All this and more happens every day, and not just in Nashville. I'm an old man. I'm worn out by it. I've had a lifetime of it. But as the song says, change going to come. When it comes, it will not be tidy. It will not be neat. It will be a mess, and we'll all be in it."

Stump had stopped nodding and was still. Pennypacker seemed to have spent his words and was quiet.

"Do you think what's coming at Vanderbilt will be a mess? Or will it be tidy?"

He turned just enough. The light from outside illuminated one side of his face. It was gaunt. The skin from below his eyes to his chin had a crease across it. Perhaps it was a scar. Maybe it was just a trick of light. "It won't be tidy. It won't be comfortable. But it won't be the storm." He turned back and his face went into shadow again. "The storm will be more than what's coming here."

His story over, he reached out and tapped Stump on the leg. "Come by more often, son. I'm always glad to see you." He looked at me and offered his hand. I took it and we shook like people who had sealed a deal of some kind. "You may not find your way back here, Mr. Go Between. But if you don't, make sure you're a fair dealer."

"I'll try, Mr. Pennypacker."

"Don't try, Mister. Do."

Effectively dismissed, Stump and I left the old man in the dark room with the single shaft of light. The domino players paid no heed as we left.

Standing outside, Stump and I lit our cigarettes. He crouched down and drew imaginary letters on the sidewalk. I leaned against the pane glass window and watched him.

"He was old when I first knew him. Already had so much life behind him."

"Quite a story he told."

"Oh, it's not a story. It's the way things were. The way they are." He stared out into the street. "I got a feeling about you, Jackson. I think you might can understand some of this. I think you can help."

I stared out into the street too. There were two boys, about nine or ten years old, throwing a baseball on the opposite sidewalk. They did it without great interest in their pastime, not throwing hard, but just passing time.

"If this was a good place, them boys would have a baseball diamond to play on. They might have a league of boys, each team with its own uniform." Stump continued to make imaginary drawings on the concrete. Then he said, "You know, like kids over in Green Hills, like kids in East Nashville."

"What do you want me to do, Stump? I can't fix these problems."

"You don't have to fix them, man. You just got to care."

"What if I don't care? What if I've got enough on my plate as it is? What if I have trouble even caring about myself."

Stump sighed. "There's your trouble. Right there. Until you've got something to care about, you ain't got no life. If you got no life, then why would you care about yourself?" He stood up. "Look, man. I did a little checking on you. You've done a good thing or two for folks. And not just Rodney Glenn. But you spend half your time in the bag."

"I have that under control."

"Maybe you do. Maybe you don't. But I need your help. I think you can see what's at stake. If Mr. P didn't convince you, I don't know what will."

"I can see."

"Then I need you to clean up, at least for a while, and help a brother out."

"You saying we're brothers, Stump?"

"I'm saying that I need you on my team, Jackson." He held out his hand. "How about it? We on the same team?"

I reached out. He took my hand firmly and we shook. "What do you want me to do?"

He smiled. Clapped me on the shoulder. "I got a few things to attend to. You do too, what with Tippy's business. But when the time comes, I'll call for you. And you need to be ready, Freddy. We'll have work to do."

Chapter Eight

THE NEXT MORNING, I had a bite to eat at the Krystal, and headed to Wardell Robinson's office. By the time I got there, Wardell had coffee ready.

"I have a couple of leads, Wardell. The manuscript mentions a female professor who might have been an exotic dancer in graduate school. And somebody in The Gardens who carries a gun, maybe threatens people. I can't find a third."

"That is vaguely interesting, but I don't see where it gets you." He leafed through some papers on his desk.

"Where it gets me is one short of suspects. Tippy said there were three. The manuscript suggests two."

Wardell kept his eyes on mine. "Maybe you didn't read closely enough."

"I think I did. I think there's more to the manuscript. Or another manuscript. Tippy said the one I have is just the start. Or the key." I returned my gaze as hard as Wardell gave his to me. "Did Tippy give you anything else?"

"There are limits to what I can tell you, Jackson." He was wearing a light brown pinstripe suit. He was flawless, at least in execution of his wardrobe.

"I thought we had an agreement. Besides, I don't need much, Wardell. I need an idea."

He might have wanted to help me, but he was wrestling with an idea too. Ideas always win.

I decided to let him in on my thinking. "Listen. Tippy had stuff on at least three people. He could have left a letter that said, 'hand it over to the cops and let them sort it out.' Instead, he sends me a letter from the grave."

"Yes," said Wardell. "Nothing there I don't know."

"But why? If he gives it over to the cops, they go after everybody, probably ruin a couple of lives that didn't have anything to do with killing him."

"I'm still not following you.

"But he says in my letter, don't mess with the ones who didn't do it." I made a steeple with my hands. "Why would he say that?"

"Jackson, I have no idea."

"What if he was blackmailing these people?"

"Makes no sense," and I cut him off.

"It makes perfect sense if one of them kills you. Think of it this way. You've got three people on a hook. They are renting your silence, one payment at a time. One of them gets tired of paying rent, and then kills you. If the others are playing along, paying you, you don't give them up. Not if you're honorable."

"If they're being blackmailed, then they have something they don't want known. And besides, blackmailers aren't honorable."

"Yes, true enough. But Tippy has some integrity, let's say. He only wants the killer sapped. The others go free."

"Because they're honorable?" He looked skeptical.

"Because they didn't kill him. It's not about telling the world their story. It's about finding the person who killed him."

Wardell sat, both hands on his coffee cup. He didn't move for a minute, and then he looked up at the ceiling. "This is not what I thought we were signed up for."

"Agreed. We thought there was something straightforward about this. But it's convoluted, Wardell. There's a lot going on here."

"What do we do?"

"My first suggestion is to follow the money. Which means I need to know how much is in his checking account."

"I can't do that, Jackson."

"Wardell, come on. All I want is a number."

He shook his head. "Even if I gave you a number, you wouldn't know if it was the right one. Who says he would even put money like you're talking about in his checking account?"

"All right, then, give me a number from a savings account. Or any other account. You can at least let me know if I'm on the right track."

He took off his eyeglasses and pointed them at me. "I cannot do that. I am an attorney. I am Tippy Taylor's attorney. I will not because I cannot. Ethics precludes it."

"Ethics be damned, Wardell. Tippy's dead and he asked me to find out who did it."

He looked down at the blotter on his desk. It was a rich saddle leather, chocolate brown, and matched the desk accoutrements neatly arrayed within reach. "I am an attorney. It was all I ever wanted to be, and that was because I understood the law as a way to right wrongs. To do justice, you must follow the law and the canon of ethics. If you do not, the good you might do is tainted."

"All you're saying is the ends don't justify the means. But what if you're mistaking ends for means."

He had turned in his chair and looked toward the window. "I know the difference."

"Maybe you don't. Maybe the end here is not to serve the canon of ethics, but to find out who killed Tippy Taylor."

His profile was lit by the sunlight. I could imagine him sitting in judge's robes, a Thurgood Marshall of Davidson County, passing judgment. "What else can I help you with, Jackson?"

I wasn't getting anything out of him about Tippy's finances. Maybe he could help with identifying the suspects. "Is there anything Tippy said that gives you an idea who any of them might be? Could there be another manuscript?"

"He didn't really get along with any of the people in his department. He was sure they thought he was just a flash in the pan. They didn't take him seriously."

I doubted that. Faculty take everyone seriously, especially if they sense a threat. And a black man with a faculty position and a loud voice is very definitely a threat. "What about the women in the department? Did he ever say anything about them?"

"I don't recall his making a distinction between the women and the men. He didn't cotton to any of them."

"Fair enough." It wasn't any help, but there were other ways to figure it out. "What about the mysterious guy in the neighborhood?"

"Could be anybody. Lots of people have guns."

"Not really, Wardell. A guy who's well known. Someone looked up to." I paused.

"All right," he smiled, "Maybe not just anybody. But define what you mean by a leader. Activist? Community organizer? Drug dealer? Somebody in a church?"

"Tippy called him an activist."

"There's more guns on the north side than you can count. I don't doubt half the pastors have one. And before you ask, yes, I have one at home."

I wasn't sure how much of what he was saying was true, and how much of it was that he didn't trust me. Or trust me to understand. "Give me a little something, Wardell. You have to have an opinion."

He straightened a small stack of papers and placed them in a yellow file folder. He pulled a second file folder out of a desk drawer. He looked at his wristwatch. "I have to be at the courthouse in a half hour." He reached below and pulled an attaché case up to the desk, snapped its closures open and put the file inside. Closing it, he crossed his arms on top of it.

"Look. I think your heart is in the right place. And God knows, Tippy thought enough of you, for whatever reason, to entrust you with this task. Maybe he was right to do so. But here's what I think. It's going to be hard for you to move around as you need to and get the answers you want. Maybe on Vanderbilt's campus. Although maybe not. I mean, look at you."

I got it. I didn't fit the model.

"But," he continued, "You will not be able to move invisibly through the north side. You will stand out like a pale white finger on a black hand. And people will not open up to you. In fact, they may actively make it difficult for you." He put his eyeglasses back on. "It may even be dangerous for you."

"Is this a pep talk?"

"I'm trying to be realistic. Even if blackmail were involved, and you have no proof of that, you will have considerable difficulty getting information."

I had no doubt he was telling the truth about that. I didn't think I could get much out of anyone, unless you count Stump Collins and that would be a tit-for-tat exchange. I didn't think I'd get anything without a price there. "Still have to try."

"I suspected you would say that. I admire that. But keep your expectations real. I believe the police, if they cared about a black man in a dumpster, would have a better chance. But they don't care, apparently."

"And I do."

"Yes. And you do."

He rose to leave, and I got up too. "One more question, Wardell?"

"Of course." He was shrugging into his topcoat.

"Was Tippy a user?" The shrugging stopped. "Did he use heroin to your knowledge?"

He reached to the top of his coat rack, took a fedora, and put it on his head. "I don't think he could have been productive, as he was, if that were the case." I told him about the needles, and about the packet at the bus station. "I never saw any indication of it. I can't explain the drugs and paraphernalia, but I would say no. He was not an addict."

"I didn't think so." But what was he? And why did he have things that suggested he was one?

Maybe Art Blake could tell me. He'd seen enough aberrant behavior to know.

Chapter Nine

ART AND I HAD already planned to have lunch away from campus. Despite his history of expelling students and administering discipline, Art was popular among the students. Part of it was the novelty of the handlebar mustache, and part of it was his dry way of snapping off a clever phrase. If we had lunch on campus, we'd have been interrupted every minute by a student.

We went instead to The Gerst Haus, across the river on Woodland. I got barbequed pig knuckles and Art got a pork schnitzel. We both had schooners of the Gerst beer.

I was picking apart the tender meat on the knuckles when Art asked me to tell him about the basement meeting.

"Here's the thing," I said between bites, "Metro was not prepared. I think they believed they would walk in and say how it was going down. But the news is that Stump Collins isn't having it."

He sawed off a sizable piece of the breaded meat. "They'll come around." To my questioning look, he said, "I mean Metro, but really both of them will. This isn't going to happen unless they find a way to cooperate."

My knuckle meat was disappearing faster than I wanted it to. "Won't Collins and his crew just go ahead and stage the protest anyway? It's not like they need Metro."

"If they want a parade and a loud stage, they do. You're right that anyone can show up on campus and wave signs.

But if you want wall-to-wall media coverage, you are going to need a spectacle that spans across town. For that, they'll need Metro."

"Ok," I said, "let's posit that. Why would the city want to provide that opportunity? Don't they really want all this to be as quiet as it can? Don't they want a non-event?"

"Not necessarily. There's a mayoral election next year. If the protest is a mess, or if it just fizzles, the black vote goes somewhere else. Maybe the white vote does too."

"But if the protest is notable and safe?"

"North side is happy. Law and order folks are happy. Police look good, and they're happy. That's the way you get reelected if you're a mayor."

Art had a point. He always had a point.

"What do they want from the University?"

"They were making their demands on Metro," I said, finishing the last of the meat stuck between the bones. "But to tell the truth, I don't think they see much difference between Metro and you."

"Just more white people?"

"At least, just more people not friendly to their way of thinking." I thought about Wardell's warning to me, and about my near trouble several nights before. "They've probably got a point. Nashville's getting a little hot that way."

"Look, Nashville had been like every other Southern city during the 1950s and 1960s, first a bastion of segregation, then a hotbed of ugliness, both big and small, over school integration. There had been a set of lunch counter sit-ins that had led to the bombing of a prominent home, and then to an eventual negotiated settlement where the counters were integrated. And with those victories, and others that were won nationally, there seemed to be progress." He finished the beer and his lecture. "Nashville's always been hot that way."

"Well, it's getting worse. And the Davis Cup isn't helping."

"How are the faculty holding up?"

I laughed. "Thanks for giving me the day off today. It's about as boring a duty as I've ever pulled, military or civilian."

"Learn any new chants?"

"Not a one. There's nothing new. I think it's the same signs every day too."

Blake pushed away from the table. "I've got a two o'clock meeting to discuss the new student handbook. Like to come?"

I stood and left a couple of dollars on the table for a tip. "Even when I worked for you, I wouldn't have gone to that meeting. Even if you told me to go."

"That's because you're not much for rules." He wrote a check for the meal and left it with the waitress. "You are incorrigible, though lately you seem a little better."

"I'm not incorrigible, but you've known some who are. Have you known any who were heroin addicts?"

We walked outside. The spring was waiting on March to get deeper in the calendar before tipping its hand. I pulled my jacket collar up.

"I've known some who quit coming to school, or at least that's what I heard. As you can imagine, it's difficult to stay current in your classes if you're laid out all the time." We got in his Rambler. "Why are you asking?"

"I'm trying to figure out if there's a way an accomplished person could be using."

"Professor Taylor?"

"Tippy. Yes."

We drove across the river and back onto campus in silence.

At the corner where the Beta house was, I said, "Hey, Art. Let me out here and I'll see you later, ok?"

He angled the Rambler in front of a Vanderbilt Police car driven by Don Mercer. Mercer leaned on the horn at the Dean, and Art responded with a long blast of his own. While they were occupied with each other, I got in Mercer's patrol car. Art backed up and headed back toward Branscomb.

"Just what the hell was that about?" Mercer fumed.

"I don't know, Donnie. But that Dean is a scamp."

"What if I was on a call? Or if there was an emergency?"

"What can I say? The Dean is irresponsible."

"And you. You are not supposed to open a patrol car door and jump right in. You're not a police officer."

"You are correct. Are you done now?"

Like I said before, Don Mercer is a vet. Unlike me, he is a cop, and he generally does things by the book.

"Sure. I'm done. I could be done for the rest of the day." He wore the look of fatigued persistence I'd seen on his face before.

"Bad day, huh?" I didn't have to see him agree. "Can I get a favor?"

"Depends. You want a ride to your apartment. Sure. Anything else. Probably not."

"You've got keys to Calhoun Hall, right?"

"You know that I do." He had a key ring the width of a coffee can on his belt.

"I need to get into Tippy Taylor's office." He started to say something, but I interrupted him. "I'm looking for something that Tippy left for me. It's not at his place. It must be in his office."

"I am not letting you into a faculty office."

"Come on, Don. You have the key. You know Tippy and I were friends."

"I don't know anything like that. What I know is that I could get in trouble letting you in there."

"You'll have to let someone in at some point, just to collect his things."

"That might be true. It will not be you." Don was picking a bad time to stand on procedure, and I told him so. "Nope." He put the car into drive but kept his foot on the brake. "You staying or going?"

I opened the door and got out. "Thanks for nothing."

Chapter Ten

SPRING HADN'T AWAKENED YET, but you could see the first shoots of early grass peaking their tips out, and there were premature spikes of daffodil leaves breaking the earth. Soon the place would be a riot of color, but now winter still held sway.

I walked to Calhoun Hall. It was a typical academic building, built in the 1920s with the idea of capturing what academia should look like. All brick, except for an oval stone opening leading to thick wooden doors, the four floors of the building spread in a neoclassical straight line. Economics and Canadian Studies were here, as were numerous classrooms. Here were also housed a few of the History faculty, Tippy among them.

The History faculty were all on the first floor. Willa Winter was there, as were a couple of endowed chairs. Halfway down the hall on the right, next to the water fountain, was a card that read, "Thomas Taylor, MA. Lecturer in History." No mention of office hours. No listing of classes being taught. It was there almost as if he was planting a flag, no other information necessary.

His door was one of those sturdy oak doors that are two inches thick. The original locksets were still there, complete with the small clear glass doorknob, but they no longer served as security. Rather, installed just above the original plate was a newer deadbolt. It would be easy enough to get into, but not while the building was open.

I went to the bookstore to make a purchase, then I walked across to Sarratt Student Center, and took the elevator to the top. The Overcup Oak, VU's student pub, was a convenient enough place to rest until dark. I ordered a beer, and took a campus newspaper, The Vanderbilt Hustler, from the bar.

One beer and five replays of "Margaritaville" later, I retraced my steps to Calhoun. Dusk had settled on the campus, and the last students were migrating back toward the residential parts of campus, either to eat or to go out. They would be back after dinner, but for now I had Calhoun largely to myself.

I extracted the bobby pin set I'd bought at the bookstore and stripped the bulb ends off both. I bent one into an L, inserting it into the deadbolt's key slot. I put a little tension on the L pin, then inserted the other one, unbent. I pulled the unbent one across the pins inside the lock, pushing them outward. I felt most fall on the first try, then got the rest on the second. I knew it was done when I could twist the L pin a little. Then it was just a matter of twisting the bent bobby pin until the cylinder twisted all the way, causing the deadbolt to snap back.

Three minutes and I was in.

As an undergraduate, I'd been in Calhoun offices a few times. Mostly to visit the history folks, but once or twice in Dr. Hayes' office for a Religious Studies course I was taking. Those times, the interiors teemed with books, bowing the boards that held them in old bookcases. One might have a painting he'd picked up in France. Another might have on the wall a flag from some ancient and no-longer existing republic. The effect was always to impress, usually with more than was necessary. Most undergrads, after all, would be impressed, if they were going to be impressed, simply by a tweed jacket and a pipe.

Tippy Taylor's office offered none of that. A poster of Malcolm X adorned one wall, while an advertisement for the March on Washington was taped on the opposite. A short stack of thin paperbacks, likely the texts for his courses, was piled on the edge of the desk. A couple of wire-bound steno notebooks, the kind you used to see everywhere, were there too. I flipped them open. Just some haphazard notes for a lecture.

His desk drawers were locked, but that was a simple matter for my Case pocketknife. Get the center drawer open, and the rest are unlocked. I didn't worry too much about an artful job; Tippy wasn't coming back to complain. I made short work of the lock by making a little gouge at the top of the bolt where I could wedge my blade and pop the lock.

The center drawer was empty, but at the bottom of the upper left drawer was a single manila envelope, taped along all four corners and down each side with heavy packing tape. The opening, where the metal clasp was, had been covered with two layers of the packing tape.

I flipped it over. There, in Tippy's unmistakable handwriting, and marked over twice in what looked like red crayon, was a surprise.

It read: IF FOUND GIVE TO JACKSON TRADE. And it had my address.

I guess I knew the sort of thing that was inside, if I was right about the blackmail. Tippy was a man who'd walked through life with his ears open, maybe ready for the worst, but always with an ear toward the advantageous. And after a lifetime of listening, it was not that hard to believe that he'd found a way to make listening become profitable. If the problem of a black man was knowing the price of living in the world, it was at least as true that knowledge, if you wanted it to be, could become a wealth-making commodity. Especially if you rented it, one month at a time, to the people that didn't want it out in the world.

The only problem with that way of life is that it tends to make the people paying the rent mad. And if they're mad, they don't usually stop with writing a check. They usually want you to stop, and they'll stop you if they have to.

Tippy would have needed some insurance, and that insurance would have taken the form of an envelope, maybe one he bragged about but maybe one that he simply alluded to, that served as leverage to make sure that his marks didn't get mad enough to stop him. The point is to make sure your leverage is sufficient. Usually someone -- a lawyer, another accomplice, even a lonely safe deposit box would do -- housed the proof that the blackmailed couldn't afford to come to light.

And that was what kept the equilibrium. Usually the black-mailed party believed, and the equilibrium was kept. But sometimes, the mark thinks it's worth whatever it takes to break the spell.

I'd guess Tippy told the blackmailed parties about the en-velope, and I've have guessed that they took him at his word. Tippy was nothing if not theatrically efficient. But there had to come a time, at least for one of the marks, that he or she had enough.

And I'd guess that Tippy knew that, knew that the moment had come, whether before the person who shot at him or afterward, that he needed to put his envelope together. He knew, whether he wanted to or not, that the person who'd decided to sweat, who'd decided it was worth it to try to kill Tippy, had to be held accountable.

So Tippy made the envelope.

The question was why, if that was what this was, Tippy had made the misdirection to his bus station locker and the incomplete manuscript. Why do that? Why run me in that direction if this was where he wanted me to end up?

And so the first thing I looked at, when I opened the en-velope back at my apartment, was the letter. Like the one Wardell Robinson had given me, it was typed, and carefully edited. You could see a few small traces of Wite-Out on the sheet. Whatever you could say about Tippy Taylor, he was a man who wanted to leave a clean record behind.

Hey, Jackson,

Whether you got this because it was part of my effects, or whether you did what I thought you'd do and broke into my office, no problem. You got it now.

You've read the manuscript. You can see what shit I'm stirring up. And some of that could get me killed. Don't doubt it.

But you need to know that I've been mixed up in some other things, some things not in my department. You'd think Canadian Studies would be the sort of department where cool-headedness, and not cold-bloodedness, would reign supreme.

You'd be wrong.

I've got three little dossiers inside this envelope. Each one is coded, and you can find the code in the manuscript. I've done that in case somebody gets this besides you. I don't need nobody getting into this stash who ain't trying to solve my murder. Unless you got the code, won't none of it make sense.

Here's the thing, Jackson. Like I said, if somebody hit me, it's one of these. There's a chance it's somebody in the manuscript, but these three were the ones I had the hook in.

No matter who it is, Jackson, I want you to nail them. I don't want the police to get this. All they'll do is line them all up and blow up the newspapers. Only one of them killed me. The rest played fair, by the rules of my game. They don't deserve to be in the papers.

One of them, though.

I also don't want Wardell to do this. He's too stiff, too cut and dried. He's like the police. In his mind, they'll all go down, and rightfully so.

But you, my brother, you know that there's a right way and a wrong way. And you know the right way is twisted.

I wish I could help you more. But if I'm dead, it's because I couldn't help myself. So how can I help you?

If you found the locker key, and you have the manuscript, you will read where there is a second locker key. In that locker is five grand. It's most of what I've scored from blackmailing these three fine upstanding folks this year. That's your pay, brother.

Find my killer.

Tippy.

PS: If you have been in my apartment and the bus locker, you know about my little hobby. Don't think of me as an addict. I'm not. I just like my high from time to time. Maintenance was all it was, brother.

Everyone has a moment when they commune with the dead. I've had it happen in the middle of a dark night, when the boys I served with in Vietnam come to me and speak in their voices, strong and clear as they were back then. I have heard my brother's voice, and my sister's, when I was walking down the street, or when I thought of times growing up, times standing in a tobacco field, the summer sun baking us.

And there are times when you don't commune with the dead, but you hear them, clearly, and you wonder what it was that made their voice come to you, choose you. When you wonder, for God's sake, what you are supposed to do?

And there are moments when you hear the voice of the dead, no longer dead for a moment, alive just for that second, and you believe that they are there with you. Just for a moment, a second that cries out itself, authentically, with no ambiguity.

"That's your pay, brother. Find my killer."

I cracked the office door and looked outside. Nothing. Not even a stray undergraduate looking for a classroom to study in. I took my prizes and walked away from the office, trying to look like I belonged there.

Just as I reached the center of the hallway, right in front of the exit, I heard my name called. At least, part of it.

"You there. Mr. Jackson." It was a female voice, a little unsure of itself. I turned to see Willa Winter stopped there. "I thought so."

Great.

Chapter Eleven

To say she ran toward me would be to overstate her speed, but she covered ground quickly enough that she was facing me before I knew it. "Why are you everywhere?"

She had an armful of books. Glasses perched on her head like owl eyes.

"I said, why are you everywhere I go? I've become used to your being on the Kirkland plaza. But Calhoun Hall?" She pulled the eyeglasses down and looked at me. "If I were paranoid, you would be positively frightening."

"Are you paranoid?"

"I said, 'if.' You don't frighten me. You annoy me, and I don't like that."

"Why do I annoy you?"

"Good question. I don't like not knowing the answer."

"I bet you're the sort of person who always knows the answers."

"Here." She handed the stack of books to me, and then pulled the eyeglasses into position. "Walk just a minute with me."

"Where are we going?"

"Just to my office. I'm tired of carrying those and you look perfectly capable."

"I barely know you, Dr. Winter. Making me carry your books at school seems a little forward." I shot her a glance to make sure she was taking it in the spirit it was intended.

She was.

"It is much easier to be sure you are not going to do something inappropriate if your hands are occupied."

"I beg your pardon."

She stopped, just for a second, then continued walking. "I do not mean that," and she blushed a little. "I assure you."

"Then what? If you don't mean that I would get handsy with you?"

"You are an unknown actor, as it were. For all I know you have bad intentions. You could have a weapon."

"If I had a weapon, I doubt these books would be a deterrent. And I'm no less annoying whether I'm carrying them or not."

We arrived at her office. She opened the door for me. "Just put them on that table over there."

I did as she asked. "You're supposed to be a big hire for this department. At least that's what I'm told."

"I'm like every junior faculty member in America. I need to do the things that will get me tenure. Until that happens, I'm as big-time as you."

"That can't be true. You were in the magazine."

"That only increases expectations. I would have preferred it not happen."

There it was. Underneath all the bravado and fierce posturing, she was afraid she wouldn't make it. "Anything else you need from me?"

She put the eyeglasses back on her head. She could do that a lot more. She was good looking with them. She was stunning without them, for some reason. "Tell me the truth. What are you really up to?"

Until I could decipher Tippy's message, I didn't really know, and I wasn't about to tell her. "I'm up to about 6-2." She sighed and shook her head. "Sorry. Just being a smart ass."

"You're not going to tell me. Goodbye, Mr. Jackson."

"It's Trade. Jackson Trade. And I can't tell you what I don't know, Dr. Winter. I'm not up to anything."

Her look told me she knew I was lying.

I did what Tippy told me. I correlated the manuscript with the code. I found the second locker key. Then I found the $5000 and the blackmail information. Easy as pie, once you owned all the right clues. I put the money in the bank, then made it my business to get to know his targets.

And, as Tippy said, there was something rotten in one department: the department of Canadian Studies.

The dossiers were impressive. Watkins LaSalle was a high flyer in the world of Canadian Studies. He had gone to Europe for a second doctorate and postdoctoral work, at the University of Bologna, in Italy, the world's oldest university. He had traveled far and wide across the globe, making a reputation as a scholar of Canadian immigration.

The only problem, which Tippy had documented, was that he had never gone to the University of Bologna. It had served as the launching pad for his entire career, and it was based on a complete fabrication. Tippy had the goods, a letter from the university registrar documenting that no one had ever heard of Watkins LaSalle at the University of Bologna.

Sure, he had a doctorate from the University of Toronto, and for Canadian Studies that was likely sufficient, but the lie was trouble. His tenure would have been called into question. The chance of his becoming elected chair if this became known? Zero.

His lie was foolish in the extreme.

The material on Irma Beddington took less detection, perhaps, but was more graphic. The pictures alone might not have been enough. The light in whatever motel the assignation happened were inferior to Hollywood's. There were a couple of four-by-five color prints and half a dozen clips of 8-millimeter tape that Tippy, no Hollywood producer, mostly butchered.

And even that might not have been enough for a good blackmail. A lot of folks find themselves, sometime in their lives, doing things once that they might not ever do again.

But Tippy had done his homework, for sure, and he'd documented the trail of Professor Beddington as she'd bedded her lover from one motel to the next, all over Nashville. Presumably to keep from developing a pattern. The problem was, of course, that once Tippy knew something was happening, he didn't need a pattern. He just needed to be following.

He went from one place to the next, although Dr. Beddington and her consort had a preference for places on the west side and south, nothing expensive but nothing that dangerous like the ones near the truck stops. There was one time when they almost got caught by the manager, in flagrante delicto as it were, but even then they weren't in any trouble. They were just lovers. Only Tippy knew it was a problem.

The problem was that Dr. Beddington was the chair of the tenure and promotion committee in Canadian Studies, and one of the only women who might be up for Associate Provost when the time came. But when the time came, if someone spilled the Beddington beans, becoming Associate Provost, or continuing as Chair of Promotion and Tenure, or even being employed, might get a little problematic.

Wes Willougby was a different matter altogether. He was a new Ph.D. He had a couple of years to go before he came up for tenure, and frankly, as someone with a Ph.D. from a middling regional university, he might have had fewer prospects than others.

He was a climber, though, and he wanted it pretty bad. He was active on committees. He had a book contract from Oxford University Press and was making progress on his manuscript. He presented regularly at the best conferences. And he gave his teaching enough attention so the administrators weren't going to pitch him on account of that.

But Tippy was connected still to the Army, and he somehow got wind that Willoughby had what we called a big chicken dinner. A BCD. A Bad Conduct Discharge.

They give those to soldiers who do bad things. Like shoot up a village.

And that appeared to be what Willoughby had done. Sometime in 1967, somewhere near Khe Sahn, Captain Wesley Willoughby had snapped, or he had been ordered, to cleanse a village in order to save it, as they used to say. At least that was the report. And whatever the report said, what it didn't say was what had led up to the incident.

I knew. It could have been a reaction to some action by Viet Cong. Or it could have been a reaction to an attack by "villagers" who were VC. Or it could have been a moment, fueled by Benzedrine or by something harder, something that made a captain lose his mind and go off.

It could have been anything. But whatever it was, it got him shitcanned. Got him a Bad Conduct Discharge. The big chicken dinner.

And he'd come back stateside. Somehow, he'd pulled it all together, did an MA in history at Ryerson and a PhD with a dissertation on the religious demographics of draft evaders in Canada. Then he had landed at Vanderbilt.

And no one knew his history, apparently, although how that slipped through a background check was anyone's guess. Hell, I once took off for a weekend with a girl named Eloise Wells and, by the time we got back, everybody in Nashville knew.

But nobody knew about Wes Willoughby until Tippy Thomas did. And that was a serious thing for a young up and coming scholar who needed tenure.

So it seemed that Tippy Thomas, history lecturer ensconced in Calhoun Hall, knew enough about the Canadian Studies department to have garnered a second income from the knowledge.

The question was, as he had put it, who did the crime?

Chapter Twelve

I WALKED OVER TO Hannigan's as dusk settled into evening. It was one of those nights that, when I was an undergrad, always felt like a long night studying was in the cards. There was something due, maybe two things coming due. Both of them were extra difficult. And there was nothing you could do but apply the mental energy to putting them right. Anything else, and you'd be staring down the barrel of more work later. Because the way it works is this: better get your work done today because tomorrow's work is already loaded in the chute. You were like a bull rider on an endless set of bulls. You always had to get up and ride the next one.

My life now was a succession of bull rides into the night. Most of them were bullshit rides, where I'd take my spot at Hannigan's, then ride something at the Top Hat, before spinning a stool at the High Life. And if it was a real long night, you could find me closing Linda's. Anywhere along the line you could get thrown, but I was a great bull rider. I almost never fell off the stool.

Tonight was one of those. I had a big test coming with Tippy's murder, and I was ready to hit the studying hard.

I started at Hannigan's to fuel up. Nothing fancy. Just a massive cheeseburger with fries and a couple of beers. Charlie asked me if I had plans for this night.

"Just gonna observe the inner workings of my mind, man."

"Sounds like you're gonna be tripping."

"Only trips I take are up and down the street, Charlie. But my mind goes all over the place."

After Hannigan's, I ended up at the Top Hat. It's classier than my usual haunts, with white linen tablecloths and nice flatware, but it's in a terrible spot for the restaurant business. Too far from campus for a walking date, but not enough parking, except the meters on the street, to pull in a good business from everywhere else. So despite the nice digs and decent ambition, it was always quiet, and it was a place where I could have a couple of really silent drinks.

At least, that's what I tried to do. The waiter was a guy who looked like a graduate student in some subject where you'd never get a job. He had hair the length of mine, pulled back in a ponytail, and he'd given the good old college try at a beard, which ended up being a patchwork affair.

"Another bourbon?"

"Just one. Then I have to scoot."

He lingered. "Big night planned?"

It was a weekday. "Nothing big about it."

"You seem like you've got plans. Do you have plans?"

He was either mindlessly inquisitive or annoyingly nosy. I gave him a look that leaned toward the latter. When he didn't move, I gave in. "I have no more plans than to find another bar and continue drinking."

"You could drink here."

"At the other bars I don't have to tip. Here," I waved my hands expansively, "you have rent to pay, and you, presumably, took the job for tips. I feel obligated."

He made the OK sign with his finger and thumb. "That's cool, man. Tips are fine. But you seem like a guy who'd be more comfortable with a quiet place, maybe a little music, a little conversation here and there."

It occurred to me that he might be trying to pick me up. Or he might just have been desperate to keep a paying customer in the Top Hat. "Tell you what. Bring me another bourbon and I'll think about it.

He did, and I didn't. When he was in the back I finished off the bourbon, and left a couple of singles on the table.

It was a good tip. And it was probably a tip to him that I was going my own way under my own steam.

Two city blocks up, on the other side of the street, was the High Life. This was where the bull riding would get serious, even on a weekday night, because even on a weekday night the High Life had business until 2.

I know all the bartenders at the High Life and they all know me. Their names are all "Bud," as in, "Hey, Bud, gimme a Pabst," and they all know my name, as in, "You got it, Slick."

They don't know much else, except I am allowed to run a tab, just as at Hannigan's, because I can win more on the money pinball than they've got in the till most nights. So they do know my real name, and they do know that when I get close to running out my tab, I'll head over to the Grand Casino machine and crank out a couple hundred dollars in free games.

The owner isn't that happy about it, but the bartenders don't care. They just have to keep an accurate record.

It was a pretty quiet night for the High Life. The juke box was making the rounds, which means that at least three or four different hands had pumped quarters in, and the jukebox was being diplomatic in the way it played the favorites. Somebody was Outlaw, so there was a Willie and Waylon and Tompall part of the rotation. Somebody else was a traditionalist, and so there was some Patsy Cline and some Merle Haggard. And some fool had played at least a dollar's worth of "Rhinestone Cowboy," so it came up every second or third song.

Some nights are like that.

I sat in the back corner booth when Mercer came in, got a draft, and sat down.

"You park your bike out on the street?" Don always does, even though it makes him nervous. And that's the reason he usually sits at the bar, so he can keep an eye on it.

"Not tonight. Chet dropped me off. He's got to go feed his dog before he pulls his second shift, so I am just in for a beer."

"A single beer." I pushed the empty PBR to the side and started on the next one.

"You are taking them two at a time, it would seem. Any reason?"

"Celebration, man."

"And what's are you celebrating?"

"I got a paycheck today."

"Didn't know you were working anything except Blake's gig. And I figure that doesn't pay shit."

I took a long pull. "I was paid in front. Got to figure out a puzzle. Kind of like a long final exam."

"You get more money if you figure it out?"

"Nope. Got the money in front. Doesn't matter if I figure it out or not. Got the money no matter what."

Mercer gave me a quizzical grin. "You get the money even if you don't figure it out? Even if you don't try to figure it out?"

"That's the deal, my man. Got the money in front." I finished the beer in a single gulp.

Mercer got up and tossed the last of his draft down. "Damn, Jackson. That's the kind of job you need to teach me how to get."

"That's if you want it man. It comes with some other shit that doesn't seem much fun."

"But you don't have to do it. You can just take the money."

That was the problem, of course. There was no way I could just take the money.

I spotted a familiar face coming out of the back room where the pool tables were. He went to the bar and got another beer. I motioned with my cup toward him. "There's the dink that is Willa Winter's lap dog."

Mercer nodded. "Looks a little too big to be a lap dog to me. More like a lap moose."

"Either way, he's clearly starry eyed. She wrote a book. She uses big words. She's so smart."

"More like, she's a fox. As in, foxy lady."

"Sure. There's that too."

When the moose turned away from the bar and saw me, he grinned, the kind of grin a slightly drunk guy grins. He walked toward us and towered over the table. "I saw you in Calhoun Hall tonight."

"That so?" I had to figure he saw me leaving Willa's office. He didn't figure to be tailing me.

"Yeah, that's so. What's your deal, man?" He wasn't slurring his words exactly, but he wasn't stone cold sober either.

Mercer stood as if to leave, but the undergrad stepped the wrong way accidentally. At least I think it was an accident. He backed up. Two little steps. Then halted. The beer sloshed over the rim of his plastic cup.

"You've probably had about enough tonight." Mercer was dressed in his jeans and flannel shirt, and was the only black guy in the place. He looked around. "You recognize me, right? I recognize you."

The moose peered at him, but he already knew. You could tell. "You're a campus cop."

"He's the campus cop," I said. "Lieutenant Mercer. Be nice to him and he'll be nice to you."

"Campus cops are bullshit." He looked over at Mercer. "No offense."

"None taken. But you still have had enough."

The moose drained the cup in one gulp. "Fine. I was leaving anyway." He half strode, half flounced toward the street door. "I'd still like to know exactly what your deal is," he said over his shoulder. "But that's all right." He kept talking to himself all the way out the door. I saw him turn on foot toward campus.

"Don't you wish you were twenty-one again, Don."

"No way in hell. I was in 'Nam when I was that age. You were too."

"I was younger. But we were both carrying M-16s and looking for the enemy. This one? He's carrying a torch and looking for trouble."

"With a few beers in him," Mercer said. "He's a dime a dozen down the street."

"Lap moose." I laughed. "That's an image I can't get out of my head, Don."

"Glad to help." He took his leather jacket off the seat and headed toward the exit himself. "Spend all that money wisely, Jackson."

I waved. I didn't intend to spend anything for a while. I was going to keep it on the straight and narrow until I found Tippy's killer. And maybe for Stump too, if he really needed my help.

I had one more for the road.

Chapter Thirteen

IT'S NOT THAT OFTEN that I go inside a grocery store. I can find most of my food at Hannigan's, Krystal, or IHOP. And truth be told, I don't much care, most of the time, what goes inside my body. It's just fuel. It just has to get me by.

But I do need staples like Folger's Instant Coffee and a couple of cartons of cigarettes. I sometimes have a wild hair and pick up a bag of little green apples, but they tend to go bad before I get through the whole thing.

But like I say, I do need to make the occasional trip to the A & P and roll through the aisles in a random way, looking at things I know I don't need so I can decide not to buy them.

The next day found me there in the morning. I had scraped the last of instant coffee out of the jar, and I knew I was a pack or two away from needing more Luckies. There was nothing for it except to do my duty.

I was rounding the corner into the coffee and tea aisle when I saw her. Betty Henderson. Former good friend and one time, and one time only, lover. That was on me. I'd behaved like a cad -- I guess: that's a word I know from literature -- and she'd quite properly shown me the door.

And once shown the door, you don't have to show it to me again. I know when it's closed.

But there she stood, a tin of tea in each hand, looking from one to the other, trying to figure out which to buy. She looked good, as she always did. Jeans and a t-shirt, with a denim jacket and little strappy sandals. Her hair was pulled up, like she'd just said "to hell with it" and left the house. To tell you the truth, she couldn't have looked better.

I was prepared to back quietly out of the aisle and avoid her. As I did, though, I got poked in the butt by a shopping cart piloted by an old lady. "Hey, watch where you're going." She had a cane sitting in the cart, and her hand went toward it. I don't know if she thought she would need to knock me out of the way or not, but it didn't seem advisable to argue. I tried to make a quiet apology and retreat.

But it was too late. The commotion had caused Betty to turn and see what was happening. Or rather, to whom it was happening.

"Jackson Trade." Her voice cut through the morning quiet of the A & P. "Are you bothering that woman?"

"He wasn't watching where he was going." The old lady had a loud voice too. Didn't either of them grow up in a house? They were using their outside voices.

"He is careless that way. If you don't watch him like a hawk, there is no telling what he'll do."

She muttered something under her breath. "Well, I hope not to have to watch him at all once I get past him." I moved to the side, careful to keep her in my sights. I didn't like the odds if I got brained by her cane.

"I am sorry. I didn't see you."

"Sorry is what he always says, ma'am. There is literally nothing he can't be sorry about."

The old lady coolly regarded me, then apparently decided that I was not worth much notice as long as I let her pass. She made some kind of dismissive noise with her lips and went on by.

Betty walked up to me. She had both tins still in her hands. Given the way our last conversation had gone, it was entirely likely she would throw one, or both, at me.

"Hi, Betty. Been a while."

She put both arms down. Honestly, the months that had passed had not made me think any less of her as a friend, even though I'd been insensitive. I should have called her. I should have tried to make amends. But life has its demands. It had demanded a good bit from me.

"Hello, Jackson." She smiled, her pale pink lipstick matching the nail polish she wore. "You come for the special?"

"I don't even know what the special would be. I'm not much for cooking."

"You never were. You were much better at other things. But as I recall you never turned down food."

"True. How've you been?"

"I've been ok. Sold a song to Tammy Wynette." She was a songwriter, trying to make it in Nashville. I always thought she was better suited for Memphis, had more that kind of vibe.

"Congratulations." I didn't know what else to say.

She'd been an important, but fleeting part of my life. She was the superintendent of an apartment building where a Vanderbilt coed was murdered. I met her when I was nosing around the case. She'd been an excellent ear and sounding board, and then a friend. And then, once, a lover. All that came rushing back to me, and it paralyzed my vocal cords.

"I've missed you being around." She folded her arms, the two tea tins now reversing sides of her body. "I sorta thought you'd call."

"That was the problem, remember? I didn't call. I just showed up." I shifted my weight. Being backed up against the vegetable oil, first by the old lady and now by Betty, wasn't the most comfortable position to be in. "I got the feeling that I had overstayed my welcome."

"You did. I was very angry at you."

"Like I said then, you had a right."

"But you just disappeared off the side of the earth." She didn't change expression, but her voice changed. "If you didn't want to fight for it, that's one thing."

"I just didn't want to fight at all."

"I think you have to fight for what you want. I was willing to."

"Don't take this the wrong way. All it seemed like you wanted to fight was me. I got it. I was wrong."

"Jackson." She put the tins on the shelving behind me. She crossed her arms now, in an attitude that wasn't angry but was certainly challenging. "I know you've got issues. We all do. But we can be friends." She uncrossed her arms again and smiled. "We should be friends."

"Maybe I should have called."

"Or maybe I should have. Either way," she reached out her hand, "friends?"

I took it. "Friends." I moved away from the Wesson Oil. "Again."

I found my Folgers and slid out two cartons of Luckies from the cigarette display. I stood behind a woman in the checkout line. When she turned, I saw that it was Willa Winter. At approximately the same moment, she looked at me. There was a brief confusion, and then she saw it was me.

"Again?"

"Look, it's not a big city. And it's really not a big neighborhood."

"I can go days without seeing my next-door neighbor. I see you every day." I couldn't tell if she was flustered or angry.

I had just made a new start with Betty. Maybe I needed to do that with Willa. I put my coffee and cigarette cartons on the shelf next to the conveyor belt. The checkout clerk looked at the two of us like we were a TV show playing out in front of her.

"Listen, Willa. I thought about what you said last night. About how I annoy you."

"About why I don't know why you annoy me." The clerk shook her head and went back to ringing up Willa's groceries. We weren't that interesting after all.

"It's because I have pretty consistently tried to annoy you." Her eyebrows lifted, and just as quickly her face went back to normal. Pretending surprise. Sarcastically. "I know. Big surprise. But I shouldn't have given you such a hard time."

She took the mid-sized paper bag and held it in the crook of her elbow. "People, and by that I mean generally my colleagues, annoy me without trying. I shouldn't have let you get to me."

The clerk rang up my coffee and cigarettes, and I paid her. "So, let's hit reset on this, okay?" I took my bag and rolled the top, then held out my hand. "Start over?"

She hesitated but shook my hand. "Starting over." She smiled, just a small one but it felt significant. "I know I can be a bit stuffy at first." We began to walk toward the front doors. She turned to go to the right. My path took me to the left. "I still do not know how I end up seeing you everywhere. Still seems like you're up to something."

I resisted the impulse to be a smart-ass again. "Probably just the weird end of statistics. I bet you don't see me again for several weeks. It'll average out."

"Hm. I doubt that. Because you will certainly be at Kirkland the next time I'm there. Won't you?"

"You never know, Willa."

Chapter Fourteen

IT MADE FOR A pleasanter than expected morning, but it wasn't long before I had left the Betty Henderson section of my brain for the Tippy Taylor part. It was a far larger part just now.

About three-thirty that afternoon I sat in the reception area of the Department of Canadian Studies. To say it was a reception area glorifies it. It was an office, crowded by file cabinets and a desk, staffed by a harried looking woman in her forties. Streaks of gray rifled through her black hair, the result, I'd guess, of too many unreasonable demands by too many entitled professors. At least, that's what her tightly pursed lips told me.

"Is he expecting you?"

"No. I don't think Professor LaSalle has any idea who I am."

"Then let me take your name and number and I'll let you know when. Or if. He's a very busy man."

"I think he'll see me."

"He never sees anyone. Even students have to make appointments."

"Not very student friendly, if you ask me." She pursed her lips tighter. "Tell him that I'm here on behalf of Tippy Taylor."

"The dead professor in History?"

"One and the same. Tell him that Tippy and I are in the same business."

She gave me a puzzled look, her eyebrows somehow managing to knit together and rise at an absurd angle. "Just a minute."

She walked down the hall and returned about three minutes later with a different version of the puzzled look, this one accentuated by wrinkles on her forehead, surprised. "He says you can go in. Room 342."

His office was one of the corner ones, larger and with two windows. The rich sunlight of a Vanderbilt afternoon streamed in. He had the requisite number of books, arrayed like a border around his office, punctuated here and there by paintings and pictures of places far away. The older wood of the floor was covered by an Oriental rug, probably worth more than everything in my apartment.

I had seen his picture in the yearbook. He had a leonine head of hair and a beard cut carefully to emphasize his lion-like intent. His hands were the sort that had not seen manual work, perhaps ever. The nails were carefully manicured and his hands were a rich olive tan, the sort of color you get from the ease of sitting in the sun, not from working in it. His face in the yearbook was one of calm and effortless superiority.

Now, though, his face showed a more interrogatory look. He looked like he was considering whether he should invite me to take a chair. In the end, he didn't, so I sat down.

I looked at him as he opened a gilt cigarette case and carefully lit a cigarette. "I don't understand what Mrs. Davis just told me."

"I'm an associate of Tippy Taylor. Not that hard to understand."

"You are not on the History faculty. I certainly know all of them. Besides you do not look even like a graduate student."

"I might differ on that last point, Dr. LaSalle, but you're right. I'm not employed here."

"Then how you are an associate of Mr. Taylor's, I cannot fathom." His voice was a baritone devoid of any clutter. It was rich, as if he had cultured it from a young age. No accent of any kind. I imagine undergraduates experienced it, if they experienced it as he wished, as the voice from beyond. Maybe God's voice.

"Tippy and I did business together."

"What kind of business? Mr. Taylor taught as far as I know. And wrote letters to the editor."

"Just the sort of business you get into in the neighborhood. Nothing like you." I motioned toward the bookshelves. "Very successful, I would say. Maybe top of your field, right?"

He let himself give the slightest preen. "I am respected in my field. That is what one wishes for. To be respected."

"Lots of articles. A book or two. That sort of thing?"

"Yes, those go some way toward a reputation. They most certainly do. And peer reviewed. All of them." He was quite pleased. He twirled the cigarette a little between his index and middle finger.

"Must pay pretty well. Not like at the law school or the med school. But you must make a good living."

He looked at me blankly.

"Reputation," I continued. "Yes, that's the coin of the realm in academia. That's what I wanted to talk with you about."

"I beg your pardon?"

"Mr. Taylor, as you call him, was quite reputable in his own way."

"Not to be rude, but he was a rabble rouser. He really did not belong at Vanderbilt, though no one would say it, then or now."

"And yet, he had certain undeniable skills."

"I wish you'd come to the point."

I got up and walked over to the north wall, where he had hung all his diplomas and certificates. "Undergraduate degree from Penn. Very nice. Took your Masters degree at Stanford. Are they a big deal in Canadian Studies?"

"No, but they are a very big deal in economics. That is my area. Specializing in Canadian political economy."

"Makes sense. Where is your doctoral degree?"

"I have two. One from the University of Toronto. Another from the University of Bologna. In Italy."

"Is your diploma at the dry cleaners? It doesn't seem to be here."

"See here, Mr. . . . "

"Trade. My name is Jackson Trade."

"See here, Mr. Trade. I don't have time to waste. What is your point?"

"Reputation." I ran my hand along the books on one of his bookshelves. "The kind of reputation that makes one man a respected scholar and another a laughingstock."

"I know all about that."

"Then you can imagine what it might be like to lose it."

We locked eyes. He betrayed little in the look he gave me. I doubted he ever played poker, but if he did, I don't think his face would have been a problem.

"What sort of associate of Mr. Taylor's were you?"

"Tippy was a collector of sorts. We collect the same kinds of things. Things that were out of place. Things that were uncomfortable. You know what I mean?"

"I don't. Really, I don't." The poker face continued in force.

"Tippy Taylor had some papers he'd picked up along the way. Some of them had your name on them. The important ones didn't. I thought maybe you'd like to purchase them."

There was silence between us. I gave the bookshelf another pass with my hand, and moved back toward the chair to take a seat. As I did, he got up and walked to the door. He locked it, and retraced his steps, back to his desk.

He sat and leaned back in his chair, looking at the ceiling. "So you want to pick up where he left off?"

"In a manner of speaking."

"I tried to tell Taylor this. All this," he said indicating the office, "is ephemeral. I've bought it over time. Some I've acquired from adoring students. I do not make a great deal of money."

"You do all right."

"Doing all right, as you put it, does not mean you can be bled by someone. Just enough might become not nearly enough."

"You've got more than just enough. And you've got your reputation. For now."

He leaned quickly forward and pointed a tanned finger at me. "I've worked hard for that reputation. You have no idea. A man like you would hardly understand the torture of the academic life, the difficulty. I have given everything for my success. For my reputation."

"How bad could it be, LaSalle? You spend your days and nights studying the thing you love. Your life is a passion project. How could that be torturous?"

He could not contain himself. He nearly jumped out of his chair and began pacing. "Passion? Yes, I have passion. But the scholarly life is lonely. You are the only one who can do the work. And you dare not share it before it's finished. You can't have others beat you to publication. And publication is everything. Publish or perish? Ha! Publish repeatedly or perish ignobly." He had worked himself into a lather.

"Reputation. What would it mean to lose it?"

He slammed his fist on the desk. "I will not lose my reputation. I've have worked too hard, too long for it."

"And I am offering you a way to keep your reputation."

"What is that? Are you just taking over for Taylor, now that he'd dead?"

"Depends. What was the number?"

"I beg your pardon?"

"What were you paying Tippy?"

"I thought you were in business together."

"On other things. Not on this. I'm just taking over the franchise."

"I see." He considered whether telling me the truth was the right thing to do. He decided. "I gave him five hundred dollars a month."

"See? That's not that much. Not to keep your reputation intact."

"It's not that easy, Trade."

"Sure it is. You just write a check, and it's done."

"And that's what you propose? How do I know you have anything? Maybe Taylor just told you something some night in a drunken conversation. Maybe you don't have anything."

"Perhaps if I told you that the Dean of Studies at Bologna is Dr. Emilio Ruggeri, and that I have a certified letter from him attesting that no one named Watkins LaSalle ever matriculated there. For a doctorate or for any other reason."

"I can't keep doing this." He sat back down. "It's not the money." His head found his hands. "Well, it is the money, but it's the stress. I cannot do my work. My classes are suffering. And I'm to become chair of the department. This is really too much."

"I guess you shouldn't have falsified a credential. Falsified an important credential."

"I was in Italy. I came under the tutelage of the chief of staff to the Canadian ambassador. I learned more in four years there than any degree could have given me." He looked up. His eyes wanted to plead with me, but he couldn't lower himself to that. "I am more knowledgeable, more qualified than any of my colleagues."

"If the degree doesn't matter, why not just let it be known? Do that, and the fact has no power over you? More important, I have no power over you then."

"You know full well that I cannot do that."

I might have found a way to pity him if he hadn't been so superior. As it was, I had no doubt that it was his condescension that had driven Tippy to find out something, anything on him.

Tippy, after all, had lived history. His lived history had tried to kill him, both here and in Vietnam. And in fact, someone had killed him. No wonder he might find a man so condescending, so smug, so very worth blackmailing, and not for the money even, but just to watch him squirm.

I got it. I really got it.

"Where do we go from here?" LaSalle was relenting, just for the moment. "What do you want from me?"

"I'll get back to you."

"How much, Trade?"

"We'll figure it out. Like I said, you might want to own the property outright."

"How could I possibly trust you? You might have made copies of everything."

"We'll figure it out, LaSalle." I got up, walked to the door, and unlocked it. "Next time, I'll just knock. Next time, you'll let me in."

Chapter Fifteen

I HAD MADE AN appointment to meet Irma Beddington at Hannigan's right after the dinner rush subsided. From LaSalle's office I went to the Hideaway for a couple, then made my way down Elliston to Hannigan's where I had a cheeseburger with fries and nursed a beer. The place was louder than usual because some Dekes were celebrating somebody's birthday, but they had other places to be, which is to say the keg was being delivered to the fraternity house.

In between I'd stopped at West End Methodist and went around back where the entrance to the gym was. I'd come there as an undergraduate, sometimes to play basketball and sometimes just to watch the theater, or rather the drama, of young men playing out their fantasies on a hardwood court.

I'd played enough in high school that I never embarrassed myself. But I was of middling height at 6-2, and of wiry but not particularly powerful frame, so that my game mostly consisted to getting the ball to the guys who could really do some damage.

Now, I can't even do that reliably, so I come to hear the shoes squeak on the court, see the ballet that happens when an inspired young man suddenly realizes that the move in his head has just played out in real life. When that happens, it really is a thing to behold. It is the one thing in life that really passes for beauty, and that's why I come in.

I don't come in to pray. I've got nobody to pray for and nobody to pray for me. Besides, that's in the other part of the building.

But it's the perfect place to sit and think and puzzle the world a little. If that's praying, then so be it. I sat and thought about Watkins LaSalle and his conundrum. The problem of reputation. The thoughts didn't come in orderly fashion, and if I'm honest, I don't think there was an original one there. If he'd been a poker player, I'd have been suspicious. But he seemed completely honest about his little ruse and the price he had paid so far for it.

Then again, if he'd been tough enough to put Tippy in a dumpster, he was more than clever enough to fool me.

Still, I had trouble seeing him as the murderer. For one, it was way too coarse a matter for him to get into. Those finely manicured hands, devoid of any mark of work, were a perfect instance of that. Plus, once having given in to a shortcut and paid for it, a few extra credentials would make the hornswoggling over a degree he didn't have seem a trifle. He could get a post doc on the strength of who he was perceived to be. Probably even in Ottawa with the Prime Minister. Tippy didn't have so much on him as he thought.

But that's the power of blackmail. The person being blackmailed thinks the information is catastrophic. If you just let it out, say that it's fine if the world knows it, all the power of the blackmailer disappears.

That's the way it works.

So, to me, he had a way out, if he wanted it. And he had no particular motive for killing Tippy, other than getting out from under the $500 a month.

Like I said, he didn't seem the type. Unless there was more to it than Tippy had told me from the grave.

Three professors of Canadian Studies. All of them in hock, information wise, to Tippy, and one of them did him in. Find my killer, bro. Yeah, one of them did it. But which one?

And I really didn't want to follow this trail. For one, I had enough of a troublesome gig with the Davis Cup protests. Art Blake had given me a lifeline, financially, but he'd also put me on the edge of something that might get out of hand. You could argue that with 25,000 protesters coming for Vanderbilt, it was already out of hand. It was certainly enough to keep my hands full.

And there was Stump. He was going to come calling at some point. Stay ready, Freddy, he had said.

For another, though, I was nosing around after three people, at least one of whom had the ability to get very nasty. Tippy was someone who could handle himself. He ended up underneath rotten vegetables. That's not a place I wanted to be. Metro could do a lot better job of all this, if they had the interest. The department could put some resources on this case, maybe turn up alibis, put people under the bright lights and interrogate the hell out of them. With these three, that would be enough to blow the thing wide open.

But Tippy had been insistent in the way that dead men can be. He didn't want them all ruined. Two of them played by the rules. Two of them had kept their parts of the bargain. There was no need to decimate the Canadian Studies department because one person got carried away.

I could have given it to Metro anyway, arguing that they all had done something bad, got caught, and had been paying to keep it quiet. A liar about the one thing that got him his job, another liar, at least by omission, who couldn't have got the job if his secret were known, and a woman who was sleeping with a lover all over town.

And you know what? I didn't give a shit about any of them. Maybe Tippy felt like he owed two of them the silence they'd paid for. But they hadn't paid me anything. I didn't owe it to them.

Except I kind of did. Tippy had paid me. He had paid me well. In advance, even knowing I didn't have to do anything to keep the money. Which had been their money to begin with.

So of course, I had to do what he asked.

I could always pass it along to Metro later. I could use them if I didn't get a line on the killer. But for the moment I would have to work with Tippy, see where this road led. I had seen LaSalle, and I was about to see Beddington, and by tomorrow this time, I'd have seen Willoughby. And by that time, they'll have all identified me as the new owner of the franchise that Tippy had built. And at least one of them will decide that one murder wasn't enough.

A black kid about fifteen chased down a ball as the rest of the guys walked toward the water fountain, their game over. I reached over and picked it up, flipped it to him. He caught it one-handed, nodded, and turned to head back. Almost imperceptibly he paused, then stopped. He spun on his sneaker and looked at me.

"You come in for a game?"

"Not me, man." I opened my coat, showing him the clothes of a man without basketball on his mind. "I'm not dressed for it. Why do you ask?"

"I've seen you in here before. Seen you play once. You're not bad."

"I'm not in your class, or your friends' class."

"Ain't true, man. Everybody's got something he can do. My job right now is to make sure that tall dude over there, DeMar, gets the ball every time he wants it."

I nodded. Everybody does have a role to play. Tippy gave me mine.

Don Mercer jokes that Hannigan's is my office, and Charlie acts like I should pay him rent sometimes. But the fact is that I feel comfortable there, the bourbon is all right, and they let me run a tab. Running a tab is a critical part of my business model because I don't have a reliable source of income, my current good fortune notwithstanding.

Hannigan's was part of the carriage house for a grand estate, and the only remaining part of that estate is now known as Centennial Park, home to the replica of the Parthenon. It's a local eatery that's gone through several generations of Vanderbilt students. I used to hang here when I was on staff at VU.

I still do. It's my office, remember?

I rarely saw faculty in there. So when Irma Beddington came in, she looked momentarily confused, then slightly irritated. It was clearly a townie and student kind of place, and she looked far too put together in her houndstooth blazer and her pearls. In fact, she looked pretty good for what she was, a professor in her late 40s.

She had her hair knotted in a bun that had a little maple stick through it, and she wore fashionable eyeglasses that were too narrow for bifocals. She looked like the sort that would pass up the bifocals as long as she could. Perhaps that's a little biased. Maybe she would not be vain. But vanity in a philandering wife wouldn't be an unheard of thing.

She made her way to a booth on the side of the restaurant and ordered a glass of wine. I let her sit there and get comfortable. No need to spook the horse just yet.

If she watched me walk toward her, she hid it well. As I stood next to the table, she ignored me, then finally looked up. "Yes?"

"I'm Jackson Trade."

"Good for you."

"Butter wouldn't melt in your mouth, would it, Dr. Beddington? That's a good trait to have, given what we're about to discuss. But why don't you just invite me to sit down?"

She looked upwards toward me. Closer now, I could see that she had a fine profile, and her eyes showed a kind of inelastic intelligence that would probably pass for sternness. She was the chair of the tenure committee in Canadian Studies. I had no doubt junior faculty saw those eyes and quivered in their boots.

For all that, though, she was sophisticated, even assured. All in all, her lover probably had all he could handle, and that was before the bedroom even entered the picture.

"You're just a fucking hippie." All the sophistication left in an instant, and her profile wasn't all that well-bred suddenly. "Where did you get it? From Taylor?"

"Mind if I sit?" I didn't wait for her permission. She fixed me with those eyes and their intelligence, and appeared to be considering what to say next. I waved at Katie. "A bourbon? And whatever this lady is drinking." She was drinking a Chablis Blanc, but it was easier to let her think I was just a hippie, rather than someone who knew which wine was which.

When Katie went to fetch the drinks, she continued to glare at me. Her question hung in the air. "Tippy and I were partners on several pieces of business. This is one he passed along to me when he died. Kind of a way to say thank you for our past successes."

"If you were anything like Taylor, then you're just another prick. By the looks of it, an unemployed prick."

"Sometimes pricks have more smarts than you give them credit for."

"Or maybe you're not really one of Taylor's friends. You don't look like you'd be. He was a little more particular with the people around him. You?" She looked a little disgusted. "I don't think he'd consent to be seen with you."

"If you can't stand to be around me, maybe you'd like me to show my cards to someone else."

Katie brought the drinks, gave me a look, and retreated. Irma downed the first glass and pushed it to the side. Both hands encircled the base of the wine glass. She had bright, blood red nail polish, and it set off nicely against her long slender fingers.

"How did you wind up with it?"

"How do you think? Tippy left it to me. A sort of inheritance."

"But why? I understood that I was being blackmailed. I didn't like it, but I understood it. It was a price I was willing to pay." She looked at the wine and decided not to drink it. "Then Taylor was dead. I don't mind telling you, I was pretty happy. That's the end of that little problem, I thought."

That's a pretty good motive for murder, I thought.

"And here you show up. What am I to make of that?"

I made a face appear that was the same as a shrug. Eyebrows up, briefly. A slight tilt of the head. On an older man, it probably looks nonchalant. On me, it probably looked like a smart ass.

"Tell me, Trade. What is the price? What's the going rate once we go from Tippy Taylor to Jackson Trade?"

"I'm not going to bleed you dry, Irma. I'm just going to take my cut and be a silent partner in this little deal."

"Sure. Blackmailers always have to get their pound of flesh."

"I'll settle for the same deal you had with Tippy."

She gave me a look, and then a smile. "You don't have anything. You don't even know what the arrangement was."

"I've got plenty. I've got some super 8 that looks like that flea bag motel on Donelson Pike. I've got some pretty good shots of you with a sheet that does not quite cover your assets while a man with a crew cut is kissing you."

She looked alarmed.

"Yeah, there's more of that. They're not all high-quality shots. They'll never end up in Playboy or Penthouse. But it's easy to see who is who, and what they're doing."

"Is there anything I can do to convince you to lose those copies?" She was looking at me differently now. The ice was melted and the hands, once quite white, were now turning warm. She reached for my hands. "There must be something I can do."

I looked at her. She wasn't bad looking. In fact, in a kind of older woman way, she was attractive, the way your best friend's aunt looks good. For about ten seconds, and then you realize that the idea doesn't appeal to you after all.

"I don't think so." I leaned back and made my hands move away from hers. "I'd rather have the money."

"You sure about that? You saw the super 8 reel. Must have been something there that made you a little intrigued?"

"What I saw was a married professor in bed with someone who's not her husband. It's intriguing because I can charge for it."

"You're a son of a bitch." She removed her hands from the middle of the table and put them back on the wine glass. "A total son of a bitch."

"You don't have to like me, Irma. You just have to pay me."

"You don't like me either, do you?"

"Not much, but I don't know you. What I know is that you're a big deal in a small department across the street. You got yourself on the hook to Tippy. Tippy passed it on to me. You look good for 500 a month, maybe. How's that sound?"

It apparently didn't sound too good because she made a gasping sound with her mouth. "That's pretty steep."

I knew it was what LaSalle was paying, so how steep could it have been? "I don't know, Irma. That seems about right to me. Unless you want to pay it all off at once."

"All at once? How would that work?"

"You pay me a bundle, and that's the end of it. I hand over the property to you. Even steven."

"But you would still know. You could still identify. . ." She stopped and changed course. "How could I trust you?"

I thought about it. "Maybe I give you something about me, something I can't have anybody know."

She narrowed her eyes. "It would have to be big. I don't even know you. How could I trust you unless what you gave me could ruin you?"

There's a lot of things that could ruin me. Just not a lot of them you can blackmail me with. But I didn't tell her that.

"It just might work." She left a red lipstick mark on the wine glass, a little on purpose, I thought. "I could still make it worth your time if you could give me a break on the price. How much were you thinking?"

"Twenty-five thousand."

That was clearly not a number she had in mind. She paused with her mouth on the glass, and her eyes opened wide. It might have been the first time she'd thought about what it would take to be done with this business. Unless she'd thought that killing Tippy Taylor was the way to do it.

If that was true, she was thinking about how to kill me now.

"That's more than I can lay hands on."

"Surely not. Surely you have some possessions you could sell? Maybe your husband has a business, maybe something he can offer?"

"I don't have access to my husband's business. And even if I did. . ."

"Maybe I could just sell it directly to him."

She opened her eyes even wider, then caught herself. "You better not be serious about that." There was a flash in her eyes that told me she thought she meant it.

"I don't want to do that. But I think that an intelligent woman like you, someone who has made her way through an entirely male profession to a position of power, is the sort of woman who can find twenty-five thousand dollars."

"How long before I have to have this?"

"If we're going to make the one payment, two weeks."

"I can't possibly. It would take two months at the earliest."

"I'm not crazy about an arrangement that keeps me in town that long."

"You're willing to take 500 a month."

"You can mail that to me. It won't be hard."

"I can wire you the twenty-five grand too."

"For that kind of money, I'd rather be here where I can keep an eye on you. With that much on the line, you might get antsy, do something stupid."

"I'm not a stupid woman. I don't do stupid things."

"You got caught with a lover. That's not exactly smart."

She considered her options. "Give me a day or two to consider what I have to work with. I'll try to do the one big payment, if we can get to the place where I'm satisfied you won't double cross me. Otherwise, we'll see where we are on an interim basis."

"Two days. Then we close."

"I still say we could take a little off the top. There are things an older woman knows. It might be very interesting for you."

"The only thing that's interesting to me is your money. The rest you can leave for your lover."

She called me a son of a bitch again, but she kept it quiet. Nobody who saw us would have thought we were having anything but a friendly chat. "Don't call me and don't leave messages at the office. Give me your phone number."

I did. "There's a machine. I live alone. Just give me the message."

She wrote it down in a little spiral 3 by 5 notebook. "I'll call you. In two days."

Chapter Sixteen

WES WILLOUGHBY WAS THE sort of noob that would have been a captain in Vietnam. His face had not grown into more maturity as he got older, but rather began to expand the baby face into a larger, free-form kind of bulbous mass, red at the edges and pink at the center. It was the sort of face that blistered and peeled repeatedly in the field, except when the month was spent under the canopy and no sun hit him. That would have been the best choice for his skin.

What would have been the best choice for his psyche would have been an entirely different thing, if his mannerisms were any clue. He was a fidget. It was not that he fidgeted. That might have been understandable. But he was fidget itself, a mass of jerky micro-movements that served no purpose except to disturb the air. How a man like this could have been in command was a mystery, but there were many such mysteries in Vietnam, and all of them were impenetrable to enlisted men. How you were supposed to follow orders from such men tripped up a lot of GIs.

Besides his bloated face, there was not much to differentiate him from the great mass of early middle-aged professors at Vanderbilt. He was not particularly distinguished if you saw him on the street. He didn't dress particularly well, either in the business sense or in the more haphazard academic sense. He was neither too tall nor too short, and despite his fat face, he was just a smidge over his ideal weight, possibly the result not of any physical regimen, but of not finding time to eat when he was hungry. He was, in short, inauspicious.

Which was what he was telling me. "I don't know why you want to see me about Professor Taylor. We were not friends, nor were we colleagues."

"Tippy and I were friends, though. And I inherited something from Tippy that is very interesting."

He continued to make random small movements. With his hands. With his legs. He jiggled as a matter of routine, a sort of metabolic waste burner. Maybe that's how he kept his weight down. "I still don't understand. I don't know you. What did you say your name was?"

"Jackson Trade. I'm a Vietnam vet. Same as Tippy. Same as you."

He averted his eyes, jiggling, fidgeting. I swear even his eyes were fidgeting. "Not the best time of my life. Not the best time of yours, I'd wager."

"It was tough. There was nothing that wasn't tough about it. Men did things they wouldn't otherwise do, for reasons they usually didn't understand."

"Not the best time of my life," he repeated.

"Tippy knew something about you. I don't know what tipped him off, or how he knew where to look, but he had the goods on you, Wes."

He stopped. His body went rock still.

"That's right. I inherited information from Tippy. I know about your big chicken dinner." The bad conduct discharge.

He seemed to bore into himself. Then he started talking. "It started with a night ambush." He remained still. The fidget had disappeared. "The tracer rounds. Green tracers. Red tracers. Like a light show, except the real show wasn't started yet."

"I remember."

"Then you remember that you never knew who was shooting at who. It was pitch dark. The tracers made it even more dark, if that was possible."

He was back there. You could see it in his eyes.

"We slept on the ground, ate those damn C-rats. Some of those tins were marked from the Korean War. It was dirty. It was rainy and hot. There was nothing but hardness, Trade. You remember how hard it all was? Or were you in the rear?"

"I was infantry. We were in the boonies."

"Then you know. There was an LZ where we were overrun by regular NVA. It was '68. Everything was jungle except right around the LZ. We had a mortar platoon supporting us. But the NVA knew exactly what was happening. They pummeled us with 133s, those damn rockets, and sappers, and then they sent infantry in. Through the wire, and they were everywhere."

"Sounds like you took a lot of damage."

He stared ahead, still not moving. "All night long it went. The ARVN with us were not well trained, and they mostly kept their heads down and tried to survive. Our artillery was firing into the tree line to cut off the attack."

He continued the stare. We called it the thousand-yard stare. It was what a lot of us got. I'd had it a time or two myself. Over there. Here at home.

"The next morning I went with the medic attached to our unit. We picked up the dead in a deuce-and-a-half truck. Young boys cut in half. Bodies missing limbs. It was the worst duty ever, Trade. You ever have to do that?"

I'd seen my buddies alive one minute and dead the next. "Yeah."

"How did you keep it together? How did you manage to go out on the next patrol? How could you, knowing what could happen, knowing what had already happened?"

It was a good question, one I didn't have the answer to. Instead I said, "You snapped over there, Wes."

The fidget returned, gently at first then on full bore. The thousand-yard stare left and his eyes began again to dart this way and that. "How could you not? And still be human?"

I didn't like what I was about to do. It didn't seem fair. The Bad Conduct Discharge was over something that the war caused. Wes Willoughby didn't cause it. But if Wes Willoughby had killed Tippy, I needed to know.

"Like I said, I'm taking over for Tippy. You'll make your payments to me now."

He finally turned his body so he could look at me. "How can a fellow vet, somebody who was over there, do this? How? You know exactly what it was like."

"So did Tippy. So do you." I got up and went to the door. I locked it. He looked distressed. "Don't worry, Wes. I just don't want to be interrupted."

"I don't like to be in confined places."

"I get it. This won't take long." I saw an ashtray on his desk, so I lit up. "You know that Tippy was murdered."

"That's what the newspaper says. To tell you the truth, I wasn't that surprised."

"Oh?" That was an interesting thing to say.

"He's blackmailing me. There's no telling what else he has on the line. I wouldn't do anything to him. I've got too much at stake. I have to get tenure. But other people might not be so fearful. He must have made the wrong person mad."

"So you think he was blackmailing someone else?"

"It could be. But he was in the paper a lot. He was always getting his picture taken. He was an angry man. That makes some people mad. Some of them might be powerful people."

"Were you mad at him, Wes?"

"I wasn't happy. But if you think I killed him. . ."

"Why not? You snapped and killed in the war. You got a BCD for it." I put out the cigarette. "Somebody could say you were a likely suspect."

He had a way of fidgeting that made him appear almost a blur of motion, tiny motions that evened out in a way that made him almost appear still while moving. "Not me. You know what I teach?"

"You're a Canadian Studies guy. That's all I know."

"My specialty is the Western religious tradition. I apply it to American draft evaders in the book I've got coming out. I am intrigued by the religious dimensions of their fleeing to Canada."

"What's your point, Wes?"

"Within all those traditions, all of them, is the notion of redemption. They differ. They even differ within each tradition, but it's a constant in the way that eastern religions do not contemplate. In some ways, those draft evaders all connected their spiritual life to leaving. Not fighting, in some way, became a part of their redemption. Not just metaphorically."

"So?"

"Every scholar has an engine that drives his interest, his passion. Given what you know about my discharge, is it too hard to imagine that redemption is a topic close to my heart?"

"And that your paying Tippy was just part of your payback?"

He looked tired. When I entered I would have said he looked scared, but that wasn't it. He looked worn. "The price I pay for having done what I did, and then for having wanted this career, and then having received what I wanted. They are incompatible, Trade. And so that is the price I have to pay. If I want the one, I have to pay the other."

"Just the cost of doing business?"

"Something like that."

Wes Willoughby was calm now. The fidget had left his body and he leaned forward on his desk, elbows flared out, hands supporting his too large head. I knew him as a type, the kind of vet who comes back and latches onto something, some passion, and that passion creates the structure he needs to get through the day, to get from day to day. He had clearly found his structure, the thing that would make it easier to live.

I didn't have much structure anymore, but I certainly could identify the need.

"Then we'll keep the deal the same."

"If you say so, that's the way we'll do it. 250 the first of every month. How do I get it to you?"

"Let me get back to you on that one."

He was slow to raise his face from his hands, but as he did it, you could see just a flicker of questioning. By the time he looked at me, it was in full flower. "How's that? What's to get back to me about?"

"I have a little traveling to do between now and then. My plans may change. My location may change. I'll know more later." I started to rise from the office chair. "I'll get back to you."

"Forgive my saying so, but you don't act like a blackmailer. You're a little too casual about the details. Taylor always dictated the terms."

"More than one way to skin a cat, Wes."

"But the cat is the same. Is this your first shakedown?"

I could have told him I'd been shaking things down since I got back to the States. One way or another, everything I did seemed like a con to me, even if nobody else thought that way. "No. It's not my first rodeo."

If this all went the wrong way, it could be my last, though.

Chapter Seventeen

THE PROTEST BEAT WAS less likely to get me killed, even though I might die of boredom. It was misting rain, about 45 degrees, and I'd made poor decisions about how to dress. I was cold, and that was making the boredom more pronounced.

Canadian Studies was taking its turn, although the crowd included undergraduates and a few faculty members who were not, to my knowledge, in Canadian Studies. One was my interlocutor from History, the striking Willa Winter, and there were a couple who, by their collars, were Episcopal or Catholic clergy. Either way, they all carried placards and chanted the standard protest things.

If I could stand them for another half hour, I could get lunch.

Irma Beddington was there, as were Wes Willoughby and Watkins LaSalle. LaSalle and Willoughby were sleepwalking through their march, but Irma Beddington seemed to take her duty more seriously. She had dressed in, or changed into, sensible shoes and a rain slicker, and had prepared the largest sign, which read "Immoral Universities Go To Hell."

Struck me as a little harsh, but hey, I don't get paid to have an opinion.

"Got a match?"

The voice came from behind me, and I turned to find the sour face of Stump Collins behind me.

I passed my Zippo over my shoulder and he lit a cigarette. "Come and join me."

Collins was dressed as he had been the night of the planning meeting. His leather jacket was a little frayed at the cuffs and his jeans had dragged the ground enough that the bell bottoms were frayed as well. But nothing else about Stump looked frayed at all. Despite his dress, Stump was well put together. One look and you knew it.

He lit his cigarette, handed the Zippo back to me, and came around to the front of the bench. He gave my offered hand a friendly slap and sat down. "You just got a thing about protests?"

"You know how this rolls, Stump. I watch. I report."

"In my neighborhood, we call that a snitch."

"This neighborhood they call it an employee, part-time, temporary."

"Man, you got a soft gig, then. Ain't nothing to see here."

He was right. If anything, Wes and LaSalle looked as if they'd been shanghaied into walking in a circle. From her demeanor, Irma was the likely candidate. She was having a big old time, exhorting the various marchers from outside the circle, calling for more volume.

Willa Winter was there too. If I read her expression right, Irma annoyed the snot out of her.

Let's be clear. She annoyed the snot out of me too.

"Who's that white woman?"

"They're all white women, Stump."

"The one that thinks she's the head coach."

"Canadian Studies professor. Kind of high up on the faculty side of things."

He appeared to consider what that might mean. "Why does anybody study Canada? What did they ever do? That makes her someone to call the shots?"

"No shots being called here, man. At least, none that make any difference."

"They don't seem like they're risking much, if that's what you mean. Black cat like me starts protesting, all hell might break loose."

"You got that right." I stubbed my butt out on the sidewalk with my shoe. "This is symbolic action. It's meant to demonstrate moral superiority."

He laughed. "Nothing gets in my throat like moral superiority."

We watched as the marchers made their tiny circle, over and over, through the misty mid-morning. The Kirkland clock tolled the quarter hour, then the half hour. Stump and I sat silently, watching the show.

"You know what's wrong with all this shit, Trade?" He reached for the Zippo still on the bench between us, flipped it open and lit it. He snapped the case shut, flicked it open, and lit it again. Then snapped it shut. It's a satisfying movement. The clack the Zippo makes feels solid, substantial.

"That there's nobody here watching all this? Just you and me."

"Nah, that ain't it. But maybe that's part of it. Who you think cares if these people are out here?"

"Nobody cares, Stump. That's why it's safe for them to be out here."

"That ain't right. They care. They are doing this for themselves. They make their little signs, they get up and schedule at the most convenient time for them, and they march round and round." He snapped the lighter open and shut again. "They march round and round in their good clothes, then they go get a nice lunch somewhere." He snapped it again. "The way these people work, I bet half of them go home for lunch."

"You might be right about that first thing."

"You know I'm right. This is all just for show. This just makes them feel good. It doesn't have anything to do with the Davis Cup. Or apartheid." He dropped his voice. "They don't even know there's black people in Nashville who have an opinion on all this."

"You don't think they believe they're protesting those things."

"Sure, they believe it. People believe all kinds of jive ass things that aren't true."

I couldn't argue with that. "So why am I out here watching them, Stump?"

"There's no mystery about that, brother. You're getting paid to sit on your white ass and watch something that don't mean anything." He put the Zippo down. "That's the way the white world works. But remember. Be ready, Freddy. Time is coming when you have to be real." He whistled low and quiet. "Who is this coming at us?"

Willa Winter had broken ranks and was coming toward us, this time without her khakied undergrad. She was striking an urban vibe today, with tall boots and a wool knit turban, paired with a vaguely African patterned shawl. Everything else she wore from pants to top, was black. She had topped it all with a clear vinyl slicker. So you could still see how cool she was.

"You are back," she said, smiling at me, "but this time you brought reinforcements."

"Dr. Winter." I half bowed. "This is my colleague, Mr. Collins."

Stump surprised me by standing up. "What kind of doctor are you? Because I have some pains you could take a look at."

Willa didn't appear to get the come on. "I am a professor of history. My specialty is the Enlightenment."

Stump gave her a look that could have been playful, or it could have just been salacious. "Enlighten me, then, when you get the chance."

No, it wasn't acting. She really didn't get it. She turned back to me. "And you are still just enjoying being here, in this cold mist, smoking and chatting with your colleague?"

"Yes. Mr. Collins and I were just talking about the Social Contract. It seems now to be in some peril. Wouldn't you agree, Dr. Winter?"

Her face didn't change. She continued to smile at me. "I don't know why I came over here."

"You keep hoping I'll tell you I'm up to something."

"And will you? This time?"

"Nope. Still not up to anything. But when I am, you'll be the first to know."

She looked at me, then at Stump, then back at me. "I doubt that you aren't up to something now. And I seriously doubt you will tell me anything." She began to walk back to the group. "But hope springs eternal."

"Let me know when you are ready for a little north side Enlightenment," Stump said, so no one but I could hear. He looked over to me and whispered. "I have seen her somewhere."

"She doesn't look like she would hang out up your way."

"I'm telling you, Trade. I know her from somewhere."

The circle march ran its course, I retrieved my lighter from the bench between us, and said goodbye to Stump.

"You come up my way, Trade, be sure to let me know."

"How am I going to do that, Stump. I don't have a way to get in touch."

"Go where I told you. Somebody will get word to me. You hear me, Freddy?"

I nodded. It was the way he seemed to be. Everywhere and nowhere at once. Plugged in, probably even down here in Vandyland.

Chapter Eighteen

I SHOWED UP IN Hannigan's after the lunch crowd, had a hamburger with onion rings, and sat nursing a black coffee. I'd done my duty to Art and to Vanderbilt, and Stump was right. I was mostly sitting around watching overpaid professors walk in a circle. It didn't seem to amount to much.

It would have seemed like more of a deal if my business for Tippy had gone better. But what would "better" have looked like?

LaSalle was completely ready to continue the charade. He had the chairmanship of the department at stake, and he didn't seem the type anyway. I doubted he'd ever done a hard thing, a hard physical thing, in his life.

The same went for Wes Willoughby. He was a damaged unit, to be sure. The war had done a number on him, and he hadn't really come out of it yet. I got that. But unlike me, he'd found something he cared about, and he wasn't about to let it slip through his hands. That might make him a possible suspect in Tippy's demise. Or it might not. He didn't seem the type either.

Irma Beddington was the type, but she seemed more interested in just ending the blackmail bleed. I didn't blame her, but I also didn't blame her for blanching at my cost for doing that. Getting her hands on that much money would be a stretch for her. And maybe it wasn't like her husband would notice it gone. Maybe her boyfriend had it. But in the pictures I had seen he looked more like a young Marlon Brando in Streetcar Named Desire, all sleeveless tee shirt and boxer shorts.

What had I accomplished? Perhaps I had stirred up the murderer, perhaps in such a way they'd come for me. Or maybe I had confused everyone. After all, Tippy's style was a lot different than mine, and maybe I'd seemed just a little incompetent as a blackmailer.

Or maybe I was setting up a side business just fine, when all I wanted was to do what Tippy wanted. Find my killer, bro. Twenty-five grand from Irma, plus $750 a month from the other two would be a big-time haul. Maybe that's the way it was setting up. Maybe whoever killed Tippy wouldn't have a second thought about doing the same to me.

I spent the rest of the week letting the kettle simmer on the stove. I generally hung out on a stool somewhere along West End Avenue and caused the bartenders to shake their heads when I asked for a Coke. I stopped in at Hannigan's to get a bite and put it on my tab, but I wasn't doing much else. Sitting on a bench outside Kirkland for an hour a day. Stump was silent. Probably enough on the north side to keep him busy.

I went to the Joint Universities Library and hung out in microforms, spinning reels, looking for anything on LaSalle, or Irma, or Wes. Hell, even for Tippy. Tippy's letters and op-eds were easy enough to find, but he didn't seem to surface anywhere else. And the three professors were no-shows in the Tennessean and the Banner, except for a book that won Irma an award.

I went to reference and found more. LaSalle was prolific as a scholar and had a dozen or more articles in what sounded like high-powered journals. Irma was the author of a book that seemed to be cited all the time, so it must have been important. Wes? Wes only featured as the writer of his dissertation. His time was yet to come.

Just for giggles, I looked up Willa Winter. I got a couple of hits on articles she'd written, just out of graduate school at the University of Chicago. Her time was yet to come too, I guessed.

Since I came up with nothing I went back to my routine, waiting for someone to make a move. I played through several rolls of quarters at money pinball, losing enough that I figured I'd stop until my touch returned.

I called Betty but she wasn't home. That much couldn't be surprising. She was a looker, and smart, and funny. Why should she be home? Not waiting for me, that's for sure.

The next day, I called LaSalle. He didn't sound that happy to hear from me.

"Look. I've got it worked out how we can put an end to this thing." I had to apply some pressure.

"We agreed to continue Taylor's arrangement. That's what we said. We have an agreement."

"Well, I don't like that anymore. I want to leave town. I don't want to hang around, collecting chump change every month."

"It's not chump change, as you put it, to me."

"Wouldn't you rather just make one big payment, get all of the property back and be done with it?"

He was silent on the other end. "How much would one payment be?"

"Twenty-five grand."

"There is no way I could get that much money."

"I think there probably is. That's what second mortgages are for." He was single. He didn't have a wife he'd have to explain it to.

"That's simply impossible. Besides, you could still damage me with what you know. You could just write the Dean in Bologna again."

"That's where this wrinkle comes in. I'd give you something on me. It'd be like we had something on each other, each thing could ruin the other. It's like us and the Russians, you know? We'd have too much firepower to start a war."

"Still, I cannot raise that much money. It is simply impossible."

"You can do it, LaSalle. I expect you to do it."

"You don't understand. As it is, I have to borrow money to pay this, this monthly payment."

"That's why it's in your interest to figure out how to get the big one done." I could hear him breathing on the other end of the line. "Rip the Band-Aid off, LaSalle. You know you want to. It only hurts once."

I hung up. I felt a little sorry for LaSalle, but only if he wasn't Tippy's killer. If he was, then he deserved all the heartburn he was feeling. If he wasn't, if what he was turned out to be was a guy who'd taken a short cut he didn't need to take, a shortcut that would ruin his life if it became known? Ok. Then I would feel like a bastard.

Either way, I was out of my comfort zone. I had no trouble being a bastard to someone who was that way first to me. But most of the time, even when that happened, it wasn't worth the trouble.

I didn't like making it worth the trouble, because I wasn't sure it was.

One thing was clearer now, however. He had been borrowing to pay Tippy. He couldn't borrow much more to pay me. And that might be enough of a reason for him to do the unnatural, for him, and kill Tippy.

And me too, if it came to that.

I'd been good all week. I poured a small amount of bourbon in a water glass. I drank it. There was no reason to hurry. All the pots were on the stove. I had just turned up the heat on one of them.

Chapter Nineteen

THE PHONE RANG AND I let it go three rings before I picked it up. It was Irma Beddington, and she had energy in her voice.

"I saw you at the protest. Are you following me?"

Not exactly, though I wonder if all three of them took that message away. "I'm not. I just happened to be where you were. That's all."

"That's what Dr. Winter said you would say. Although she also said you'd have a smart aleck remark to go along with it."

"I save those for her, just for fun. You and I have a different relationship.

"You and I have no relationship. At least not yet."

"I disagree. I think having the goods on you means that we have a very tight relationship."

She let a beat, then two beats intervene. "Let's get together to talk. I think we can reach some sort of accommodation."

"I've got nothing but time." I took another sip of Harper. "Where and when."

"I can see you this evening. My husband will believe I've a graduate student to attend to. Let's say seven?"

"Seven it is. Where?"

"You pick. Except not that place before." She gave a silent shudder, but I heard it anyway. "So many undergraduates."

"You know the Top Hat? Little place down West End, on the north side of the street?"

"I can find it."

"Make sure you part in the little lot in the back. Street parking is scarce, and people don't know there's a few spots in the back."

She hung up. I thought she sounded happier about meeting than she should have.

I also thought it was time for me to figure out what my dinner was, and where I was eating it.

Hannigan's looked like it was in the process of being over-run by the very undergraduates Irma Beddington seemed to despise, despite being dependent on them for her livelihood. I took a pass and walked back up Elliston to the little gyro place and had a pita with fries. The tzatziki was a little runny, so I ended up licking my fingers clean. It wasn't very couth, but it was effective, in the same way that eating with your hands is. And if there's a problem with eating with your hands, then the problem only came about in this century. It's a natural thing to do.

What wasn't as natural was trying to turn myself into a convincing blackmailer, three times over. I had the feeling that Wes and LaSalle were pushovers. That is, I could probably steamroll them. Irma, however, was not the steamrolling type.

I went back by my apartment to wash my hands and brush my teeth. No need showing up with pita fingers. As I got ready to leave, the phone rang. I half expected it to be Irma, calling the meeting off. Instead I heard an unfamiliar male voice.

"Jackson Trade?"

"Depends. Who are you?"

"Don't be an asshole, Trade. You're screwing around in things you don't want to be screwing around in."

"Oh, yeah? How would you know?"

"Don't try me, Trade. You keep going like you are, you're going to make people very unhappy."

"I'll ask you again, nimrod. Who the hell are you?"

"I'm a man you don't want to meet in the dark, mother fuck-er. You want to keep playing games, you might find yourself in a dumpster, you know what I mean?"

"Sounds to me like Tippy Taylor's killer. Just tell me who you are and we'll figure the rest out."

"I've already got it figured out, bucko."

And the phone clicked silent.

I got to the Top Hat a little before seven, and there she was, decked out to the nines. She had on a flowing dress with a slit up the side, and her bare leg looked long and elegant. She had on very high heels, and her top was a shimmery affair, with a frilled bit to it.

She wasn't looking as I approached her. "You dress for all the graduate students that way?"

Her head gave a graceful, practiced turn. She had let her hair down, and even though it was brown, she'd done some-thing to it to make the light play on it. She'd also ditched the eyeglasses, so she looked different. A lot different.

"It's good to see you, Mr. Trade. It turns out that the Cana-dian Studies Institute was to have a reception for a visiting scholar tonight. I'd only just remembered this afternoon." She smiled and looked down at the drink she was sipping. "If you know what I mean."

"I think I do." What it meant was that she could lie at the drop of a hat to her husband. And probably to her lover. And certainly to me.

I ordered a Makers Mark, neat. I'm usually a "whatever's in the well" bourbon guy, but I seemed to be riding a hot streak with the cash. I could afford the premium stuff. For now. And it was just one. For now.

We settled in. She took out a cigarette and waited, coyly, so I lit it for her. Then I lit one of my own. It was the sort of pantomime that the other tables would have thought little of, if there'd been anyone at them. We had the place all to ourselves, except for the waiter. He was a different one from the other night.

"Do you like the way I look?"

There was only one appropriate answer, so I gave it. "You look like you took a lot of care to look nice. You succeeded."

"That's a pretty thin affirmative." She was smiling, but you knew that she was not pleased.

"You know damn well how you look, Irma. You put a lot of time into it. I wonder what your husband thought about all that effort."

"He wouldn't notice, even if he were home."

"So you just left a note about where you were and why. Aren't you afraid he'll check up on that?"

"My husband hasn't checked on anything for years and years."

"That makes it pretty easy to sneak a lover under his nose." Very convenient for her. Maybe for him too.

"Yes, it is." She took a drink of what looked like a gin rickey. "Maybe other things could be sneaked past him."

"Such as a large sum of money?"

"Well, there's that conversation we were having, of course." She played with a hoop earring while her other hand dabbed ash into the ashtray. "Tippy Taylor and I had an arrangement."

"Yes, you told me. A monthly arrangement. That's not the kind I'm interested in."

"What I didn't tell you is that Tippy was sometimes very forgiving on the terms."

"Oh?" That's not the sort of blackmailer that tends to get killed, at least in my experience. That's the kind of blackmailer that doesn't make any money.

"Yes, that's right." She put the drink down. Her hands reached for my hand. I felt the cold moisture from her glass on my hands. "Sometimes, when I couldn't make a payment, Tippy took his payment that month in another way."

I pulled my hand free of hers. "Then Tippy missed the point of holding information. Or at least, he devalued it."

"I can assure you that what I offered in substitution was of considerable value."

I tried to gauge her. She looked sexy. I gave her that. She was intelligent, which was a turn on too. She gave off the vibe of knowing what she was doing. But she could be lying about Tippy and any arrangement, and I wouldn't have the slightest idea.

"I'm not interested in anything but the money. We had that conversation already."

She stubbed the cigarette out. "Why are you being so difficult about this?"

That was a good question. Any other time, if what she was offering was to go to bed with me, I'd have at least given it some thought. Sometimes, in the past, I hadn't given it enough thought, but that's the way it goes. Now, though?

"Did Tippy make a practice of forgiving your payments?"

"Not as a rule. He'd say that he had to eat too. Although he was paid more than he should have been, if you want to know the truth, for what he did. But over the course of a year and a half, we made a substitution three or four times. Each time with the vow that he would never do that again."

"Why did he go back on his promise? Seems to me he had the goods on you. And, nice as you look, Irma, it's not like the way you look drives the other fish out of the sea."

"You don't know. I might have skills that are hidden." She leaned forward on the table with her elbows. "My husband is out of town on business tonight. I could show you. Then you can decide."

"I don't think so, Irma. Tippy might have had his reasons to give you a break. But I don't. I need the money, and I want the money." I pushed away from the table. "You work on figuring out how to pay me. I'll be in touch."

I dug into my wallet and tossed a ten on the table. "This is the last time that this is on me, Irma."

Chapter Twenty

I LEFT IRMA BEDDINGTON where I found her and walked a block west before crossing the street to The High Life. It's not cozy like Hannigan's or shabbily elegant like The Top Hat. It's just a dive bar with money pinball, pool tables, and a long bar where people sit and look at themselves in a mirror until they can't see what they look like anymore.

I knew what I looked like. Why was I back here?

I spent too much time there on a bar stool, but tonight I took one of the six booths that lined the wall opposite the bar. Everything was as it should be on a Friday night. Jukebox wailing. Laughter. The occasional wild yelp, either in joy or surprise or anger, there not being a bit of difference when it came right down to it. I suspected you could get all three, a kind of redneck trifecta, twice a week if the right people were there.

Bobby the bartender had circulated back from Linda's next door and was the formerly old, now new-again bartender. He was working the bar with a kid I knew by sight, and Bobby nodded to the kid and came from behind the bar, bringing me a bourbon and a draft chaser.

"You're a good man, Bob." I took the bourbon and drank it off. "Glad to be back?" He should have been. High Life was a dive bar, but Linda's was like a litter box that three cats used.

"I don't know, Slick. Seems anymore like it's just a matter of pulling beers and biding time. One's about the same as the other."

I took a sip of beer. Cold. Smooth as a small sting, which is to say it was cheap draft.

"I just came to tell you there's a man over there at the bar." He lowered his voice and indicated with his head a tall guy with his back to us. "I heard him ask about you. If we'd seen you around."

"Who is he?"

"Damned if I know. All I know is that he looks like bad news."

"Everybody is bad news in here, Bobby, except for me and thee."

"I'm serious, Slick. He's not from around here, I'm sure of that. Wrong accent."

"Nashville draws people from all over, Bobby. Maybe he's here to become a country star."

"Not this one. He looks like hired muscle, the kind you see in the movies."

"Well, there's your problem, Bobby. Nashville isn't the movies."

"Whatever." He got up. "I'd say watch your back."

If it was a normal day, I might have walked up and said something smart, like, "Looking for me?" You never know. It could have been an old Army buddy. But given that I was trying to get a blackmailed murderer to come out into the daylight, it didn't seem the thing to do.

So I waited, and watched on the sly.

He didn't seem to be drinking much. If Bobby brought him another in the half hour he was there, I didn't see it. Just shouldered in between a guy I know who runs a hauling business and an old guy who drinks a can of Pabst every hour for three hours and then goes home, he towered over both of them. I figured him for about six foot five, and shoulders that, from the back, looked pretty chiseled.

Thirty minutes after the first, Bobby brought me another draft and bourbon, and sat down again. "What do you think, Slick?"

"How the hell can I tell? He hasn't turned around. He hasn't moved. As near as I can tell, he hasn't talked."

"You got that right, Slick." He leaned over. "He's got a wild look. Like he's out of his mind."

"I don't even know what that means."

"They're scary eyes. Not much color in them, and he's all bug eyed, like he's mad and about to bust."

"What about the guys on either side? They scared of him?"

"Fletcher doesn't look at anything but his Pabst. And I don't think Jerry's got enough sense to be scared of anything."

"Come on, Bobby. You've worked at some of the worst joints in town. What's got you so spooked?"

He wiped the table with a dishrag. "This ain't one to mess with, Slick, and he was asking about you."

I figured I would make the big man come to me. And if he didn't, I thought it might be a good idea if he left before I did.

I didn't want the son of a bitch following me. Of course, you could also say he'd be waiting for me. Either way, it seemed like I could manage to leave with somebody easier than I could get an ally on the spot.

It turned out that I didn't have to wait much longer. The big man pushed his plastic Hamm's cup forward, then without glancing at me walked to the door and out into the street. He was certainly big enough, but that wasn't the thing that caught the eye.

What was most noticeable was his gait, a sort of easy, loose-limbed saunter that communicated a fair amount of power. He walked on his toes, so that each step had a barely perceptible spring, cat like, so that your overall impression was that he was an athlete, an ex-athlete for sure, one who had not lost much off his fastball and could probably deal some damage.

If he was looking for me, I was betting it wasn't to see my dance moves.

I stayed in the booth for another hour. Bobby brought me one more Bourbon and beer chaser. I nursed it the way the big man had made his beer last. If he was waiting for me, I didn't want to be too wasted to fight him off.

But the longer I sat, the more I became convinced that, even if he was the murderer, he wouldn't be coming for me tonight. He had called me at home. He had asked about me. People had seen him. If anything happened to me, there were at least a few people, notably Bobby, who could give the cops a good description. No, nothing was going to happen tonight.

But who could he be? It was unlikely he was connected with LaSalle. Where would the lonely scholar hook up with him? It was possible he was Irma's lover. After all, she was with me tonight, and probably intended to be with me all night. But he didn't fit the pictures I'd seen. Wes? Like I said about me, it could be an old Army buddy.

Or he could just be a freelance asshole. God knows, I've turned over enough trash cans in the past couple of years that any number of people might want a piece of me.

It was about 2 a.m. when I finally settled with Bobby, nodded to the last solitary drinker at the bar, and stepped onto the sidewalk. I looked west and east, then across West End Avenue. Nobody there. I gave myself mental credit for checking, and a mental checkmark for being correct. The big man wasn't an idiot. He wasn't going for me tonight, if he was going for me at all.

I began my walk toward home. Twenty minutes and I should be back in the garage apartment, behind a dead bolt and safe from anything else tonight. I had kept a clear head. I had taken my own advice.

But while I'd been in a number of scrapes in the last few years, I'd suddenly become aware just how I'd placed myself in the target zone. My reaction to the big man was different than usual. This time, I'd outwaited the danger. Next time I might not be so lucky.

I got to the convenience store right before the park. There on the sidewalk was Fletcher, the old man with the Pabst cans. He was splayed out like a cat who'd spent his ninth life.

I leaned over him. "You ok, old man?"

He groaned. "Lift me up, son. Sidewalk reached up and tripped me."

I saw a small cut on his cheek that oozed blood, but otherwise he seemed unharmed. "Anything hurt? Might need to be careful how you get up."

"Hit my face and skinned my knee. I don't think anything's broke."

I leaned over again. As I did, I heard a squealing of tires and, after that, a shot. Instinctively I fell on Fletcher, who gave a small fart and cursed. I could hear the car racing and, as I looked, I saw a dark Plymouth sedan speeding away. I could make out the first few numbers of a TN-2 tag. If that was the big man who'd taken a shot at me, he was local.

"Get off me." Fletcher was wriggling with a fairly inefficient impatience.

We had that in common. The impatience, I mean.

I never know whether it's the training, the experience, or just plain, dumb luck. I had leaned over Fletcher, then had dove onto him. Had I done it after I heard the crack of gunfire? Or had I anticipated it, ducking down at the best moment, cheating the shooter of his prize?

Out in the boonies, walking point, it happened more than once. Something in the jungle air wasn't quite right. Or there was a silence where there should have been a sound. With a platoon counting on you to understand where danger was, you had to be right. And you had to be right before the enemy was.

And so I dove on Fletcher and the shot went high. Who knows? It could have gone wide too. If I hadn't dove, it could have gone right through me.

The car was well gone down West End, into the late Nashville night. I got off Fletcher's back, dusted him off, and set him on his way.

"Wonder why they shot at us?"

I gave him a fake smile. "Probably just a couple of rednecks, one beer over the line and having a little fun. I wouldn't worry about it." I patted him on the shoulder. "Go on home and get some peroxide on that cheek, old man. Don't want an infection."

He walked heavily to 31st, then heaved himself north, toward wherever he lived.

The rush of adrenaline was over for me, and I felt suddenly a wave of cold wash through my body. I felt like I might be sick and choked it back. No need to puke in the street.

But I was rattled.

I made the twenty minute journey in about ten, climbed the stairs to my apartment, went in and bolted the door. I poured myself a double in the water glass, and I drank it like medicine. It burned all the way down to my gut.

I found an old notebook and wrote down the numbers I remembered from the Plymouth. Then I pulled the shade down and drew the curtains tight. I stripped the light down to a single, small desk lamp, and I poured another drink. I held it in my hands. I didn't drink it. It was there in case the fear made me want to puke again.

After a while, the phone rang. I let it go four rings before I answered it. I knew who it would be. I wanted to be ready.

"You're lucky to be alive, shitbird."

"And you're lucky I don't know where you're staying. Yet."

"For a guy who could have been in the morgue, you sure do have a mouth on you. Better stop what you're doing. Next time, you won't be lucky."

"Come for me again, and you won't be lucky at all." I slammed down the phone.

Funny how fast fear goes to anger.

I drank the bourbon, checked the deadbolt, cut the light and went to bed. I pulled the covers up around my ears. It took a half hour to calm the beating of my heart but, once I did, I slept without dreaming.

Chapter Twenty-One

I WOKE TO AN insistent cardinal chirping some inane bird nonsense. At first, I thought he had managed to get inside the apartment somehow. That's how loud he was. But it may just have been the hangover.

Standing inside a shower with the hot water ratcheted up to steam level, I played the night out again in my head. A warning from an unknown player. Could have been Irma's lover. Could have been a friend of one of the other two. Then the big man made his appearance, a man with no accent, according to Bobby. But that wasn't the phone caller, who'd made his second call after the shooter. He had a Southern accent, very heavy, and sounded like someone who wouldn't have been familiar with a Vanderbilt professor unless he serviced her, or his, car.

That indicated that the big man was not the shooter. But there was certainly another player.

It also indicated that, as a novice blackmailer, I'd stirred up enough hornets to nearly get stung. And that was what the ruse was about, after all: to draw out the hornet that had stung Tippy, while leaving the other hornets be.

And it indicated that there were two to take care of, one way or another. The shooter and the big man were not the same person, but they might be on the same team. The question was: whose team were they on.

I didn't go far for breakfast, given that my head was pounding and my legs still didn't feel up to a sprint. I ended up at the Krystal, with two square burgers and metallic tasting coffee, reading the morning Tennessean. There had been a fire at a tire storage facility south of town in the night, and every Metro fire unit from downtown had been there all night. While that was happening, a girl found a body on the east bank of the Cumberland River, and it sounded like half of Metro police had responded. Busy night in the city, and it was a good thing the shooter hadn't been successful. I would have been missed in the excitement.

I walked down a worn path and ended up in front of the little campus bungalow that housed VU's campus police. I was taking a chance that Don Mercer would be there, and the dispatcher out front, Mercer's sometimes girlfriend, smiled and jerked her thumb toward the warren of offices that used to be bedrooms, now all jumbled into a rat's nest of desks and chairs and typewriters.

Don Mercer sat behind one such desk and typewriter, staring at the small Royal machine as if it had done something horrible to him.

"I figure if you just talk nice to it, everything will be all right."

He looked up and glared at me, his nostrils flaring. "I have spent an hour typing up this report. An ever-loving hour. And I just realized I'm on a form we discontinued two years ago."

"Nobody will notice."

"The hell they won't. New chief is spit and polish. The new form is his baby. He'll notice."

Vanderbilt PD had gone through a chief, an interim chief, and a new chief in less than three years. The interim had been a lieutenant better connected than Mercer, so he'd got the call. He was a disaster. It wasn't clear yet that the new chief was an improvement.

"Sorry, brother. Life ain't fair like that."

He ripped the form out of the carriage, balled it up and threw it with emphasis into a trash can. "Damn waste of time."

Paperwork for a cop is always a waste of time. I'd heard Don say it over and over. But it was also the one thing a cop did every single day, if he was working at all. Paperwork made the history, and without the history, cops couldn't get others to do their jobs.

"What are you here for, Jackson? I never see you in the station unless you want something."

"That's not true, Donnie. Sometimes I come to flirt with the dispatcher."

"If you do, then you're only doing that because you want something. Like I said."

I sat down in the chair on the other side of his desk. Don's office, even as second in command, was a claustrophobic affair, about six by six. There was a two-drawer file cabinet, one drawer of which held various accoutrements that helped him get through shifts. Peanuts. Crackers. Slim Jims. None of them particularly healthy when eaten in the quantities Mercer consumed them.

"Have a seat, Jackson. Make yourself at home." Don had leaned back so that his chair was balanced on its two rear legs. "And tell me what it is you want this time."

I didn't believe there was much profit in telling him about Tippy. Cops generally hold a dim view of blackmail, and that was what I was pretending to practice. But I was also working for the University, watching out for protesters. I took that angle.

"Somebody took a shot at me last night." It seemed like a reasonable gambit.

"The places you drink in, it's a wonder more people don't take a swing at you. You can be obnoxious."

"Not a swing, Don. A shot. As in, from a firearm."

That got his attention. The chair came down with a thud onto the front two legs. Mercer lowered his eyes and looked directly at me. "Did you just say that someone fired a weapon at you last night?

"Indeed I did."

"Who the hell have you pissed off, man?" He moved papers on his desk, looking for a notepad, which he found. "This happen on campus?"

"Not really. Up West End, beyond 31st."

"You were at the High Life then. Or Linda's." His face when he said "Linda's" was the kind you make when the john hasn't been flushed for a day or two in a public toilet.

"High Life." Now it was my turn to look directly at him. "But nothing happened there. This was out of the blue."

"I don't know anything that happens out of the blue. There's always a reason. And people almost always know the reason, too."

I knew the basic reason, but I swerved down another trail. "I don't know, Don. Seem like there's all kinds of people involved in these protests. Students. Faculty. Town people. Hell, citizens of every color and stripe."

"That doesn't compute, Jackson. As far as I can tell, you're just sitting around, watching."

I could have brought up the organizing at the CME church, but I didn't need to get somebody hounding Stump. "That's all I can figure. Except for that, I'm as well behaved as a choir boy."

"If choir boys live on bourbon, I guess that's right."

We sat quietly for a minute. I didn't let the remark about choirboys sink in too much. Don and I did not agree on my choices of life conduct. That's fine. He doesn't have to like what I do.

I pulled out the paper I'd torn from the notebook. "I got a look at the car he drove. He took one shot, I dove, and he peeled out, rubber squealing."

Mercer took the paper. "TN-2 86. There's two more numbers on a plate."

"I know. You're lucky I got those two. I was lying face down on a sidewalk, on top of an old man." He gave me a quizzical look. "Fletcher, the boozer who drinks Pabst after Pabst at High Life."

"Could he have been shooting at Fletcher?"

"Be serious, Don."

"All right. Let me call downtown and see what Motor Vehicles says about this. Make and model?"

"Plymouth Fury. 73? 74? I don't keep up with their models."

"No reason to. They're shit."

"Even the Barracuda?"

"Especially the Barracuda."

Don called and was waiting on hold, so I went out to the dispatcher. Her name was Ann. She and Mercer had been on and off for a year. One of them would decide that the relationship had run its course, and they'd split up, and then the other would convince the splitter that they needed to try again. I'd lost count. Four or five times? It was never the same one who did the breakup. I told Don it probably meant they were made for each other.

"How can you stand that fat little black man, Ann?" I was leaning on her desk.

"He's not so bad most of the time." She was a darker woman than Don. He was milk chocolate. She was straight coffee, no cream.

"I don't know. He seems pretty uptight if you ask me."

She smiled a brilliant smile that was probably why Don came back when he broke up. "Uptight is not a bad thing in this world, if the alternative is crazy. And Jackson, there sure is some crazy out there in the world."

Yeah, don't I know it. "Let me know when you're ready for a change, Ann."

She laughed because she knew it was just idle flirting. "You need to find your own, Jackson. You don't need anybody else's."

I had that once. But I held my tongue. I smiled back, not as brilliantly, and certainly not as honestly.

Back in Mercer's office, he was finishing up a call. "All right. Yeah, sounds fine. We'll get together some time." He hung up the phone and looked at the receiver. "When hell freezes over, we will."

"Friendly call?"

"Just Lonnie Forbes."

Lonnie Forbes was a Metro officer who'd gone through the academy with Don. They were the only two black guys in the class, and Lonnie had attached himself to Don then, and kept trying to now. The problem was, where Don was an efficient and effective officer, Lonnie was a perpetual screw up. Don didn't like to be associated with that.

"Why'd you call Lonnie?"

"Because Lonnie has been moved over to the Central Records Division. There's less he can do to screw things up. Christ, Records was screwed before he got there. What else could he do?"

If there was a way, Lonnie would probably find it. "And what about the Plymouth?"

"You had it about right. 74 Plymouth Fury. TN2-8644. Registered to Rebecca Nolan out in Green Hills. Reported stolen last night," he looked at his notebook, "at 9:45 p.m." He put the paper down and glanced toward the door over my shoulder. Satisfied no one was outside, he asked, "She somebody you messed over? Or related to somebody you messed over?"

"More likely some clown with a gun and a bad attitude is also a car thief. But since you asked nicely, no, I don't know anybody named Nolan."

"Well, here's something interesting. It wasn't reported stolen from Green Hills. It was stolen from, get this, the D lot at Vanderbilt."

"Why didn't you guys get the call on that?"

"Who knows? Maybe she doesn't know we've got police here. According to Lonnie, the report says she was in Benton Chapel listening to an organ recital."

"Sure. That's what all the cool chicks do in Green Hills."

"Not everyone is out all hours of the night, Jackson." He leaned up and put his chin in his hands. I've seen him do that late at night, in a bar, when he's about to get philosophical. He didn't look philosophical now. "So let's try it again. What's this person, this Nolan lady, doing getting her car stolen from Vanderbilt, and then the car thief having some kind of hard on for you? Who have you stirred up, Jackson?"

I held my arms out, palms up. "Swear to God, Donnie, I'm as clueless as you are. Somebody took a shot at me. I didn't put them up to it."

"There's something you're not telling me. I don't know what it is. I don't know why you're not. But you'd be better off getting it off your chest, Jackson. Secrets aren't good for anyone. Especially where guns are involved."

I didn't necessarily disagree with him on that one. But this was a secret I was going to keep, at least for a while.

"Thanks, man. I appreciate knowing it was a car thief who took a shot at me. Or at Fletcher."

"Nobody took a shot at old Fletch. You're right about that." Don leaned back on two legs again, the chair making a small, disturbing creak. "Don't bother Ann on the way out. She doesn't need any grief from you."

I waved as I left. As I passed Ann's desk, she was on the phone, handling some irate parent. I made a kissing noise with my lips, she smiled her brilliant smile, and I left the bungalow.

Chapter Twenty-Two

At Hannigan's I splurged for a steak with some fries. Instead of my usual, I had a cup of coffee. I needed to think.

I knew that of my three marks, only LaSalle lived in Green Hills, and a quick look at the Nashville phone directory showed that he and a Leonard Nolan lived on Red Bird Drive. That had to be more than coincidence, right?

I doubted that LsSalle had either a way to hotwire a car or a propensity to burn rubber and fire a gun in the night. So there had to be the two of them. And number two had to be the voice on the phone as well. And if LaSalle seemed not up to killing Tippy, well, this guy, whoever he was, certainly could.

While Don thought the key was that the car was on campus when it was stolen, it seemed clear that it was really the neighbor connection that was the key. I needed to spook LaSalle enough that he would give up his accomplice. There was no doubt he would do it. I could break him.

I got to Calhoun Hall by 2 p.m. LaSalle was in his office with the door shut, talking on the phone. His voice sounded measured, that kind of silky baritone that's meant to convey authority. It's the voice I wanted him to stray from.

I walked down the hall to the department secretary's office. Her face fell a little when she saw it was me, but she recovered. "What do you want?"

"Professor LaSalle."

She pushed her chin up in the air a little. "He does not have office hours today."

"Just go down and tell him I'm here. He'll want to see me."

"I'm not at all sure ... "

"I'm sure." I looked down at her nameplate on the desk. "I'm very sure, Cynthia. Just go tell him. Give him this note."

I handed her a folded piece of notebook paper on which I'd written, "I know you took a shot. And one before last night too." It was folded in that way we did in high school, when we put a little lock fold on it, to make sure it wasn't too easy to peer inside.

She rose from her desk and took the paper, looking at it doubtfully. "I'll see."

She left and was back in under two minutes. "He said to ask you to wait. He'll come get you."

"Did he read the note?"

"Yes. That's when he said you should wait."

She didn't offer me a seat, and so I stood. Her office window was cracked open, and there was a steady breeze of early spring air. It was chilled, but in the sunlit office it felt good.

"I hope you are not bothering Dr. LaSalle. He's been under so much pressure lately, what with his publishing deadline and all."

"And becoming the chair of the department too."

"That too." She caught herself. "How do you know about that?"

"He told me. Very stressful, all of it." I tried to look vaguely understanding, as understanding as a guy who had no idea could. "I imagine it's been hard for you too. All this pressure."

She smiled thinly. "Oh, I don't know."

But she didn't finish whatever she was going to say. From down the hall came the sound of what could have been many things, but to someone who'd heard it the night before it was unmistakable.

Cynthia froze at her desk, eyes and mouth both wide. I ran down the hall and burst into Watkins LaSalle's office.

There he sat at his desk, slumped back in his chair and leaning to his left. In his right hand was a pistol, one that looked like the kind of Saturday night special you can get if you just ask the right person.

And Watkins LaSalle had put it in his mouth and eaten a bullet.

Behind me, Cynthia sobbed. And then she started screaming.

Cynthia stopped screaming when I put my hand on her arm. It was like a switch flipped, something that hit her just in the right place, in the right way, and she re-set. Her emotional contact points must have been on her arm. She closed her mouth, sobbed twice, then ran back to her office.

"Call Campus Police," I said to her back.

Somebody would, even if she didn't. I went into LaSalle's office, careful not to touch anything. I hoped he had left my note somewhere in plain sight. It would be a bitch if he'd landed on it. But I found the note, after a moment of moving around the motionless body, at the edge of his desk, near the inbox he used as an organizer. I took the note and put it in my jeans pocket.

I waited by the door, keeping various faculty and students from looking inside. "Just let the police get here. Until then, there's no good reason to assume anything." That didn't make any of them go away.

What did make them go away was Mercer and a couple of VUPD officers, Bentley and Crain. I knew the two officers as pretty dependable and strait-laced. Mercer went in, motioned me inside, and shut the door. I heard Bentley say, "Y'all need to disperse now. Get along." And I heard mumbling and shuffling.

Don set about looking carefully, much as I had, careful not to touch anything. "Metro is on the way. They'll do the scene. But it looks pretty clear. He committed suicide."

"Looks that way."

"I don't see a note."

I almost started, then I realized he meant a suicide note. "They don't always, do they?"

"I'd have thought this one would." He motioned at the bookshelves. "He likes words."

Metro arrived and talked with Cynthia first. By the time they got to me, they asked about the note I'd sent in to him. Cynthia had let that cat out of the bag.

"Just to tell him that I couldn't locate a student he was looking for."

Mercer gave them a sideways look. "We sometimes give Jackson a little work when a parent wants to know what junior is up to."

The Metro officer grinned. "Kind of like a skip trace?"

"Except I'm not a private investigator. I used to work here. I know all the haunts."

"Easy money, then. This professor knew to call you?"

"He said a parent had told him. He called me up." I nodded toward Mercer. "Some money's easier than others. Didn't expect to come in on this kind of mess, though."

"Secretary says he's been under pressure. You sense that?"

"I mean, I didn't know him before. Some of these guys are wound pretty tight. But, yeah, he didn't seem comfortable when I was here before. Not to diagnose, but he seemed depressed."

"You only saw him twice then?"

"Once. I came today, to tell him I couldn't find the student. I might have had the name wrong, though. You never know."

"Secretary said you sent a note in."

"Just said, couldn't find him. Need a quick chat."

"And he kills himself. That seems kind of an odd sequence."

"Look, who knows how depressed people will react? He hired me, but he seemed to think I was somehow out to get him."

"Paranoid?"

"Yeah, something like that, I guess. He insisted on having the door open the last time. He stood the whole time. Kind of gave me the creeps, if you want to know the truth."

"Why'd you work for him, then?"

"Easy money, right?"

The Metro officer looked at Mercer, then at me. "I think it fits together. He was having trouble. Depression. Pressure. Maybe paranoia. Maybe he was having a bad day on top of that. You coming with bad news, or if he's paranoid, you coming to do something to him. I mean, it doesn't make sense to us, because we're not in the shape he's in. But he's got a gun. He keeps it here because he's paranoid. And then, you're coming, he doesn't want to see you, and before you know it, boom. I mean, who can even understand why people do what they do?"

Chapter Twenty-Three

WE LEFT IT AT that. I'd go by Metro in the morning and give a statement, and they'd take care of getting Cynthia sorted out. Mercer and his two officers left, but not before Mercer said something about my luck. He meant bad luck, but I thought it was pretty good luck.

LaSalle must have been the one who'd taken the shot at me. He took a car from his neighbor. Maybe he'd managed to lift a car key from his neighbor's house. He'd tracked me down and shot at me. I didn't think he was the main guy in this, because he didn't sound like the caller. But he must have been either the shooter or the mastermind. Why else would my coming here put the fear of God in him enough to end his life?

But that was Tippy's business.

I left campus intending to put as much distance between myself and the idyllic pastoral that is Vanderbilt as I could. The sound of the shot. The lifeless body of LaSalle. The sight of his blood, his disfigured head. All these were things I was familiar with. Any soldier who's been in combat can hear those things, see those things, even smell them, and be immediately transported back to worse times, scarier times, more dangerous times.

I knew vets who take immediate cover, reflexively, when a truck backfires.

And I knew me. I have enough trouble walking around every day, keeping myself moving, that anything can put me off my game, can make me want to crawl up inside a bottle and drown.

I didn't want a bottle now, but I wanted a drink. I cut down 19th Avenue, made a left and headed toward The Hideaway. I went in, had two shots, and left. That settled the chills.

What I needed was to sit and think. Some people use the library for that kind of thing. I know others who go sit in a church pew. I go to a church too, but not for the sanctuary. I went around back of West End Methodist, to the church gym entrance, and climbed the little set of bleachers to the top. I leaned back on the cinder block wall and shut my eyes.

The sounds of basketball played joyously if not always expertly rang in my ears. Shouts to give me the ball. The thump, thump of a ball handler who was taking a little too long to set up a teammate. Little gasps of profanity when an opponent got by for an easy layup. I could hear all the things I knew. I didn't have to see them.

Just like I didn't have to see blood, or death, to know them. In my mind's eye I could hear and see the swish of the jungle canopy. I saw the face of an Aussie digger I met on R and R, a guy who disappeared just before another GI was shot. I saw a silent Huey Slick turn and glide out of sight. I knew them, but I didn't want to associate them with LaSalle.

LaSalle was just a killer who'd been caught, a killer who wasn't going to hang around for the ending.

And true to Tippy's wishes, the other two candidates for blackmail were scot free. I'd tell them later. That would be interesting.

I sat listening, reconciling my mental accounts, past and present. They didn't balance, but they added up. And what they added up to didn't make me happy.

Watkins LaSalle was Tippy's murderer, or at least the man who put the money in the pocket of the man who did, the big man. And LaSalle must have been the man who called me; if he could produce his velvet tones, maybe he could change his voice on a whim. Like Don said, he liked words. He knew how to use them.

For all that, Tippy would certainly say, he should pay. And he had. But my part in all this was problematic. I had put him in the position where he had killed himself. I had made it inevitable that he would. I found a weakness, and I pushed hard. I set him up, even if I didn't realize what I was setting him up to do.

I've killed before. Not as much as people think, but it has happened. But that was in combat. Outside, in the world? Never. Not even close.

But I'd killed Watkins LaSalle as surely as if I'd pulled the trigger myself.

That made me sick to my stomach. And when I'm sick to my stomach, I don't go for Rolaids. I go for a drink. And more than one.

I kept it going at a steady pace. I walked all the way downtown to Printer's Alley. I went to Oscar's. I pulled a shift at Dusty Roads, then worked through the dive bars over by the bus station. I didn't stay long at any of them, but I drank a little at all of them. Most people looked at me and gave me space. If my expression was as black as my mood, I didn't much blame them.

I was back at The Hideaway around nine, and the evening crowd was beginning to swell. The bartender, who'd served me earlier, nodded, pushed a bowl of bar snacks toward me, and motioned with an old-fashioned glass and a raised eyebrow. "Yeah. Double."

I had slowed enough that I only took a sip at first. At a certain point, there's not a reason to drink more. Once I get to an equilibrium, a place where my head isn't about to explode,

I like to maintain that buzz. Some days it just takes more than others. Today it took a lot.

"Hey, fella." The bartender was in front of me, polishing an already dry hi-ball glass. "Lady back there in the corner booth is asking about you."

"Ladies don't ask for me, buddy. They might ask for me to leave, but that's about it."

"Tonight's your lucky night, then. First time for everything." He pointed over my shoulder with the glass.

It was Betty Henderson. She smiled when I turned around and waved me toward the booth.

Before I knew it, I was standing in front of her. "I'm not great company tonight."

She patted the seat. "Don't worry. My girlfriend and I came in for a drink. We were just leaving, and I saw you. Come sit for a minute." At my quizzed expression, she said, "She left. Keep me company for a minute."

I sat what I thought was a discrete distance from her. "You look good." And she did. Hip-hugger jeans with some kind of heels. A ruffled top that looked a little more like what a Playboy bunny would wear, definitely not what your Aunt Tilly's ruffled top would look like. Silver hoop earrings, with her hair doing a really fine cascading thing. Yes, she looked good.

"You had a rough day. Or a rough night. Want to talk about it?"

"I killed somebody today."

Her eyebrows went up, but she composed her face quickly. "Are you drunk, Jackson?"

"Been trying all day. Haven't managed it yet." I noticed that I'd stopped drinking the bourbon in my hand. "My brain won't let up enough to let the alcohol take over." It was true. I could feel the world disoriented, but it was from inside my head, not from anything I was putting into my body.

"Why?"

A simple enough question. It was one I had an answer for, but should I tell her?

She put her hand on mine. "What's going on, Jackson?"

I didn't think. I just started telling her. About the shot at me. About the reason I thought it was taken. I left out Irma and Wes. They were out of it now, just as Tippy would have wanted. I concentrated on LaSalle.

"I pushed him pretty hard, Betty. I wanted him to crack, to break. I was sure he was at the center of it. So when I sent the note in, and I heard the shot, I knew I'd been right."

She left her hand on mine the entire time, only changing once to hold it in both her hands. She was looking at me, not as if she were sorry for me, but as if she didn't know what she could do to help me.

"Let me take you home, Jackson."

"I don't live that far. I can walk."

"Let me take you home. With me."

I squeezed her hand and then extracted mine. "I don't think that's a good idea, Betty. We did that once before, and I screwed it up. It's taken us this long to get to a conversation. I'd just as soon not mess up again." Because I was pretty sure that I would mess it up again if I went home with her.

"You need a friend tonight. You don't need a lover."

I wasn't sure either would do me much good, but it was a cinch that bourbon wasn't working. "I don't think I'm much of either right now."

She smiled. "Let me take you home. We can talk. Or we don't have to talk. We don't have to do anything." She patted my hand. "But you shouldn't be by yourself. You're not being very friendly to Jackson right now."

She had a point. "All I really want to do is sleep. Maybe if I sleep long enough, all this will leach out of my head."

She scooted around on the vinyl bench so that our legs touched, from hip to knee. She put her face close to mine, and pulled our hands back together, close to our faces. "Listen," she whispered, "you're too hard on yourself. Come. Relax. Whatever you need to do. Just not alone."

She shoved me with her hip. It was notice that this conversation was over, and she'd had the last word.

I complied.

Back at her place, she made a pot of decaf and we sat in her living room, mostly quiet. I remarked that she'd finished painting the living room since the last time I'd been there. She pointed out the new curtains, green with white translucent panels between. We let Otis Redding spin, sitting on his dock at the bay. I began to feel the tension loosen.

We spent an hour like that. Companionable silence, broken by innocuous chit chat.

"Why are you beating yourself up about this?"

It was another simple question, asked quietly.

"He killed your friend. He took a shot, or had someone take a shot, at you. You let him know the jig was up. And he took his way out." She leaned forward on the couch, put her hand on my knee. "You didn't give him the gun. You didn't pull the trigger. You didn't decide for him."

"He was a little, deceitful man. Petty in his way, even."

"See? There you go."

"That's not what I mean, Betty. Because of the way he was, I didn't expect him to make that choice. Too vain, maybe. But it's a neat solution that doesn't feel that neat. You know what I mean?"

"You can't stand being right. That's what it sounds like to me."

Maybe that was it. I had primed myself for a big set piece with three flawed people, each of whom had a reason to mess Tippy up. I had put my plan in motion, and I'd executed it so well that someone had taken his shot at me.

But he'd messed up by taking a car from his own neighborhood. When I pressed hard, he cracked. She was right. Why wouldn't I take "yes" for an answer?

I stood up. "You're probably right, Betty. I need to sleep on it. Or sleep it off. Whichever is the right way to think about it."

She leaned back and draped her arm on the back of the sofa. "You don't have to go."

"Yes, I do. We said friends, not lovers."

She threw both hands in the air. "You have a literal one-track mind. You can stay as a friend. I can hold you as a friend. Nothing else needs to happen."

But I know that road. There's the place where you start, and then there's the place where you end. "Not tonight, Betty. I appreciate the coffee and the support. You may trust me, but I don't trust myself. Not where this friendship is concerned."

She rose and put her hands around my waist. "Ok. That's the right answer tonight." She tiptoed up to lightly kiss my cheek. "That's a friendly kiss. Be a friend tonight and take care of yourself."

Chapter Twenty-Four

THE SLEEP DID ME little good. I woke up with a hangover I hadn't worked hard enough for, and a memory of the night before that should have made me glad but didn't. The only thing I could say for sure was that Betty and I were still friends. That counted for something, but it didn't make today any easier.

I would have to find Irma and Wes and take them off the hook. I supposed they would be glad, but who knows? People react to the truth in all kinds of strange ways.

First though I had to give my statement downtown, which I did, and then do my time at the protest. As the Davis Cup grew nearer, the student body was taking a little more interest in the faculty's circle march, to the point where there were almost as many students as faculty. And not just the long hairs, the ones who could be counted on to wave signs and chant about any damn thing. Lately, there'd been an increasing number of students who bore the traditional marks of frat boys and sorority girls. And that meant that it was growing in the campus's consciousness.

Maybe the faculty were doing more than walking in a circle.

I had resumed my perch on the nearby bench as Willa Winter, accompanied by her student lackey, walked up directly and sat down without ceremony.

"Yes?" I gave her a harmless smile, as if I was happy to banter but not insisting.

"You are a bad man, Mr. Trade." She said it with a little feeling, but without much volume.

"Why do you say that?" I shifted so that I could face her directly. She was sitting, angled toward me, legs tightly together, feet under the bench. Prim. Proper. Her very light blond hair, almost white, pulled severely into a ponytail that made the heart shape of her face more pronounced. Overall, anybody would have to admit, she was good-looking. Her student towered over her, his mouth set in a frown.

"The word is all over campus. You had Cynthia Reeves take a note to Watkins LaSalle. He read it and then killed himself."

"As a connect-the-dots, that is correct in sequence."

"Are you suggesting that there's more to it than that? Because I hardly see how it matters."

It was clear the campus rumor machine had cranked up and manufactured a story that, while it might be partly true, was not as wild as the real truth. And whether Irma or Wes had connected the missing dot to the sequence was anybody's guess.

But I had no doubt they'd keep it to themselves if they had connected it.

"I don't see that it matters in any case, Dr. Winter. It's true I had the secretary take him a note. It's true that it explained why I wanted to see him." I pulled a pack of cigarettes from my shirt pocket and offered her one, which she refused with a slight shudder. I shook one out, flipped open my lighter and lit it. "But here's the problem with your sequence, Dr. Winter. You assume that he got the note, then shot himself in the head. You assume that he did that because of what was in the note."

"Of course."

"When I was an undergrad, in Dr. Murray's logic class, we called that a fallacy. I don't remember which kind. But you are assuming that, because he committed suicide after being handed my note, he committed suicide because of what was in the note."

I took in a lungful of smoke, breathed it out so that it didn't go in her face, but wafted toward her Topsider'd lackey. She waved her hand, trying to dissipate it. He blew toward it and glared at me.

"But you can see how there are plenty of other ways to construct that scene. Let's say he was about to do the deed when interrupted by the secretary. He could have taken the note from her, and then resumed what he was doing. In that case, it has nothing to do with the note. Or with me."

She flushed a little. "Well, then, why was the note not in his office?"

I kept my gaze steady. "I have no idea. Was it not there? I don't know that it's relevant. Maybe Metro took it. Maybe Housekeeping cleaned it up."

"Housekeeping has been nowhere near the office. It's a crime scene."

I wanted to tell her that, once the police declared it a suicide, it was just a sad place where a guy died. But that wasn't what interested me.

"Either you or someone else has been very diligent. Or nosy." I smiled again. I didn't want to become a smart ass again, but I did want her to back off. "You ought to let the police do the work, instead of running around constructing theories that don't hold up to the smallest amount of daylight."

She shot a look at her student, as if she wanted to invite him to refute me, then thought how strange that would be. "There is no earthly reason that Watkins LaSalle would have killed himself. He was respected in his field. He was about to be made department chair. He had everything he could have wanted." Her hands were encased in expensive leather gloves, and the hands had knotted the gloves into little fists. "You are here, watching our every move. You were there when he took his life."

"That's another fallacy. Just because I'm somewhere and you don't like it? That just means you have a problem with me. It doesn't mean I'm doing anything wrong." I let the smile fade from my face. "I thought we had agreed to let bygones be bygones."

She stood up unexpectedly. "You are not a good person, and you make me furious." As if to prove it, she gave a stomp with one high heel. It came across as stereotypical, staged. Although maybe that's just what she was in real life--staged, a stereotype. Or maybe I wasn't giving her enough credit. Sometimes cliches are cliches because they're just too true. Maybe she was furious, and I was the easiest target.

I finished my cigarette and flicked it out into the street. "I'm sorry you feel that way. But you're welcome to believe what you want, Dr. Winter. I'll believe what is true."

If the stereotypical move was to spin and mutter a sort of feminine harrumph, well, that's what she did. Her student watched me as he retreated behind her, then turned to catch up with her. His jaw was set in a very unattractive way.

It was just the sort of thing to make my morning. If a faculty rumor could have this approximately right, what else could I expect?

As the faculty organized themselves, I felt a tap on my shoulder. Actually, it was more like a pop, but one that was deliberately more like a tap than a shove. "JT, my brother."

It was Stump Collins.

"Stump. You just showing up to watch this? Looking for tips on how to protest?"

He spit, then sat down. "Hell, man, don't need no instruction from the teaching folk. Ain't nothing they got to tell me."

"How's the planning going? Metro come across?"

He shook his head. "We're hitting roadblocks. Metro has a new reason not to cooperate every time we talk. Vandy is just sitting on its ass."

"Sorry to hear that."

"Might be it's about time for you to make your move. Might be that you could shake Vandy loose."

"You see what Vanderbilt thinks of my talents, Stump." I motioned toward the protesters. "I just watch and wait."

He looked at me up and down, as if he was searching for something. "I don't know that you are on their side, though."

"Got that right, Stump. I'm on my side. Right now, the rest of you are just outside my concern."

"That the reason you got canned?" He grinned at my surprised look. "Yeah, I asked around. You used to have to behave so you could get paid. Now?" He made an exaggerated shrug with his palms. "You tell me, man."

"I got canned because I messed up a guy who was sleeping with my wife." He whistled quietly. "That's right. And so, my allegiance is not to the University."

"All right, all right." He reached over and pulled my cigarettes out of my pocket. "Where's that lighter?" I gave it to him, and he lit up, elbows on knees, watching the faculty start their circle walk.

I took the lighter from him and lit up too.

"There she is." He took the cigarette and pointed toward Willa Winter.

"Yep. It's her day to be here."

"You remember I told you she looked familiar? Well, she does. What'd you call that look she's got? Unique? Sort of thing you'd not forget?"

"I guess. She's a little bit of an ice queen, but that could be memorable."

"Ha," he snorted, and coughed a little bit of smoke. "Ice queen. That's pretty good. Girl's name is Winter, right?"

"Willa Winter." Alliterative, like an ice queen might be.

"What if I told you I could show you a picture of that girl? Something that would surprise you."

"I don't know, Stump. Friend of yours got a camera?"

"Not a friend of mine. But I got a magazine back at my place that she's in. Miss Winter, they called her. Two-page spread, brother. Miss Spring, all light and springy. Miss Summer. That's a looker, like she's about to put some heat on you. Miss Autumn. And Miss Winter. Our girl right here. Looking so cold your tongue might stick on her if you licked her. Looking like she might like ripping your tongue right off you."

A professor who did some dancing in graduate school. Some lingerie modeling. "You sure, Stump?"

"Sure? Hell, I'm certain. That's the girl right there." He stubbed the butt out. "Tell you what, brother. She's aged pretty good. Girl's still fine." He gave a low wolf whistle. "Damn fine."

So this was the history faculty member in Tippy's manuscript. I wondered if she knew that Tippy knew.

And then I wondered, not for the first time, if Stump was the community enforcer Tippy wrote about. "Off the subject, Stump?"

"I don't know why you want to leave this one. Just look at her. All righteous now. But she used to take her clothes off for money." He looked at me, then back at her. "Sure. What you want to say?"

"You ever kill a man, Stump?"

His head snapped around. His mouth slightly open, slightly snarled. "What the hell does that mean?"

"Just what it sounds like. Did you ever kill a man?"

He seemed to think it over. "Let's see now. Kill somebody. I mean, there's people I haven't seen in a while. They might be dead."

"Don't play me. I'm just asking. I'm not planning to tell the cops."

"I don't know what you're trying to do. Let's just say that I haven't and leave it there." He puffed derisively. "You ever kill anybody, JT?"

"Yes." I didn't say, even yesterday. "I was in combat. I didn't want to die."

Stump nodded, his lips pursed. "Yeah, sounds about right. If you don't want to die, you might have to kill. I can see that."

"Tippy Taylor was writing a book. Did you know that?"

"No big surprise. Tippy was writing all kinds of things."

"He didn't name her by name, but he was on to Willa Winter."

"He put her in the book? That'd be pretty damn cold."

"I think he also had you in the book, Stump. He talks about an organizer who is judge and jury in the neighborhood. Someone you don't want to cross."

"Sounds like a bad mother fucker."

"When I think back to that night I went into Tippy's place, it made me think of you." I ground out my cigarette. "What'd you say? You let me know when you come to the neighborhood. I can take care of you. Sounds exactly like the man in Tippy's book."

"Just because I'm the unofficial mayor of The Gardens don't mean I'm in Tippy's book. Or that Tippy knew shit."

"Like I say, Stump, it doesn't make any difference to me. I just need to know if there's another mayor on the north side I need to be worried about, now that I've got Tippy's manuscript."

"Hell, man. You don't have to be worried. Rest his soul, Tippy don't have to be worried no more either." He had said all this while looking sidelong at me, as if he was barely able to tear his gaze from the marchers. Now he returned his full attention to them. "So you figure Miss Winter has gone all stuffy? Or you figure she still can get down?"

"I have a feeling we won't ever know."

"What's that supposed to mean? You never know. Miss Winter might like a big black breeze to warm her up."

He laughed. It was a double hoot, like an owl who grew up on the north side, not like his brother owls. "That's right. Warm her all the way up."

And with that he rose, clipped me again on the shoulder, and strode off toward the parking lot. "Stay ready, Freddy. I may be needing you soon."

Chapter Twenty-Five

FROM HANNIGAN'S LATER THAT afternoon, I called Irma Beddington. My message was pretty simple. I needed to see her.

"That's not possible. Besides, you said I had some time. I haven't had enough."

"I need to talk. Tonight at eight."

I could hear the tension in her voice. "I am already committed."

"Another graduate student soiree?"

"It may surprise you to know that I have quite legitimate evening commitments for the department."

"Not everything is reserved for your lover?"

"You're a snide man."

"Listen, it's not exactly about the money."

"Then what?"

"I don't want to discuss it over the phone."

She silently considered. "I can't tonight. Really. How about tomorrow? If it's absolutely essential, I can move things around."

"All right. You know The High Life down West End."

"For God's sake. That dive? Why not the Top Hat, where we were before?"

"I don't want people getting used to seeing us together. I'll see you at The High Life at eight."

Maybe I should have told her she could have a good evening, don't worry, it'll be a pleasant conversation. But she was, after all, cheating on her husband and she was, despite that, a complete ass about it. Another day of worry wouldn't hurt her.

I called Wes and got his answering machine. I left a message that told him I'd see him during office hours tomorrow. I was vague. There's no reason to leave things where the wrong people might find them.

Katie was working the day shift and had floated by the phone booth a couple of times, looking like she had a question. When I emerged and found a clean booth, she was over in a couple of minutes. She stood by the table, apparently waiting for me to speak first.

So, I did. "And you wanted to know. . . what?"

"I didn't want to know anything. Your friend from the other day? The distinguished gentleman in the nice suit?"

Wardell. "I remember."

"Was that who you were talking to?"

I shook my head briefly. No reason to go into who I was talking to, or why.

"Well, he came by looking for you." She handed me a business card. "Wants you to call him."

I think I sighed. Maybe I did. I certainly had news for Wardell Robinson, but I had put off telling him. Or rather, I'd put off calling him. Maybe I was a little guilty about LaSalle. Maybe it was just that it closed Tippy's case. Tippy was all the way dead now.

"Thanks. I'll get right on it. After you bring me a beer."

"No bourbon?"

"Just a beer."

When she brought it, I took it and the card to the pay phone, dropped a dime, and listened to the twirling sound that was supposed to mimic a bell ringing. It always struck me as the sound a bird makes when it's confused. I waited five rings and was about to hang up when I heard a deep baritone.

"Robinson Law."

I announced myself. "Heard you're looking for me."

"I wanted to know what progress you'd made. The last I heard, you had possible suspects."

"Three." I didn't tell him I could have had five. It missed the point now. "But I put the press on the most likely one, and he caved."

His voice was astonished. "He gave himself up to the police?"

"He put a gun in his mouth and pulled the trigger."

The line went cold. Finally Wardell said, "You were there?"

"I was in the building." Now my side of the conversation went quiet. "Anyway, it's over. Tippy's killer is dead."

"Are you absolutely sure? It seems a little tidy."

There's a word I don't hear much in my life. Tidy. Everything in its place and well-ordered. Put together the right way. Perfect.

"Might be tidy, but it all makes sense. I can fill you in on details when I see you."

"When would that be, Jackson? We do not travel in the same circles."

"Fair enough. But you know who's been traveling in my circles these days? Guy named Stump Collins. You know him?"

Wardell was having one of those days where he had to think before he spoke, I suppose. There was another gap in the conversation before he said, "I know him."

"Trustworthy guy?"

"On some things, I imagine. On others, perhaps not."

"That's so much help, Wardell. Any chance you can be more specific."

"Just tell me why you are asking, and I'll be better able to help."

"Stump is coordinating the Davis Cup protest that's coming from the north side. I'm watching the campus protests. We have been thrown together a little. He seems to think we're partners in all this." I thought back to my initial meetings with

Stump. "Plus, when I went to Tippy's place, he warned me off one time, then bailed me out a second time when a couple of 38 specials tried to give me trouble."

"And is he friendly to you, or do you rub him the wrong way?"

"Like I said, he seems to think of us as partners in the protest business. He told me to let him know when I came north, so he could help me out." I didn't tell Wardell that Freddy needed to be ready, whatever that turned out to mean.

"I see."

This is the problem with telephone conversations. You can't see the other guy thinking. And I wondered what Wardell was thinking.

"I'd say you would know if Collins was antagonistic to you. I believe it would be clear. If he says he will help you, I think, and I emphasize the word "think," that he is inclined to help you. I know him to be sincere, at least in that way. If he is wanting to partner with you, I'd take him at his word."

"Does he have a record?"

"If you mean, has he been arrested? Many black men in that neighborhood have been arrested. If you mean, does he have a record of convictions? I don't know. But I doubt it."

"Why do you doubt it? Because he's the mayor of The Gardens?"

Wardell chuckled, a sort of low, breathy articulation. "Yes, I've heard that. I am fairly certain it was made up by Collins himself. And enforced with some fairly assertive actions."

"Like using a 44 Magnum to make a point?"

This time, the time it took Wardell to compose his answer was a longer patch. I waited.

"If you know the gun enough to name it, I assume you have seen it."

"That's right. In person. And in Tippy's manuscript."

"And how did Tippy feel about it?"

"Tippy said the user was the neighborhood's judge and jury. He was distressed about it."

"Jackson, listen to me. I represent the laws of the State of Tennessee and the United States of America. I am sworn to abide by those laws, to give the best counsel, and in some cases the best defense, I can."

"Sure. That's the way you roll, Wardell."

"As long as that's clear. I have spent my life doing what's right and doing it for my community."

"Without a doubt."

"All right. I am not at all surprised if Tippy saw something that gave him pause. There are things that go on in The Gardens that I do not condone. That I do not approve of."

"Same all over town." All over everywhere, I thought. Everywhere I go, there are things I don't approve of. "What's it got to do with Stump? And Tippy? What's your point, Wardell?

"Just this. Nashville Metro only comes this way when it's in their interests, and they never come as quickly as they should. If the neighborhood has developed a system for informally policing things that they suspect the official law can't, or won't understand, well, there's a place for the Stump Collins of the world."

"Tippy said he had executed. Not the law. I got the impression it could have been a person."

"I have no knowledge of that."

"Would it be unrealistic to believe he did, Wardell?"

"There is nothing realistic about living in The Gardens. And it's especially unrealistic, with the Davis Cup bringing South Africa right into our city, to think that north Nashville won't look to protest."

"And Stump and I are in the middle of it."

We talked a minute more. He more or less congratulated me for bringing Tippy's assignment to a close. I told him I'd buy him a lemonade when he was in Hannigan's. He more or less told me he had lemonade where he was.

I'd been leaning, draped over the pay phone to keep my conversation from anyone who walked by. When I hung up and turned, I came face to face, or as face to face as most could, with Art Blake.

"I hope that was a long conversation with an attractive and available woman."

"It wasn't that long. And it was no woman."

I followed Art back through the aisle of booths and to a back table in the corner, far from everyone. Katie brought a plate of ribs with potato salad for Art, and a fried chicken dinner for me. I started to dispute that I'd ordered anything, but Art said, "I ordered for you. Eat."

The only sound for a few minutes was the clinking of flatware on plates. The chicken was as it usually was, crispy on the outside, slick like it was lightly oiled on the inside, a perfect marriage of things that may not be good for your body but are good for your soul. The fact that there was also fried okra and mashed potatoes made it a winner.

Art wiped his fingers on the third napkin of the meal and leaned back. He reached for his beer and drained it in one gulp, belching slightly. "Mighty good. I don't think there's better ribs in Nashville."

"There's not better ribs, or chicken, in walking distance. Loveless might give it a run."

"Hell, Loveless's chicken beats this by a mile. But there's no need to drive all the way out there with Hannigan's in your backyard."

Katie came and got the plates. She brought coffee for Art, a double shot of bourbon for me.

"What have you learned from your rounds, Jackson? Are we going to have an orderly protest? Or a riot?"

I took a sip and immediately looked for Katie. Usually, I drank what was in the well, which would burn in the back of my throat. I think it might have been Old Crow. This was way too smooth. It covered the chicken fat on my tongue like dark amber heaven.

"I'm buying tonight. I told her to bring you the good stuff."

I toasted Art a little too elaborately and took another sip. "I've learned that the University has not acceded to all the protester's demands."

"Of course, I know that. Things take time."

"I've become an acquaintance of the guy who seems to be in charge. He comes on campus occasionally and we talk."

"He comes to you? That's not what I'd expect."

"Put it this way. He comes and sits with me while I watch the faculty and students march. He could be just killing time."

"I don't know why he'd kill it with you. And kill it there."

"I didn't say it made sense. It's just what's happening."

"And speaking of what's happening, Mercer tells me you were on the scene when Dr. LaSalle killed himself."

"I had nothing to do with that, Art."

He looked surprised. "Why would I think you did?"

"Faculty rumor mill says that Jackson made him do it."

Art shook a toothpick from the little glass container on the table. He worked some bit of rib from a lower molar, chewed it, and swallowed. "I don't listen to faculty rumors. They change too fast, and they're almost never right."

I didn't tell him this one was dangerously close without knowing why. Instead, I asked him, "This north side guy, the protest leader, is named Stump Collins. You ever hear of him?"

Art frowned. "No. Was he a student?"

"I don't think so. He doesn't seem the type. More of an up from the streets guy, if you know what I mean."

"And you're on good terms with him? Up from the farm meets up from the streets?" He laughed at his own joke. "You must make an intriguing pair."

"I'm intrigued myself." I let it drop. If Art knew him, it might have meant something. It might have meant there was a reason Stump was stalking me that had to do with Vanderbilt somehow. Now it just looked like he was keeping an eye on me, staying in touch.

Chapter Twenty-Six

I LEFT ART AFTER another bourbon and began to walk toward the west section of West End, where Top Hat, The High Life, and Linda's all held sway. I would see High Life tomorrow with Irma, and Linda's was not the sort of place you wanted to be right after a full meal. At least, most nights that was true. It had too much of a sweaty, musty, dive bar odor to it. So I crossed to the south side of the street and headed toward Top Hat.

It had begun to rain and the wind picked up, enough that I pulled my jeans jacket tighter and buttoned it. It was only March, but somehow Nashville should have been warmer by now. It still felt like winter, or at least like winter's ugly cousin who wouldn't take the hint and leave.

I put my head down and walked, eager to get inside at Top Hat. Somewhere between 29th and 30th, I became aware of footsteps behind me, moving quickly, catching up. I looked over my shoulder and saw a big man with a baseball bat moving rapidly.

It was the big man from the bar.

"Stay right there, Trade." His voice was raspy, the sort that comes when you've screamed too much.

I backed up. "Whoa, fella. You're coming in a little hot."

I'm not short at six-two, but this guy was closer to Art Blake's size, bigger than I had thought, maybe even six-seven. He had the broad shoulders I'd seen the other night. His chest was broad too, and his arms, even in the raincoat he wore, looked to be big as well. He looked like he knew his way around the inside of a gym.

He got two arms' lengths away and stopped. He had me trapped against a concrete block wall, part of an old auto parts store that had sold out earlier in the year. "Come on, man. What gives?"

"You know, Trade. I'm tired of hearing about you. That's not why I'm going to do what I'm going to do. But let's just say it'll be a pleasure to mess you up."

"Maybe you haven't heard. LaSalle killed himself. There's no need, man. It's all good now."

He twirled the baseball bat in one meaty hand. "LaSalle? LaSalle who? I don't care about any LaSalle."

Maybe it's just that Nashville isn't safe anymore, if it ever was, but this was taking an unexpected turn. If he wasn't LaSalle's collaborator, then who was he? And how had I pissed him off?

"Look, brother. I don't know what I did to you. Maybe we can set it straight."

"Not a chance," he snarled. "Brother." And with that, he took a swing with the bat, one-handed. I slid under it, but it was too close.

"Come on. If you intend to kill me, you can at least let me know why."

He kept me pinned against the building, still twirling the bat. "Maybe I'll just bash your brains in, Trade. All they're going to find is a bloody mess."

I had no doubt that's what he had planned. I could see the eyes that had worried Bobby so much, eyes that suggested there was no heart, soul, or remorse behind them. "Who are you working for?"

"That's nice that you have to ask. It tells me you're screwing so many people over that you don't even know. That's fine. I'll be doing it for all of them." He grinned and showed a gap in his teeth. "That's just fine. A public service."

With that, he flung the bat toward my head, once again missing but not by much. But instead of caroming off the concrete to him, it landed flat, and came straight down. I grabbed it.

But if it bothered him, he didn't show it. He simply reached into his pants pocket and pulled out a knife. It was a switchblade, and he flicked it open. It locked. "Yeah, that's right. You have the baseball bat. I have the knife. I think I'd take my odds, but you're welcome to place a bet, Trade." He circled to my right, giving up a little advantage in order to get fully on the sidewalk. "What do you think?"

"I'd say let's don't and say we did. You can still walk away from this."

"I don't walk. I finish what I start." He made a feint toward me with the blade. I held the bat in both hands.

I thought about running but didn't like the idea that he might be somebody who could throw a knife accurately. I didn't like the idea that he could, for all I knew, have a gun on him. Mostly, I didn't like the idea of taking my eyes off him. He had enough anger boiling inside that he might do anything.

I waited for him to make a move. He kept talking, though. "You have been playing games, boy. That's a no-no where I come from. You wouldn't have lasted there. Long-haired hippie. I bet you protested people like me."

"You're a vet?"

"That's right. Does that make you afraid now?"

It didn't make me afraid, but it sure did make me curious. "Sergeant Jackson Trade, Alpha Company, 54th Infantry." I kept the bat ready.

He didn't relax, but he narrowed his eyes. "All right. I had that wrong. You don't look like one of us."

"Nobody's supposed to look like we did over there."

"Doesn't matter." He shifted the knife to his right hand and began to shift his weight like a prizefighter. He was big, but he was also athletic.

"Tell you what. Let's put the bat and knife down. If we're going to have a go at it, let's just do it. You and me. No weapons. No hardware." I didn't know what good it would do, unless he prided himself on his hand-to-hand skills.

He showed the gap in his teeth. "You'd like that? I bet you would. I put down my knife and you run like a coward?" He shifted his weight so that he was on his back foot, like he might mount a charge. "Or you really think you could get the knife in a fight?"

"I just thought an old soldier like you would go hand-to-hand."

"You're not a vet, then, Trade. If you were, you'd know that the only reason to fight is to win. You don't give up your weapons."

"Then why give me the baseball bat?"

"Because that's not worth a dime in this fight. See, I'm going to get in close quarters. I'm going to stick this in you as many times as I want. That bat won't do you a damn bit of good."

I mirrored his footwork. "Why even bring it then, dumbass?"

He faked toward me but backed up. "Might have had the pleasure of splitting your skull with it. Might have had to bolo it at you if you'd run." He made a helicopter motion with his free hand. "Bat gets between running legs and all kinds of bad things happen."

His deadened eyes were staring at me, waiting to see an opening. He started and stopped twice, feinting with the knife. I stayed balanced, one foot back, bat at waist level.

And then he made his move, screaming, those blank eyes bugged out. It was as good a specimen of crazy as I'd seen in a while, and it happened so fast I didn't have time to plan.

I thought I could swing the bat onto his arm and dislodge the knife from his hand. I stepped into the swing, trying to launch the knife.

But there is always the law of unintended consequences. He adjusted his arm, or I miscalculated the path, and I missed completely.

Or rather, I missed his arm. But my uppercut, the swing that wanted to launch the knife into the bleachers, connected with his jaw. The sound of wood against bone didn't make a crack like it does with a baseball. It was more like the sound of a cork popping, if it popped inside a well, a pop that has depth and resonance, one whose sound lingers a little longer on the air.

The big man looked surprised, and I thought, just for a moment, he might shake it off and come hard at me. But his eyes glassed over, shut, and he keeled over backwards, halfway out into the street. His top lip bled from where the lower teeth had lacerated it, and there was a trickle of blood behind his head where he'd fallen.

He was out cold, still holding the knife.

It was then I heard the breathing.

"Christ's sake, Jackson." Don Mercer was doubled over, looking like a man who'd run for miles. He had his hands on his knees and looked up at me, one eye sideways. "What was that about?"

The short answer would have been, I don't know but I can guess. But that would have turned into a long question. "He wanted a piece of me."

"Why?" Don was still breathing hard, but he straightened up now. "And where'd you get the baseball bat?"

"Can we disarm him first?"

Mercer took his .45 out and moved toward the big man. "You stay where you are, Jackson."

"You bet."

He circled the body, staying out of range of any leg kick, in case the man was playing possum, and gradually made his way into the street, above the prone man's head. He then nimbly cross-footed his way to the man's right side and, with a deft kick, sent the knife flying against the concrete wall. It fell into the grass quietly.

The big man never moved.

Chapter Twenty-Seven

IT WASN'T MUCH OF a statement. I knew that. So did the detective who took it, a tired, hound dog looking guy named Winston. All I said was that the big man had come for me, first with a bat, then with a knife, and that I had no idea why. I didn't have a weapon until he threw the baseball bat at me and, no, I had no idea why he'd do something like that.

"He knew you enough to say your name, right?"

"That he did."

"You didn't put that in the statement." He scratched an itch under his forearm, didn't like the result and did it again. "You also said you'd seen him before."

"Once. He was looking for me at High Life, just down the street from where we were tonight."

"All right. I don't see a lot in this. You don't know him, but he knows you. He's got a beef, but you don't know what it is."

"Could be a guy who looks for beefs."

"Yeah, could be." He scratched his forearm again, going faster, as if that would be more effective. "I assume you want to hang around until we run the prints, see if that jogs something loose?"

"Might as well, right? See if he's got friends I know."

Winston put the statement down on the desk and leaned back in his chair. A smile formed as he looked across at me. "You already know some things that aren't in the statement."

"Me? About this guy? Not at all. In fact, there's a lot of stuff that I just don't know at all."

"Come again?"

I took my time answering. I didn't want to let anybody's cat out of the bag, but a little help might not be a bad thing. "At the end of this, I think you'll know who killed somebody else."

"Who?"

"I can't tell you that. Not yet anyway."

"Listen, Trade. . ."

I held up my hand. "Not yet." I reached in my shirt pocket and got my pack of Luckies. I lit one as he glared at me. "Give me a little time to work this out, Winston. I can give you a little, but nothing that sets the machinery into motion. Besides, this little dance tonight is wrapped up. A witness, a cop for God's sake, saw what happened. It was self-defense. If the guy dies or not, it was self-defense."

"So what?"

"So he wanted to kill me. When we get who he is, I may know who he's associated with. And because of that, I'll know that either he or the associate killed someone else."

"You're a vague one, Trade. And you sound like you already know."

"Except I don't. And I don't want you arresting the wrong person."

He reached across the desk and shook loose one of my Luckies. As he lit it, he said, "I know a little about you. You end up in the middle of some bad stuff."

I shrugged. "Wrong place, wrong time."

"Yeah, most likely not." He stood and looked around the bullpen. "Guys like you find trouble."

I could have told him that Tippy Taylor found trouble, but that I could stay out of it. Except he would have replied that I found enough of it tonight. I just let it go.

"They're running his prints now. You didn't think he was local, so we'll probably see what the FBI has and that'll take a while."

"I hear you. It could be morning."

"Right. That means you can go home."

I stubbed out the butt. "All the same to you, I'll just hang out here."

"I figured." He pointed at a closed door with a frosted glass window. "Go catch a few winks in there. Captain won't know you slept on his couch because you'll be up and at 'em before he gets here."

I was out cold before I knew it, and didn't wake easily when Winston shook me a couple of hours later. My eyes opened, but felt sticky.

"He's not local."

"I told you that."

"But you don't know him, right?"

"I heard his voice. Not a Southerner."

"Yeah, well, there's lots of Yankees in town. You could make this a lot easier by spilling what you know."

"Nothing easier than seeing what the Bureau boys say."

Exasperation sounds different on everybody. On Winston, it was the sound of a loud exhale punctuated by a raspberry at the end. He stomped away.

I went back out into the bullpen and looked for the coffee pot. When I found it, the remains of the night were down to the last inch. I was too tired to sleep, so I poured the last of the thick liquid into a Styrofoam cup and found an empty chair.

The big guy had to be Watkins Lasalle's partner. It couldn't be any other way. Either he or LaSalle, or both of them, had killed Tippy Taylor. LaSalle knew I was onto him, so LaSalle sent the big guy after me. Maybe the big guy didn't know

LaSalle had blown his brains out. Or maybe he knew, and he came after me in anger. It had to be one of those things. It didn't matter that he claimed not to know LaSalle.

Or else, I'd miscalculated badly.

I hadn't lied to Winston, at least not yet. And I had to figure I was right. It added up to Watkins.

So, there I sat, drinking really bad coffee and looking at yesterday's edition of the Banner, all the while trying not to think what the implications were if I was wrong. Somewhere in the early morning Winston said he was ready to cut out and handed me over to a crew cut detective he introduced as Bobby Flood.

Flood and I stared each other down. I knew him from the year before, when he and a few of his crew served a search warrant on me. They hadn't found anything, and I think it made Flood just a little angry. He was the sort who was always right, even when he wasn't.

"Yeah, I've met him." Flood was a fit five foot ten, and you could see his muscles through his white shirt.

Winston looked from one of us to the other. "Doesn't sound like there's much love lost, then."

I stood up and put out my hand. "No hard feelings, detective. You were doing your job."

He took my hand and bore down. "It turned out all right for you, I guess." He was referring to the fact that neither I nor my brother had killed anybody. He was probably not too happy about that. I wasn't all that happy that he was trying to crush my fingers.

"Truth comes out, Flood." I extricated my hand.

Winston waved a sheet of paper. "This just off the teletype. We have a make on your boy. I want to read it before I go. You mind?"

He sat at his desk, reading. Flood gave me one more dirty look, and we flanked Winston who began reading off the sheet. "Barton. William Thomas. DOB is 25 December 1950. A

Christmas gift for his mama. Place of birth listed as Milwaukee." He made a clicking noise. "Whole list of arrests here. Assault. Assault with a deadly weapon. He is not a friendly person."

"I told you that."

"It's a trail of trouble, all right. Also a notation here that he had a bad conduct discharge from the Army. Vietnam. Something went strange in the jungle, I reckon."

I felt a chill in my blood. Something had gone wrong in the jungle, and I knew only one person who had a similar BCD. Someone who had as much reason as Watkins to want Tippy dead, and to want me silenced.

It meant I'd picked the wrong professor, and I'd panicked him into killing himself.

I looked from Winston to Flood. "Get somebody who can take dictation. I'll tell you what I know."

I gave them everything. Wes Willoughby had somehow outrun his BCD to become a tenure-track professor. He'd gotten religion, literally. Maybe he really had. But Tippy Taylor had pieced together enough of his story to research the rest and put the squeeze on him.

"I have no doubt that Taylor pushed him just as far as he could. Willoughby makes ok money, but he's not getting rich. And he's already under a lot of pressure trying to get himself tenured. I've talked to him, and he is a walking case of nerves."

"Why were you talking to Willoughby?" Flood asked as if he thought there was a secret motive. I guess he's a good detective after all.

"Tippy left me a letter, asking me to figure out who killed him."

"He knew he was going to get murdered?"

"Blackmailers assume the risk. People don't like it when you make them rent your silence. Murder is a way to make the information secure."

"Go on." Winston had stayed to hear the story. He didn't look so tired anymore.

"I didn't really figure Willoughby for a killer. Too addled. But I knew what the info Taylor had was about. He had a bad conduct discharge. It was for taking out a village."

"Like My Lai?" Winston was leaning into the story. Flood was glaring at me.

"Something like that. It wasn't just him. It was several in the platoon."

"And so you think Barton is part of that unit that took out the village?" Flood was still looking hard at me, but he was tracking the conversation.

"That's right. Somehow they connect, and Willoughby tells his old buddy the score. And while Willoughby has turned into a trembling mess, Barton has kept his rage and has been using it in a professional capacity. First, he offs Taylor and tosses him in a dumpster. Then when I start asking around, he tracks me to a bar, and takes a shot at me."

Flood and Winston spoke at the same time. "What?"

"At least that's how I figure it now. He left the bar after asking for me. Then when I close the place down and start walking home, a car peels out of an alley and a gun fires. Didn't hit me, but my guess is that's what was intended."

"And then he comes for you tonight. Baseball bat and knife. Seems like he hadn't thought it through." Flood was playing detective again, and in his theory of the case, I was telling a flawed story. "Baseball bat. Knife. Gunfire. Seems like he'd pick one and go with it."

"Who knows why people do what they do, Flood?"

"Good thing he gave you the baseball bat, though. Pretty inconvenient for him."

"Or convenient for me?" I took a step closer to him. Six-two beats five-ten, all other things being equal, if you're trying to intimidate. It wasn't going to work, but I'm damned if I won't at least try. "You got something to say, Flood, spit it out."

He squinted. "I didn't say anything, Trade. Just that it worked out for you that he gave you the bat. I'd say you're a lucky SOB all the way around."

Winston intervened, his voice all of a sudden sounding like he was past the end of his shift. "If I leave, are you boys going to act nice?"

"I am always nice." Flood looked anything but. "I guess we'll head out to bring Willoughby in. Why don't you go home, Trade? Unless you have anything else you didn't tell when you should have."

I thought about giving him a piece of my mind, but he knew he was right and I knew he was right. There was nothing to be gained by protesting my innocence.

And I had places I had to go. Somebody I had to let off the hook. Nobody could let Watkins LaSalle off the hook. He took care of that himself.

Chapter Twenty-Eight

BUT FIRST I HAD to have some breakfast. And some real coffee.

I called Mercer from the pay phone outside the bullpen and asked him to meet me at the IHOP on 21st. By the time I got there, he had already ordered and was on his second cup of coffee.

After the pancakes arrived, I told him about Barton. About the BCD. About Willoughby. I didn't tell him about LaSalle. Or Irma. All the time he nodded, shoveling blueberry pancake into his mouth. When I finished, he put his fork down.

"Pretty tangled web. I'm guessing Canadian Studies is about to be two men down." He dabbed at his mouth with the napkin, found a sticky spot and rubbed it harder. "If I connect these dots, there's another one."

"What's that, Don?"

He leaned up so that his face was over the plate, and he crooked his finger, telling me to lean up too. When I did, he shook his finger at me. "You, Jackson. You are in the building when LaSalle kills himself. You are in the mix when Willough-by goes down. Barton tried to put twenty holes in you with a sharp knife. The only thing any of this has in common is you."

I leaned in closer. "And Tippy," I whispered. "Tippy is in the middle of this. And he gave it to me."

"What are you involved in?" He pointed his fork at me. "You know something, and you kept it from Metro. What are you working on? What didn't you tell Metro?"

"Oh, I told them, Don. Tippy Taylor was blackmailing Willoughby. He left me all the info.'

Don whistled slowly.

"But here's what I didn't tell Metro, because they have the goods on Willoughby and Barton. Tippy was blackmailing LaSalle too. He wanted me to find out which did it." No need to give up Irma. She wasn't in it. And LaSalle had taken himself out of needing protection.

"So, you just go up and ask them?"

"Not at all. I told them I was taking over the brief. They'd pay me from now on."

He choked on his coffee. I slid a glass of water toward him and he managed to stop hacking. "That's blackmail, Jackson."

"If I took any money, it would be. I'm just trying to smoke the killer out."

"That's how you ended up in LaSalle's office."

"Correct. I came to put the push on him, planned to go pretty hard. He confessed with his pistol. Or so I thought."

"These are things that any ordinary person would report to the police." He dragged an already wet pancake piece through more syrup. "Or at least tell a cop who they know."

"They might. Or they might play the string out. I told LaSalle in a note that I had him figured out. The car that shot at me was stolen from his neighborhood. I put one and one together and got LaSalle and the man we know now is Barton. Like I say, LaSalle put himself out of the story. And now it turns out that Barton belongs with Willoughby instead."

Don finished his stack and picked up his coffee cup. It was lukewarm like mine. He drained the cup, then poured another from the brown thermal carafe they'd brought us. "If you've really located Taylor's killer, you are out of work."

"Not really." He raised an eyebrow. "It doesn't matter to the murder. But there's a loose end still to tie down."

Don opened his mouth to say something, but he shut it. "I know. You'll let me know if you need my help. And you damn sure won't take my advice."

"Not true, Donnie. I will always listen."

"Yeah, but you do what you want."

Chapter Twenty-Nine

I'D CALLED IRMA AND reset our appointment. She'd heard about Wes, and she said to come to her office.

By the time I was done talking to her, I was pretty sure she was rightfully the most powerful faculty member in Canadian Studies.

She realized, as soon as I sat down, that she would be well served just to listen. She saw the look on my face, I guess. I'm pretty sure I looked humbled. Or at least apologetic.

What I had to say, the bits about Watkins LaSalle and Wes Willoughby, were probably a complete surprise, but if so she had the poker face of an expert player. She just sat there looking at me, the only color on her face put there by a brush of some kind.

Cool customer. Like I said the first time I saw her, butter wouldn't melt in her mouth

I told her she was off the hook, and that in fact she'd never really been on it. I told her that I was no blackmailer, that I was a friend of Tippy's, and that he'd asked me to find his killer.

But he wanted no one else exposed. Her affair, no matter that he'd taken advantage of it, was safe as long as she wasn't the killer.

I told it slowly. I didn't want to answer questions afterward. The look on her face suggested an interrogation might be less pleasant than the one down at the station.

She just sat there, nodding once or twice. Mostly she looked intently at me, as if she was trying to decode some encrypted message.

When I was finished, she nodded one last time, this time ending with her eyes on the floor. After a few beats, she finally looked up and said, "How bizarre."

"I couldn't give you any different treatment than the others. I couldn't know who the killer was."

She laughed. "It wasn't the pressure. It was you. You were such a prick."

"I didn't like it. It's not my style."

"Oh, I think there was plenty in it that was your style, Mr. Trade. You were morally superior to my indiscretion." She raised her eyebrows when I raised mine. "All right. Once is an indiscretion. You were morally superior to my affair."

"I didn't like when you propositioned me. But I understood."

"Yes, I suspect you did." She reached across the leather blotter on her desk and picked up a silver cigarette case with a bit of filagree engraving. It was the sort that had a lighter incorporated into it. She took out a long, slim cigarette, and lit it. "What about the proof?"

"I destroyed all of it. I don't need it anymore."

She exhaled a plume of smoke. "I guess I have to take your word for that?"

"Yes, you do. Remember, I'm not a blackmailer. I have no use for proof of your . . . indiscretion."

"I suppose. You are telling me all this. That means I am, as you said, off the hook."

"You are. And listen, I thought of bringing you the picture and the film. But what if I got mugged? What if a car hit me?" She looked through the smoke at me, not smiling but not expressionless. "You wouldn't want that stuff out in the world. So I burned it."

She waved me off with her cigarette before she took another drag and put the butt in the ashtray. "You are either brilliant or stupid. You could have been killed doing this."

"I almost was killed twice. It was the second attempt that led to Willoughby."

"And you did all this for Tippy Taylor?" She started to lift the cigarette to her mouth, then thought better and stubbed it out. "Why? What was he to you?"

"Just a guy who asked me to help him out. Plus he left a little money so I would do it."

Irma shook her head. "No. You could have kept the money and not done a thing. Why did you really do it?"

"Call it a character flaw. I get something in my head, and I can't get it out."

"Very well. I could have given you a shortcut, had I known more about what you were doing. As it was, I thought you were only blackmailing me."

That was a new twist. "Tell me more."

"Both my lover and I had rock solid alibis for the night of Taylor's murder. In fact, so did Wes Willoughby and Watkins LaSalle."

"I suppose you were all in the same place."

"Indeed we were. We were in Vancouver at the international conference for our discipline." She smiled now, but it was a superior smile, the kind I must have had when she judged me. "So it is a good thing indeed that you located and captured Wes's accomplice."

My mind raced to get in front of her information. "Let me get this straight. All three of you were out of town."

"All four of us. Remember Paul, my lover."

"All four of you were out of town that night."

"So you somehow pressured Watkins to take his life, and you were pressuring me." She leaned back and crossed her legs. "And pressuring Wes must have been torture for him. Although I do believe he enjoys torture."

She was right. If the big man hadn't come for me, Wes's plan would never have come to light. He had it set up perfectly. Until the big man lost his temper. Or whatever it was that he lost.

"I must congratulate you, Mr. Trade. You were successful. But at what cost? Watkins' life. This Mr. Barton. It sounds as if he won't make it, but perhaps that's all right. And Wes, of course. He is behind the murder, no doubt, but he might get off with a few years, a career ruined. I must say, even though you have spared me somehow, you have chopped my small department in half."

She rose. I knew the interview was over. I got up as well, and we converged on the office door. She arched an eyebrow. "It's Shakespearian, really." She paused next to me. "Do you know Henry VI, Part 3? It's a horrible play. But there is body count. There are dead and ruined galore. That's what Shakespeare's audience loved."

"This doesn't feel Shakespearian, Irma."

"No, I suppose it doesn't. In fact, it feels rather like a farce." She opened the door. "Thank you for letting me know, Mr. Trade."

I walked into the hall. She shut the door firmly. I heard the deadbolt turn.

Chapter Thirty

LATER IN THE AFTERNOON, it didn't feel like Shakespeare or farce. What it felt like was absurdity. Epic absurdity, if that's a thing.

I sat in Hannigan's nursing a bourbon. About fifteen minutes into it, and less than half of it downed, I pushed it aside and left.

I walked over to Centennial Park, climbed the steps of the fake Parthenon, and sat, leaning against one of the columns. Tourists came and went, taking pictures. One came up from the side of my column and nearly tripped over me. She gave me a dirty look, and I gave one back.

As darkness fell, I walked further down West End Avenue. I ended up at Linda's and ordered a draft. It tasted flat to me and it was warm.

Either that or I was just not in a drinking mood.

I tried for the next two days to lose myself. I walked all over town. I walked to the Cumberland River and back. I went to the bus station and watched the buses come in and leave. I walked all the way out to 100 Oaks Mall, bought a pack of cigarettes at the pipe store, and walked back. Not once did I go to Hannigan's, or Linda's, Top Hat, or Hideaway. I didn't darken the door of any of my usual haunts.

Everything felt finished. Everything felt empty. Tippy was dead. LaSalle was dead, for no good reason. Wes was finished. Maybe Barton was, too.

Nothing tasted good. Not food. Not bourbon. Not beer. And about all I'd had for two days was nicotine and walking.

Friday morning my phone rang and knocked me out of the soundest sleep in weeks. It took me a while to realize it wasn't ringing in my dreams. I got up too quickly, and dizzily walked to the small table it sat on. Funny, when I'm drinking I'm never dizzy. I knocked the phone off the table, and picked up the receiver.

It was Flood.

"You're hard as hell to find. Didn't you get my messages?"

I looked at the answering machine. It was blinking. "I didn't notice."

"I've been looking for you for two days. We have to talk."

The clock by my bed said it was eight o'clock. "Can it wait? You woke me up."

"It couldn't wait two days ago. I'll be over in thirty minutes."

"What about?"

"I'll tell you when I get there. See you in thirty." His voice was annoyed. Insistent.

"Make it an hour, Flood. I need to shower and have some coffee."

"An hour. Just be there when I get there. I'm tired of chasing around after you."

I boiled some water in the hot pot and spooned Instant Folgers into a cup. What the hell could be so important that Flood insisted on seeing me? The water had not been hot enough, and the beige skin on top tasted like dirty rags.

I splashed the coffee into the sink and went to take a shower. I stood and let the stinging hot needles hit the back of my head. I soaped up good and then got a handful of Prell, scrubbing it through my hair and beard. The past two days had left a lot of street smell on me. The smell of soap and shampoo washed it away from my nostrils. I assume it did the same for my body.

It felt like it washed me clean. Of LaSalle's suicide. Of the sleaze of blackmail. I climbed out of the shower dripping but feeling better.

Maybe I should have done that two days ago.

I toweled off, then shaved my neck and dried my hair. I dressed in jeans and a red plaid flannel shirt, put on socks and slid my beat-up Tony Lama's on. I was as presentable as I get.

The second boil of coffee produced what instant coffee does best: an unsatisfactory tasting vehicle for caffeine delivery. I sat at my table and waited for Flood.

He arrived on time. He was wearing one of those cheap polyester suits you get at JC Penny's. You could see his shoulder holster and the bulge of his gun. It didn't matter. One look at his crew cut and you knew he was a Metro cop.

He sat in the chair opposite me. "I wanted to talk with you after we brought Willoughby in. He's a burnt unit."

"He's a sad case. A lot of vets find themselves that way."

"Nervous Nellie, if you ask me. Couldn't sit still." He lit up a Marlboro. It was the last in the pack and he crumpled the cellophane, left it next to the ashtray. "Anyway, he can go be nervous somewhere else. He's out of jail."

"That's what a good lawyer will do. Get you bailed out."

"He's not bailed out."

"I don't get it."

"He alibied. He was in Vancouver."

I could have told him I knew that now. I didn't. "So? Our friend in the hospital did the actual deed on Taylor."

He shook his head. "No score there, Sherlock. He was locked up all that week. In Milwaukee. Assault. Has a court date we had to move until he's out of the hospital." He continued to smoke, continued not to look at me. "Willoughby makes a pretty good case. He felt guilty about the thing in Nam. He just thought the blackmail was what he deserved." He flicked an ash into the ashtray. "I mean, that's a real sad case. He figures he deserves what he's getting."

"They all have alibis."

"All?"

I caught myself. "I mean both. They both have alibis."

He looked at me and nodded. "So maybe Willoughby had someone else. Maybe, right? But that wouldn't make sense. He wouldn't have one person do Taylor and somebody else do you. Do you think that's logical?"

"But he went after me."

"So what? Willoughby tells an old Army buddy that you're harassing him. It's not like the guy isn't violent. Not like he wouldn't drive down just to take his shot at you. But Willoughby says he was just venting to the guy over the phone. He says he didn't even know he was in town."

"And you believe that?"

"I have to. Son of a bitch insisted we polygraph him. You know what? As nervous as the guy is, he passed with flying colors." He grinned. "The way our guys do it, if you're fool enough to let us administer the test, nobody passes. Nobody. You understand? But he did."

"Good God."

"So, there's nothing to tie Wes to the attack on you. There's nothing to tie Barton to Taylor's murder. All you can prove is that these two guys were in Nam together and they had a phone conversation. Willoughby admits that. There's nothing here that would even rouse an Assistant DA to carry a message to his boss."

"You're sure about the Milwaukee records."

"Sure as I am that the sun comes up in the morning."

Flood kept talking. He was running down the details of the interrogation. I suspect he was trying to impress me. I wasn't impressed. I was pissed.

And then I slapped the table with my hand. "The car. That couldn't have been Barton."

Flood stopped in mid-sentence. "What?"

"The car the night I got shot at. It happened the night Barton was looking for me at the bar. A car burned rubber out of an alley and somebody took a shot at me."

"You thought it was Barton."

"Wouldn't you? I figured he was waiting me out. But Barton is a physical SOB. Like you said, he had a baseball bat and a knife the other night. If he was a gun guy, I wouldn't be here talking to you."

"Yeah, that sounds right." We sat in silence. "Then who?"

"Tippy wrote that someone took a shot at him one night."

"North Nashville, man. That happens every night."

"It didn't happen to Tippy every night. And I've been getting phone calls. Somebody trying to spook me."

"This is all well and good, Trade. But you're not connecting your dots. You're just lining them up and looking at them."

"I know. But that's all I've got."

"Maybe Taylor just met up with a bad apple in the neighborhood. He got on somebody's bad side."

"Nothing in Tippy's writing suggests that."

He stood up and poked a finger between the blinds. "I've been a cop a while, Trade. When all the suspects alibi out, you've probably got a one-off. A robbery gone bad. A drug deal didn't work out. Sometimes even just a vagrant who came along at the wrong time for everybody."

"You're saying to let it go."

"I'm saying it's letting you go. You played your hand. And all you got is a busted flush."

Chapter Thirty-One

IT'S A HELLUVA THING to invest yourself completely in something you know should make a difference, and then find out it makes no difference at all.

Flood was right. I played the hand that Tippy had dealt me, and it had come up empty. Three perfectly good suspects, all of them with reason to kill, and all of them conveniently out of town. You could make your case that they had someone else do the deed, and that was in fact the argument for Wes's friend, Barton, but there was no disputing an alibi. Not one given by the city of Milwaukee. I was out of ideas. I was out of luck. I was out of time, and I didn't care.

Except I did care.

There was no getting around it, though. I was done. Tippy's murderer, whoever it was, was going to get away with it. There was nothing I could do about it.

At least I still had the job monitoring the protest.

I sat smoking a cigarette on the cold stone bench outside Kirkland Hall. I could feel the cold in my fingertips, especially my left index finger, the first knuckle. It's not been the same since I got back from Vietnam. And when it does hurt, when the humidity is just right, or just wrong, I can feel the pain all the way to my eye teeth. I put the cigarette in my mouth and cupped my other hand around the knuckle trying to warm it up. It was going to be a long day.

The usual suspects were marching and chanting. The history department had lately begun to take the lead from the Divinity School. For whatever reason, the history folk had attached themselves to the cause of the Davis Cup and were not letting it go. First and foremost among them was Willa. Since our brief detente and subsequent argument, Willa had begun to change. She had abandoned the stylish and fashion forward look. In its place, she had substituted a still attractive but more utilitarian style. Jeans, albeit ones cut to flatter her shape. Sweaters and boots. She didn't exactly look like a Black Panther. It would be hard for a white woman of her age and general look to pull that off. But she looked more usable. More ready. Perhaps even as we used to say, more rough and ready. Spoiling now for a fight and maybe a fight she could win.

Her acolyte had followed along with her. While he still wore his khakis and his Izod shirt, his topsiders without socks, he had at least put a sock cap on his head. He looked a little like a fraternity boy with a head cold, but at least he had made an adjustment.

I became aware of a figure in the bushes behind me. When I turned, I saw Stump Collins, leaning against a lamp pole that shot through and above the bushes. He saw me, but he put a finger to his lips. I stayed quiet and turned back to the protesters. Whatever Stump was up to was none of my business.

It soon became apparent what Stump was watching. Moving through the entryway to the campus was a group headed by a rather stern looking young woman. She was followed by about twenty other folks of various ages and heights and weights. They moved with the steady step of a military unit, as if they had found their rhythm a mile ago and were just hitting their stride. The woman in front stopped when she reached the faculty.

"Who's in charge here?"

The history faculty were unaccustomed, egalitarian as they were, to acquiescing that anyone was in charge of them. They were leaderless.

Willa stepped forward. "I don't think we have a leader," she said. "But we all are on the same wavelength."

The black woman was in her mid-20s. She wore black bell-bottomed slacks and a camouflage jacket buttoned up to her neck. Her hair sported a colorful piece of fabric that went down her back. She looked Willa up and down, as if measuring her. Whether she was measuring her for a role or for a box in the ground was anybody's guess.

"My name is Arletta Jones. I lead a group of civic-minded people from North Nashville, and we have come to lend our support to your protest. May we join you?"

Willa looked puzzled for a moment at the formality of the address, then smiled. "Of course. We are delighted to have you."

The North Nashville group watched as the faculty arranged themselves in such a way as to make room for the new participants. Somehow, they managed to get themselves sufficiently interspersed so that it seemed they had imperfectly but completely blended. It should be said that the volume got louder. It should also be said that it began to seem like more of a protest.

I leaned back and protected my aching knuckle. Just as I was getting comfortable in the sun, I felt the familiar clap of Stump Collins' hand on my shoulder. I reached into my pocket and pulled out my Zippo. "Here. Feel free to light up."

Stump took the lighter and proceeded to flick it open and shut several times. "You know what I like about this lighter?"

"I imagine you like that I give it to you anytime you show up. Although you play with it more than you light cigarettes with it."

"What I like about this lighter is how solid it is. It is one beautiful piece of metal work. It does what it is supposed to do, and it does it every time with a satisfying and substantial click." And as he said that, he clicked it shut. I had to admit it. It was satisfying.

"And did you bring this group to Vanderbilt's bucolic soil?"

"This is a group I'm working with. Arletta Jones is the daughter of one of the north side's most influential citizens. Arletta is a hard case, but she is a damn fine protester."

I looked to the side of the group. Arletta and Willa had separated from them and were deep in conversation. Arletta was pointing her finger and stabbing the air with it.

"It looks like your friend is giving Dr. Winter the what-for."

"Arletta gives everyone the what-for."

We sat on the bench in silence, watching the two women as they seemed to negotiate some point. Soon they were back in line and beginning to march. Now the group of protesters had stopped their chant on Willa's order and a young black man, about six four, skinny as a rail and wearing a houndstooth pork pie hat, began singing. "We shall overcome," he sang, "someday." When he got to the part where the song intones "deep in my heart," the entire crowd of protesters had joined in and, though the history faculty's voices provided a slightly nasal and reedy background, the overall effect was not unpleasing. The song rang against the brick of Kirkland Hall and, as the hour struck 11, it seemed that the meter of the song had set itself inside the bells of Kirkland. As they reached the last "someday," the last bell of the hour rang.

"Pretty neat trick," I said. "Ending the song as if the bell tower was keeping the time."

"Maybe it's the other way around, Jackson. Maybe the bell tower is just trying to keep up with the song. Maybe Vandy is trying to keep up with us."

We watched a few more minutes and then found ourselves face to face with Willa Winter. She had her acolyte, Alex, in tow. And she stood in front of Stump with a face like a question mark.

"What can I do for you, Dr. Winter?" Stump's voice was a low, friendly rumble.

"Are you responsible for these folks who have joined our ranks today?"

"I don't think I'm responsible for anybody, lady. I try to keep up with myself, but I don't try to keep up with nobody else."

Willa smiled. "Then Ms. Jones and her friends are not known to you."

"Oh, I didn't say that. I have known Arletta since she was a young 'un. But if you are asking if I put them up to joining you, I did not. No, I'm afraid it was their idea. Entirely their idea."

"Well, I think we all appreciate the reinforcements. So if you had anything to do with it, thank you."

Stump nudged me with his elbow. "Jackson and I were just saying how this protest could get a lot bigger. Just saying that it will get a lot bigger. Especially when all the TV cameras show up."

"I wonder," said Willa, "if we are sufficiently well organized for that. I worry that this will get out of hand, that our message will get lost."

Stump's voice rose a little. "Why do you say that? Are you afraid that a lot of black people coming on this campus will somehow turn this into 1968 all over again? Like the Black Panthers and Huey done showed up again, and there'll be gunshots, police? You think they got too much dirt on their shoes for this to be a good protest? Like maybe all these black people will ruin your nice little protest?"

Willa was calm, but her undergraduate was fidgeting. "There's no need to be ugly," he said.

Stump laughed. "Ugly? You think I'm being ugly? Here's all I'm saying. This protest is our protest. This cause is our cause. We are certainly happy to have good folks along who agree with the cause. But if I have to be a well-mannered house servant, if we all have to behave according to white people's idea of what is proper, well, then I'm afraid that ain't going to happen."

"The police will shut that down," said the acolyte.

Stump laughed again. "Police got less to do with this than you think, little man."

The undergraduate tensed. I noticed he had a tendency, when challenged, to ball up his fists. It was unclear whether that was the balling of an infant's fist, or an invitation to get rough. One look at his face and you would have to go for the infant theory. But at his size, the other could be true too.

Willa held her hand up like a traffic cop at a stoplight. It was intended for Alex, but it got Stump's attention as well. "That's enough, Alex. Go back to the group."

Alex began to protest but Willa's look silenced him. He walked back with his shoulders slumped and his head down. He brushed a lock of hair from his forehead, and it stayed in place. He picked up a sign and began to walk again, not without having a look at the three of us on every revolution.

"Here's all I meant," said, Willa. "I want to help."

"You want to help? How?" He motioned toward the marchers. "This is what you do, right?"

"I believe in what you are trying to do here. But you know that most of Nashville doesn't see it the way you see it."

"Most of white Nashville, you mean. Black Nashville sees it pretty clearly."

"That may be so. I have no way of knowing that. But I do know that what I can do is less involved with marching and more involved with what I do for a living. The theory of natural rights. A way to talk to people who are not on your side. Yet."

"I don't get you."

"My research turns on the philosophy of the Enlighten-ment, a sense that there are natural rights that every human possesses. Regardless of his race."

Stump waved his hand dismissively. "You're talking about old guys. Old guys who didn't think black people were humans."

"Old guys who were creatures of their moment. If they were creatures of this moment, though, they would agree with me. That is our great Enlightenment inheritance, that everyone, all humans, enjoy natural rights." She leaned toward him and lowered her voice. "I would like to tag along."

"Let me get this straight. You want to tag along? Some kind of shadow? I don't get your drift."

"It would give me an insight into the way that you organize, the way you think, the way you construct your argument. I admit, I don't have that. Look at me." She stepped back. "I'm a white woman with a PhD." She pointed toward the protesters. "Arletta Jones has more savvy about the theory of natural rights as it applies to black Americans than I could ever have. Her knowledge is pragmatic and real. Mine is theoretical. I want to make mine less theoretical and more real."

"So, you want us to help you. What? Write a book?"

"I won't lie. There could be a book involved. But what I really want to do is to give credibility to your work. To your movement. She looked from Stump to me, then back at Stump. "I didn't know anything about this until Tippy Taylor told me."

I felt my heart jump. "Tippy? What's Tippy got to do with this?"

"Tippy was my colleague. He was one of the most interesting people I've ever met." She looked toward the marchers, as if comparing them in her mind. "We used to meet for lunch, twice a week after our Tuesday and Thursday classes. We would go over to Rand Hall and drink coffee for hours and talk. Tippy helped me understand."

"What did Tippy help you understand?" Stump did not growl the question, but it was not an entirely friendly one.

"Tippy helped me understand that I don't understand. It began with me trying to give an exposition of the history of rights and it usually ended with Tippy showing me that the lived experience of not having those rights is not one easily communicated to someone like me. Everything I accept as real and usual is foreign to someone who does not live my life."

Stump stood with his arms crossed. The protest continued, this time with the North Nashville group leading "We Shall Not Be Moved." I watched with interest. Suddenly things had changed. The protest on campus had begun to feel more real. Willa Winter had made a move. And she had known Tippy, perhaps better than she was letting on.

And like a tree that stands by the water, Stump was not being moved.

He continued to look at her, his light-colored eyes deep set in his face. His lips were set with the top one just inside the bottom as if he was thinking hard.

Finally, he uncrossed his arms. The upper lip emerged and joined its partner, and he allowed them a small smile. "All right, lady. We need all the help we can get. If you are going to tag along, you were going to have to work. And I don't mean your go-to-the-library kind of work. I mean help-us-get-organized kind of work."

"Perfect. I look forward to that."

"Then you need to be here, right here, at 7:30 tonight. Jackson will bring you where you need to go."

That got my attention. "Really? What do I have to do with this?"

"Freddie, you just need to bring yourself and this woman to Hope CME tonight at eight. We will get our whole thing on when you get there."

"Freddie?" Willa looked at me.

"It's my middle name. Stump likes to call me by my middle name."

But right now, my middle name was Confused.

Chapter Thirty-Two

I WAS THE FIRST to arrive. I looked at my watch. 7:20. I had a habit of being early, probably ingrained by my childhood on the farm. The sooner you get started, the sooner you're finished.

Kirkland Plaza was lit by a single streetlight, the kind that evokes 19th century London but that are manufactured by the thousands down the road in Tullahoma. It had grown colder when the sun faded. I was happy I'd overdressed. My knuckle still ached.

I stood by the stairs to the building. Last year, I'd watched as a man fell to his death just a few steps above me. As I looked, I knew I would not see a trace of the blood that was there that night. That's the way it goes. Time moves on. Your pain, or the proof of it, doesn't matter much. We all get on with life. The signs of the past, the visible ones, are erased, and the deadly steps are sanitized.

I heard footsteps from the alcove to my right, but as I turned to see who it was, I caught sight of Willa Winter coming from the other direction. She had changed out of the professor garb, and had on a heavy, knee length wool coat. Boots, a dark knit scarf, and leather gloves completed the ensemble.

"You are certainly ready if snow comes tonight."

She eyed me and decided not to answer. "Where is Stump?"

"He's living on Stump-time. He'll get here when he gets here." I burrowed my aching knuckle in my pocket. "Can I ask you a question?"

She had set her mouth in such a way that I couldn't tell whether she was tense or simply perpetually suspicious. "I suppose so."

"Were you and Tippy an item?"

I half expected an outburst, but she stayed calm. "Define item."

"Romantic item. Lovers."

"I'm not sure that's any of your business, Mr. Trade."

"Call me Jackson, Willa. And it's not any of my business."

"Then why even ask?"

"Tippy was a friend of mine, in a way. He left me his manuscript. He had a feeling he might be killed."

"Is that why you've been shadowing me?"

"I've not been shadowing you at all. Until you told Stump and me about your lunch conversations with Tippy, I didn't know you knew him more than casually."

She put a hand to her cheek and seemed to consider the question in a different light. "We might have become close, I guess. Close, in that way. But we weren't. He was someone I believed was a challenging colleague. If fact, I wasn't sure he belonged here on the faculty at first."

"He changed your mind?"

"Look, Mr. Trade. . ."

"Jackson."

She started to protest but didn't. "He was adored by some students. He was that sort of man. He was charismatic, or he could be. But he was also sensitive. He felt the brunt of envy for his popularity." She looked away. "Why do you ask all this?"

We were so involved in our own conversation that we hadn't noticed Stump's arrival. "You're asking my question, Willa. Don't anybody know what my man Jackson is up to."

She nodded hello. "I'm puzzled."

"There's no need to be. Tippy believed he might be killed because of something he knew. He appointed me his post-mortem investigator."

"But the police?"

"Tippy knew that there ain't no police going to be interested in finding his killer." Stump sounded convinced. Because he was.

"And you are here every day watching us. Do you think a faculty member did this?"

Stump had his arms crossed. He seemed to be enjoying himself. "Go ahead, Jackson. Explain yourself. I'd like to hear it all come out for once."

"All right. It's simple enough. Vanderbilt wants me to monitor protest activity. Here at Kirkland, it's been simple. I show up and watch the faculty march. Where we're going tonight, I listen to what's being said, what's being planned."

"And you report back to the Chancellor? I can't believe this." Willa gave her head two swift shakes, dismissing me from her thoughts. We were enemies again.

"The Chancellor doesn't know me from a stray tom cat."

"Then who?"

"Dean Blake. His office seems to have been the unlucky winner in the draw."

"The Dean of Students?"

"I believe the focus is there, yes. Because students are most likely to be impacted by the big protests. On campus. Right on Greek Row."

"Blake's interest is not political, then?"

"The Dean's interest is in the students."

Willa sat down on the third step, looking more than a little like an abandoned store mannequin, her legs straight out in front of her. She said nothing. Stump still had his arms crossed, but now he looked down at her without the same smile. "What do you say, Willa? You look like you lost your best friend."

"I don't know what to say."

I knew what to say. She used to have a way to understand the situation. I was a cop first, in her imagination, then I was an investigator, then a tool of a corrupt university. And then I wasn't. I was working for someone who was only looking out for the students. I got it. I don't give people a very clear picture of who I am. Ever.

I'd parked on the traffic circle in front of Kirkland. The night was one of those March nights where a front had come through and it was warmer in the dark than it had been all day in the light.

"You go. I'll meet you there." Stump was already walking away.

I opened the passenger door for Willa and she hesitated a moment, shook her head slightly, and got in.

The old V-8 rumbled to life, and I pulled around the circle to West End Avenue, turned right, and kept going for a block, then turned left up toward the river and headed to the north side.

The defroster was having a hard time keeping up with the condensation on the windshield so I was constantly wiping the back of my hand against it, trying to keep clear enough that I could see.

"That doesn't seem to be doing much good."

I could've told her that nothing I did seem to do much good. I could have told her this is what happens when it's colder inside the car than outside. But I didn't. Instead, I said, "Do you really think you can make a difference in this business?"

She sat silently, then leaned up and brushed a handkerchief against her side of the windshield, leaving streaks. "Have you ever felt like you were on the outside of something important and needed to be let in?"

"I was in Vietnam. I felt I was in the middle of something important, and I wanted out."

"That's not exactly what I mean."

Behind me, I could see the stream of headlights. There were fewer and fewer as we got closer to the north side. Just not that many people, I guess, feel the need to drive from West End to the north side.

"What I mean," she said, "is this still seems like the most important fight we have. I was a little young for 68, even though I was in Chicago during the convention and the riots. That seemed important. But in a general way. This seems specific. And because it is specific, it is important to get it right."

"Uh huh." There was a car shadowing every move we made about two blocks back. I kept my eyes on it. "Sounds like you just don't want to miss out."

"If by missing out you mean blending my voice to something I think is important, you're right. It's taken me a while to figure out why I do what I do. Now that I know, now that I believe what I do as an intellectual can be linked to what I do as a citizen, it's incumbent on me to do the right thing."

I could've asked her about going to graduate school and dancing and modeling. But that didn't seem really to have much to do with what she was talking about. What she was talking about was nothing less than growing up, becoming the kind of person she always thought she could be. I understood that. I couldn't do it myself, but I understood it.

"You keep looking in the rearview mirror. Why?"

"It's what good drivers do. Defensive driving. You've seen the commercials."

"Defensive driving usually means keeping your eyes front and to the sides. You seem preoccupied with what's behind us."

"I'm always preoccupied with what's behind me. I thought you would be too. Isn't that what historians do? Look backward?"

"Historians only care about the past as it informs the present and the future."

"That's why I'm looking in the rearview mirror, sister." Just in case it informs my future.

By the time we got where we were going, what was behind me was an empty street and what was in front was just asphalt. I saw Stump's car already parked in front of the church. I was a gentleman, let Willa out, and we went into the church.

Hope was modest. If you wanted higher-falutin' AME or CME or Baptist churches, you could find them. But Hope seemed to be a less aspiring church; it didn't get out on a limb. The façade had a central, front-gabled entrance, flanked by a short wooden tower, atop which a small cross stood. On the other side was a second, gabled roof, which housed a cloak room for the choir. Both the cloak room and the tower featured matching windows, which gave Hope the illusion of watching the world as it passed by, two unblinking eyes, neither welcoming nor condemning. Simply watching. Waiting.

Once inside, Hope became more familiar without surrendering its simplicity. Ten pews on either side, clean without ostentation. A bare wood floor and bead board walls, painted in a soothing green. In front, a simple chancel rail behind which, to the left, was a chair and lectern and, to the right, another folding chair. Behind it all, in the one accommodation Hope gave to flamboyance, was the choir loft, though it was only lofted two modest steps. However, it was fronted by a rail that gave meaning to the idea of baroque, with grand twists and turns of a yellow wood shined in a way that the wood of the pews was not. Even in the relative darkness of an early evening, the choir rail shone like a golden gem. The aged piano just behind it mundane by comparison.

No doubt, the choir was the pride of the church, and Hope was a community that rose on the wings of its singers. And the rail was the defining feature.

It was a piece of architecture that would have been more at home in a cathedral. It ringed the loft and the lectern space and could not have been more at odds with the rest of the church. Where the sanctuary was modest, the rail was extravagant. Where the rest of the church was utilitarian and comfortable, the rail was ostentatious, even forbidding. And where the rest of the church was a familiar maple, burnished by age, the rail was some sort of wood more blond than brunette, and varnished heavily so that it shone with a kind of unnatural brilliance.

It was carved such that it consisted of a series of chapel-like openings, each one exact and identical, except for the figures inside. One clearly was a Nativity scene, and others were familiar enough. The figures of Thomas the Apostle reaching for the hand of the risen Christ, seeking the nail wounds as proof, or the figure of Zacchaeus, up in his tree. But others were suggestive simply of a people who had wandered in the wilderness. Moses was there with his tablet of commandments, but there were others I thought that were less Israelite and more African, and African-American. One figure might even have been Harriet Tubman.

All in all, it was remarkable.

"Fascinating."

I turned to see Willa staring at the rail. "More like something you'd see in Europe, right?" I'd seen pictures. But she had probably been there and seen them in person.

"Yes. The sort of altar rail you'd expect if there were an elevated lectern for the priest. But that would be far too Catholic. Not Protestant at all."

"Y'all don't think black folk do their own church art?" Stump's face was hidden in the unilluminated church, but I could imagine what it looked like. Stern. A little dismissive.

"It just stands out so much." Willa didn't know Stump enough to worry about what his face looked like.

"If a person comes to the altar, to be saved or to take communion, might be that what a person sees might ought to be special." Stump moved toward the door to the basement.

"That is, if their salvation or their repentance means something to them."

I motioned to Willa to follow him. "Damn, Stump. I didn't have you figured for a theologian."

"Ain't no preacher if that's what you mean. But I know why you'd want a stand-out rail. No secret there."

We went downstairs where the leadership was assembled. Arletta Jones and her father, George, were there. A young man named Elijah, who was introduced as the conduit to the north side clergy, was there. He was a small round man with a ready smile and a bald head. He had raised up quickly to shake my hand, then sat back down, as if an invisible rubber band snapped him back into place. Also, there was a man named Monitore. He was the conduit to north side businesses. He was the one who spoke first.

"Here's the problem. This here is a weekend event, and most of our merchants make their living on Saturday and Sunday. They're not real keen on supporting something that carries all their sales across town for a weekend."

"This ain't about their business." Stump was glowering at Monitore. "This is about something bigger. You know that."

Monitore nodded. "I know that. You know that. They know that. But they all know that baby needs new shoes. How you going to get them past that?"

Arletta groaned. "How is anybody supposed to get out of this mess if all they think about is their baby's shoes? If we aren't free, baby's shoes don't mean nothing."

Elijah leaned forward, testing the invisible rubber band. "I get the same kind of thing from the preachers. They are in favor of the idea. But they are not in favor of anything that looks like it might turn violent."

"You told them, right? There is not going to be any violence. Didn't you?"

"Saying it and making it so ain't the same thing, brother man." The invisible rubber band pulled Elijah backwards.

"So, you were saying that we have gone to all this trouble. We have got permits. We have done pissed off City Hall. We've got Metro police ready to slap us down if we do the least little thing wrong. We even got Vanderbilt to play right. And you are telling me that we can't get our people to come out? What the hell kind of thing is that?"

Willa and I were seated at the far end of the table. We exchanged glances and knew we needed to say nothing. This fight was not our fight.

George Jones, unlike his country music namesake, was a very dark man. He had wrinkles in his face that had become folds. He looked as if moving to speak might be painful, as if it might crack his face open once and for all. In the same way that Willa and I had glanced at each other, George glanced around the room, his eyes moving, his face stationary. He gave the impression of someone for whom movement was a treasured commodity, not to be spent lightly. Finally, he moved.

He held up his hand, then both hands. "I've been around this town a long time. I've been here at least as long as Penny-packer has, and he knows everybody. I know everybody too. I know what the merchants are saying. They're saying, how can you believe that this will make any difference? I know what the preachers say. They're saying, since we all know this won't make any difference, what will keep people from getting mad and acting up? What they are saying is that you, all of you, are riled up over something that ain't going to work."

"It's going to work." Stump beat his fist lightly on the table. "It has to work. We have to make this point."

"And what the merchants and preachers are telling you is that your point is already made. But not the way you think. They believe that you are making, what do they call it, a moot point."

If anyone was surprised by Jones using legal language, no one betrayed surprise. Or rather, the surprise was not in his language choice. To say that there was no good reason to protest the Davis cup, to protest Vanderbilt, to protest Nashville's history, was like cold water in the face.

George Jones' weary face told the entire story. There was no need to get fired up because there is no change coming.

Monitore stood up. All eyes went to him. I thought for a moment he was getting up to leave. But he was not leaving.

Monitore was a man who would pass on the street without notice. He was average height and average weight. His skin was average black. He had no distinguishing features that would call attention to him. I don't say that as a white guy for whom all black people look alike. I say that as a guy who served with a lot of black guys in the Army, someone who knows they all have distinguishing characteristics.

But Monitore was a cipher. You could no more tell what he was about to say or do than you could fly. I could see it on Stump's face and in Arletta's body language. They couldn't read Monitore. George's face didn't move, but because it didn't move, I assumed he didn't know either.

"It seems like brother Jones is telling us that this boat is sunk before it set sail. Is that right?"

George Jones nodded his wrinkled head slightly.

"And it sounds like brother Elijah says clergy are afraid this is gonna be more Stokley Carmichael than Martin Luther King. That right?"

His rubber band allowed Elijah to nod.

"Then it seems to me that what's got to happen is for us here locally to find a way to link up nationally. We need us some NAACP. We need us some Congress on Racial Equality folks. We need us some people with national name recognition, some people who will bring enough heat to light a fire underneath the clergy and the businesses."

Stump leaned forward and put his face in between the steeple of his hands. "How do you figure on getting those people down here? How do we get them to care about what we're trying to do?"

Monitore's face remained impassive. "Those people, as you call them, already know. They already care. They may in fact already be coming. But no one has taken the lead to organize their participation."

He looked around the room. I did too. I began to see a lightbulb on each face, a little at a time.

"That's right. They are not organizing. They are waiting for us." Monitore allowed himself a smug look.

"Who do you know, Monitore?" Stump was tapping his index finger on the bridge of his nose as he leaned forward. "Do you have an inside line to somebody? How do you know this?"

Monitore sat back down. "I don't know anybody. But I am saying what's plain as the nose you're tapping on your face. We are the civil rights center of the world right now. If the NAACP is going to be involved, if CORE is going to be involved, if you want black cats from Congress down here on a stage, well, they all are waiting to see how serious you are. They can make a racket. But they ain't gonna make no racket unless we got our pots and pans out and are beating on them already."

"And nobody round here is beating on pots and pans unless they see the national racket coming." Stump was nodding. "I see what you mean. But it may be too late."

Willa raised her hand, and every eye went to her. "I can make a phone call," she said.

Arletta snorted. "Who can you call? Do you even know a black person?"

Willa ignored Arletta and Stump's attempt to shush her. "I know the Chief of Staff for the state NAACP. He was a student of mine. I wrote him a recommendation to get the job."

Arletta was unmoved. "Looks to me like the state NAACP would already be here if they were interested."

Willa shook her head. "If what Mr. Monitore says is true, they are waiting for us."

"Don't make sense." Arletta was shaking her head. "We ain't heard nothing from them. Why is that? Why is that, Monitore? Ain't this their fight?"

"It is their fight. But they will not put resources on the ground unless they believe there is a point to it. Right now, all they see is a small group of Vanderbilt faculty marching every day. I have it on good authority that they know we have been meeting and planning. But given that you are an unknown. Given that Stump is an unknown. . . " His voice trailed off.

"Our problem is me? That's pretty rich."

"The problem is not you, Stump. The answer is you. Be the answer to their question." Monitore looked down the table. "Let the woman make her phone call."

Suddenly, a crash came from near the stairway to the basement and there was a brief sound of tumbling and cursing. Everyone leapt to their feet, even George Jones. Stump leaned to his right and flipped a switch which illuminated the entire basement.

At the base of the stairs, amid boxes of Easter decorations strewn everywhere, lay Alex. He was briefly stunned and, as he lay there, a cross of artificial sunflowers sprayed across him.

"Alex!" Willa shrieked. "What are you doing here?"

Stump stood over the undergraduate, his feet balanced in case he needed to move quickly. "It's a good question, boy. What the hell are you doing here?"

Alex cleared his head and blinked his eyes. He thought about getting up, then thought better of it. "I didn't know where you were going." You could barely hear his voice. "You got in the car with him. I didn't know if it was safe."

"You followed us here? You snuck into a church? At what point didn't you think I was safe?"

"I don't know these people. You don't know these people either." He waited a moment. "We don't know any of them."

"Actually, Alex, these are good people." She looked at me. "Even Mr. Trade is okay. We are working for the same cause."

Alex had pulled himself to a kneeling position. Stump still waited in case he needed to strike. "You can say that. You can say that about all kinds of people, that you know them so they're okay. If these people are okay, why are they meeting in secret, in a basement with no lights on. It doesn't seem safe at all. Not on this side of town."

"You just think it ain't safe because it's on our side of town, boy. Maybe it ain't safe, if you're not welcome. This professor here is welcome, Jackson too. I can't say the same thing about you."

Alex put his hands in front of him, as if in surrender, and got to his feet. He was a big kid, but I would've bet on Stump eight days of the week if it came to a rumble. "Okay. I'm not welcome. Fair enough. I'll go."

Willa made her voice softer, more understanding. "We're on the same side, Alex. If you want to stay, you can. We're trying to make the protest work."

"You can have your protest. You can have all these people. I'm not welcome here, and I don't want to be here. I only came for you."

"I'm safe, Alex. Honest, I am."

He took one last look around and then, keeping his eye on Stump, he began to move toward the stairway. Once there, he bounded up two steps at a time. He looked back. "You're not safe," he said.

"I am, Alex. You have to believe me."

His face darkened. He pouted. "Right." And with that, he bounded the final two steps and was gone into the darkness.

"That man's got problems." Arletta said it as a statement of fact. "Prob-lems."

Willa's face was far too pale. "He's just a boy."

"Don't matter," said Stump. "We have a plan. The doc is going to call her student, and we're going to get this thing moving."

Chapter Thirty-Three

AND THAT IS WHAT happened. Willa made a call to her former student, and he reached out to Stump. Stump gave him the low down and the wheels began to turn.

The local NAACP let the national know and the national reached out. Then the National reached out to the Congress on Racial Equality, and they in turn reached out to the people in their network. The Congressional Black Caucus was alerted, and the various members of Tennessee's African American political apparatus got on board.

Two weeks was not a long time to make arrangements, but not many arrangements needed to be made. What was needed was bodies, and bodies could come to Nashville by car or by bus. There would be a crowd. But maybe not until Saturday, the second day of the protest. The first day was entirely on Nashville. Entirely, it seemed, on Stump.

The morning of the march, Stump Collins sat on the parade stand, oblivious that the rainwater was soaking the pants he would wear all day long. He glared at sheets of paper as if they somehow had failed him. He scratched out something and then furiously wrote something in its place.

Stump was not the most likely choice to give the keynote, the speech that would start everyone walking toward Vanderbilt, getting them ready for two days of protest. It would've been a minister, or government official, or even George, who would've made a more likely choice to give the speech. But in the end, everyone knew that the success or failure of the protest sat directly on Stump's shoulders. He was the one who had made the biggest noise, he was the one who had taken all the meetings with Metro and with Vanderbilt, and he was the one who, in the end, had the most at stake. Because if he failed, everyone would look to him. And they would blame him.

Willa Winter stood to the side with Arletta Jones. It was interesting how, through a couple of weeks, the two had become thick as thieves. Arletta had softened her face whenever Willa was around, and Willa had taken on something of the approach of the student. She asked questions, and then she listened to the answers. She even took notes. It's likely Arletta had never had that experience in her life. And she liked it.

The sound system played Sly and the Family Stone. A crowd began to gather, and I stood near enough to Stump to hear him mumble, "This is awful."

"What's awful, Stump?"

"This damn speech. I can't get it to sound like me."

"Don't look at it, then. It'll screw you up. When you stand up, just tell the people what you think. Don't hold back."

"That's not the way anybody does it. Preachers always plan out what they are going to say."

"You're no preacher, Stump. What you are is one fired-up dude. Let them see that, and they will see you."

The music stopped. What had been a festive atmosphere grew quiet. George Jones was fiddling with the microphone. The crowd grew restless.

"Come on, old man." They weren't there to watch a 70-something year old man learn to work the sound. "Let's go."

There was an electronic screech, the kind that makes everyone wince. I don't know why it seems to be a requirement with a public sound system. Everybody does it, every single time.

George's voice came across too loud, then as a mumble while Elijah worked on the soundboard.

"Come on. Let's go." The crowd was booing now.

I looked at Stump. "You better get up there, big man. George is going to lose this crowd before you can win it."

Stump nodded. He uncurled himself from the hunker he was in and strode toward the microphone. He was large enough, imposing enough, and enough people knew him, that the quiet began to spread again from the front, near the stage, toward the back of the assemblage.

He took the mic stand from George and adjusted it so that it fit his height. He held a hand aloft, silently, waiting for calm. Slowly, beginning at the front of the crowd, one by one people began to raise their own hands high. Two by two, and then group by group, the hands began to rise. And when the crowd had mostly raised hands, and when the rumble of voices was only a murmur, Stump began to speak, with his arm still upraised.

"I was raised in the church. But I'm no preacher. We'll have a preacher when we get to Vanderbilt and ask him to pray over this matter."

A light murmur rose, as if the crowd didn't know what to expect.

"And I was raised on the street. Some of you were too. But the justice of the street is not what we look for today."

He surveyed the crowd, his hand still upraised, their hands still upraised.

"Today we take to the street to make a point. For too long, Nashville has ignored us. Nashville has taken us for granted. Acted as if the black community was expendable."

The crowd bubbled. I could hear a chorus of "That's right" crash on the wave of Stump's speaking. Stump was warming to his task.

"You know that we're supposed to stay in our part of town. You know that we're not welcome in their part of town, unless we are there to work for them. And you know that when they want something of ours, they find a way to take it."

The murmur grew louder. Some hands came down and began to clap. "Yes. That's right. Tell it, brother."

"And now, into all this comes a great university, and its leaders invite South Africa to come and play tennis. South Africa," and his voice ascended toward his upraised hand, his hand became a fist, "South Africa, where they do not bother to pretend that black folk are equal. No. Where they make it crystal clear."

"What do they do, man? Tell it."

"Where they divide the country. All this over here for the white folks. All this nothing over here for the black folks. They call it," and Stump brought his fist down, opened his hand and pointed his finger at the crowd. "Apartheid."

He had warmed the crowd up, and he was pretty warm himself. But he found a moment to gather himself, take a breath, and then begin to say what he wanted them to hear.

"We must make known our unhappiness with this. For while the university can do what it wishes, it should not do so without a clear understanding of what its actions mean. Because its action means this: they do not care that they have invited a terrible wrong into our midst. They are not here just to play tennis. No. They are allowed to be here, representing a foul, illegitimate, and evil regime. Pretending they are just here to play tennis is to lie about what is really at stake."

He paused. The crowd was quiet.

"And this is what is at stake. If you pretend that something foul, something illegitimate, something evil is a normal thing, that it's just being represented here by some tennis players --

as if tennis was just the most necessary and bland thing in the world -- if that is what you're willing to put up with? Then how far will you accept the evil? How far will you let it go? And will you be content with how things are here, right now? Or will you decide you want to push your black brothers and sisters further down the hidey hole of history?"

I had to give it to Stump. That first night over in The Gardens I thought he was a tough customer, somebody I didn't want to fight unless I had to. Now, though, I realized he was a customer I really wouldn't want to fight. He was pretty damn formidable, and it didn't have a thing to do with his 44.

"Here's what we want to do. We want to make ourselves into a march. We want to march from up here at the Capitol, down to West End, and then down to Vanderbilt. There will be others who meet us there. We expect 20,000 folks before the end of the weekend." He was pacing, kicked an imaginary object out of the way. "Our national organizations are coming, or they're here. They'll be here, and they'll speak. But this is our protest. This is our statement. We are glad to have the NAACP. And CORE. But this is the people's protest."

The crowd noise grew. Stump raised his hand again, and it subsided.

"I need for y'all to understand this one thing, too. This march is going to be peaceful. We've got police standing by and they're going to protect us. But they need to believe that we are worthy of protecting. We can't be doing anything illegal." He surveyed the crowd. "If any of you have anything illegal on you, or if you're thinking of doing something that could get you arrested, I have to ask you to not come with us. This has got to be righteous, or it is not worth doing."

Willa stood next to me. She was gazing up at Stump, not in admiration so much as what I'd call wonder. She saw me looking at her. "He's got it. That something. I don't think he knew he had it, but he does. He's a leader."

"He always knew he was mayor of The Gardens. I think what he's finding out is that he has a vision of what he wants done."

She looked from Stump to me. "You're a surprise too. But I don't know what to make of you."

Stump had given the crowd time to assimilate his message. "We are going to sing. We are going to chant. And by our size we are going to make the Man uncomfortable. Because we are large and because we are mostly black. But we cannot do anything illegal. And if you see one of us, and you think he is moving toward the wrong thing, I want you to personally stop him."

The crowd was his. It was silent, awaiting his terms.

"Nashville will hear us. Vanderbilt will hear us. Say it loud. Apartheid, no."

The crowd returned a louder echo. "Apartheid, no."

"Equality, yes."

Again, they responded. "Equality, yes."

"Apartheid, no." And they answered.

"Equality, yes." They answered again.

"We know, brothers and sisters, what we mean. We mean South Africa. But we mean Nashville too. In Nashville, Apartheid, no."

The crowd understood. And they roared when he leaped from the stage onto the ground.

I said to Willa, "Looks like we're on the move."

She didn't notice. She had her fist in the air. And she was already walking.

Chapter Thirty-Four

I STAYED IN THE back of the march. The crowd cycled through chants. Their favorite seemed to be that the people, united, would never be defeated, but they also seemed to have settled on Stump's improvised one as their second choice. Or maybe it wasn't Stump's at all. Maybe he borrowed it.

I didn't know. It was my first big march, and all I knew about protesting I'd learned from Ph.D.'s. Not exactly the best education on the matter.

It was turning into a windy day. Forecasts had called for rain later and, if this wind kept up, it was going to be a raw one. Regardless of the weather, the march continued to gain followers as Broadway turned into West End. True to his word, the Chief had Metro units out in force, both officers who'd been dropped off and lined the street, some twenty yards apart, except for places where Metro motorcycle units were parked. It was not what I'd call a show of force, but it was noticeable. Metro had no intention of letting this get out of hand.

Along the way, small knots of onlookers were on the sidewalks on both sides. Mostly white, they seemed to regard the spectacle with a bemusement, maybe even a boredom. It wasn't the sort of thing you saw every day. An almost entirely black, very large group, marching down the main thoroughfare. But the crowd was only chanting and carrying signs.

They posed no visible threat. And therefore, they were simply unusual, not scary.

That didn't keep one guy from shouting at me, loudly asking why I was affiliating myself with such a black group, whether I was a lover of the group.

Ok, that's not what he said exactly. He asked me why I was a phrase I won't dignify by repeating. I asked him if he kissed his mama with that mouth. I think he might have answered me at closer quarters if his friends hadn't laughed.

It was that kind of day. The people marching knew what was at stake. The ones watching didn't seem to know there were stakes at all.

By the time the tail of the march reached 25th Avenue, the crowd had swelled, and it was no longer all or even largely black. The two-block area between West End and the arena was elbow to elbow. Hardly a space existed to move forward or back. I retreated one block, cut between the two high rise residence halls, and made my way down 23rd. It was crowded, but nothing like the morass that was at 25th.

I lit a cigarette and positioned myself so that I could see the main stage that the university had erected. A young man wearing a knitted cap was exhorting the crowd in front of the stage, enumerating the evils of the South African government. He was followed by a group that had brought drums of various sizes, and they performed with gusto and a flair that told me they viewed this not only as a political moment but likely a commercial opportunity as well. They seemed later to be selling cassette tapes and booklets.

I moved closer to the corner where the Sigma Chi house stood. The crowd was thicker here, but still navigable. I looked down the street. I could see the SAEs were clustered on their front porch. The Phi Delts were on their roof, peering down. A few guys who I knew to be Sigma Chis were standing on their front stoop. Everyone had on their winter coats. The Phi Delts wouldn't be up there much longer as the rain was beginning now to pelt with icy insistence. I wondered how long all this would last if the weather got worse.

I felt a pinch in my side that made me react. It was Wendy Williamson, my former running mate as Assistant Dean. "That's a good way to get a black eye. I was about ready to brain you."

She dug a couple of knuckles into my side. "Good thing you didn't. No telling what I'd do back."

"Any news here?"

"We've got groups of student ambassadors in the crowd. Trying to be helpful. Make sure people know where there's water, bathrooms, you know."

"Is that really a good idea? Putting undergraduates in the middle of all this?"

"It's the best idea, Jackson. They're all trained. They all have orange jackets that identify them as friendly." She pointed one out. "See? Just having a pleasant conversation and being helpful."

"It just takes one mistake. Or one unpleasant conversation."

"It's fine. It beats having Metro wandering through the crowd."

I had to give her that. Or give Art Blake that. It sounded like something he'd come up with. "Is Art here?"

She pointed toward the stage. "He's over there. Some-where."

"I'm going to see if I can find him. Coming?"

She shook her head. "I've got another team over in Branscomb to suit up and get out here. We're running in shifts."

I left her there and made my way through the crowd toward the speakers' stand. Whoever had run this operation had done a good job. You'd never know that this wasn't something put together for visiting dignitaries. It wasn't just a bare stand. It was classed up. It didn't have bunting, because that would have been completely inappropriate, but it did not look like your bare wood stage that had been slapped together so that protesters could speak. And the sound system was impressive. As were the lights that had been erected, presumably in case they wanted to carry this on into the night.

I was proud of my old employer. Say what you want about not disinviting the South Africans, they'd done right by the protesters.

I spent the afternoon circling the crowd's perimeter. It was, as Stump had hoped, a well-behaved gathering. There were more people than might have reasonably been expected, and yet there was room, still, for the more who would come tomorrow, when the national organizations arrived.

It was a good effort nevertheless, and the stage stayed full, whether of preachers or businesspeople, many of whom had been among the north Nashvillians who had doubted the wisdom of getting involved. But the event had become self-fulfilling. It was like a flywheel; once enough folks were all in, the flywheel spun of its own accord. You just had to get it moving.

I had not seen Art all day, and I began to look for him in earnest. The day's events would soon be over, and I wanted to get a read on how Vanderbilt thought tomorrow would go.

Before I could find Art, I found Stump. He was sitting on the side of the stage, obstructed from view by the fabric that had been attached to the front. "How you doing, fearless leader?"

"I can't tell Jackson. Look around us. Half the people I see are people who don't give a damn about what we're doing here. Look over there. Fraternity boys drinking beer. Look here. Here's some sorority girls, it looks like. Any of these people seem like they care that much about apartheid? And if they don't, how the hell can they care about Nashville?"

"I don't know, Stump. It's hard to tell what anybody wants these days. The best you can hope for, I think, is that people will take it seriously. That people will listen. That they'll give it a chance."

"I don't know. Looks to me like all these people are doing is having kind of a fun day."

"Not much fun to be in this cold. All this rain coming down. Plus, you're not looking at what I'm looking at, in front of the stage. If you look up there, you can see all kinds of folks taking seriously what's being said here on the stage."

"I reckon it's true."

"Damn right it's true. You didn't have a whole bunch of people walk down West End Avenue with you just to have some fun in the cold rain. These people are serious. They're taking you seriously. What are you going to do about it?"

Stump thought for a minute. His brows knotted together. He rubbed his hands. And then he looked at me. "Yes, you're right. Somebody needs to talk to these folks and let them know what's really going on."

"I think if that's what you want to do, Stump, then you better go get on the microphone. You did it once already today. I bet you can do it again."

Stump stood and stretched his entire length toward the sky. He looked toward the speaker stand where a young man about 5 feet tall and maybe 12 years old was squeaking into the microphone. He was standing on a stepstool. And not many people were paying much attention to him, except for the people right in front, and as far as I know that may have been his mama and his aunts.

Stump came over and thanked him for his words. He helped him stand down from the steps. And then, in what could only be described as thunder, he began to speak.

"We've come too far, all of us, not to admit what is going on. We've come too far, each one of us, not to recognize that we have a kinship. Our kinship is not based on our skin color. It is not based on the amount of money we make or don't make. Our kinship is based on the blood that runs through our veins, and in our shared humanity. We do not accept, any of us, that one of us is less than another."

He scanned the crowd with his voice. It had the desired effect. People had stopped. They were listening. Again.

"And so, what I want to say today is that we mass here together to make a statement to the University, and to South Africa. Our statement is simply this. We see you, and we know what you were doing. You do not do it in the darkness any longer. You do it in the light, and that light is the light we shine on you today. You may think you were doing something that we can't see. But we see you and we know you for who you are. And who you are must change."

Once again, I felt I was in the middle of something powerful. It wasn't Stump, or rather it wasn't only Stump. The air was charged with excitement, anticipation, some strange and different stamp on the moment. The crowd, far from being angry, was charged too, as if each had breathed in the air, charged as it was, and become electric themselves. But that electricity was more a change in perception, in the way they understood the moment, than it was a change in action. While they may have come with some notion of anger, and some even with violence, they seemed now to be more in line with Stump's call: They saw the enemy, if enemy it was. Or if it wasn't the enemy, they saw it clearly as the enemy's enabler. And they looked resolved to hold it to account.

I was standing on the second step of the stage, ten feet from Stump. He was still talking to them, broadening his speech to include Nashville and Tennessee, indeed the United States, in his brief. But he was talking calmly, seemingly careful not to bend the speech into particulars he'd have to walk back later. Now, he was only demonstrating that those who enable evil may not be evil themselves, but they are responsible.

He paused and looked out over the crowd. It was a lively spectacle, but it was respectful, especially of Stump. His pause did not cause any lowering or raising of the ambient crowd noise.

When he finished, a wall of applause rose and the noise engulfed the stage. He looked at me and smiled. I smiled back. He had got through day one. Mission accomplished.

And then a crack, maybe of gunfire, echoed. At the back of the stage, away from the sight of the crowd, Stump went down, whether by instinct or because he'd been hit, I could not tell.

I jumped over the top step and rolled toward Stump, shielding his body with mine. "Let's go." I pushed him over the back of the stage, and he fell onto his good side with an oomph. I hit the ground about the same time.

"What the hell?"

I ripped some fabric from the stand and tore it. I pointed to his shoulder. "Let's get that stopped."

"It's not bad. Just grazed me."

"May be. But it's bleeding."

A couple of students crowding around us. The protest had grown loud, but it was now a noise of anger. There was a palpable feeling of danger now, partly from the unknown gunman, and partly from a group that was already tense. Now they had reason to be if they didn't before.

"Are you ok?" I recognized the voice of Art Blake.

"Can you take charge of this, Art?"

Even kneeling, Art was large. He nodded. Looked at Stump. "Let me handle this."

"Ain't nothing to handle." Stump was adamant.

"Then it won't take long." Art looked across the stage, then at me. "Any ideas?"

"Not a one." I slapped Stump on the knee. "They'll take you to VU ER. Don't leave until I get there, OK?"

"Do what I damn well please."

"Good. Be pleased to wait for me."

He narrowed his eyes, but I knew he would wait.

Chapter Thirty-Five

The crowd had roared and then, the danger unknown, had started moving in all directions at once. George Jones had walked decisively to the microphone and, still not knowing the danger, began to speak in a calm, firm voice.

"Nothing to be concerned about, brothers and sisters. It was just a noise. Noises are meant to frighten us. But we are not afraid."

Someone near the stage shouted, "They shot that man."

"No one has been shot. Brother Collins jumped out of the way when the noise came. We all have our reactions. We have our instincts. But he is fine. And we are all fine. There is nothing that can make us afraid. Nothing that can divert us from our goal."

The crowd was quieting, but it still moved, directionless, back and forth in front of the stage. "Somebody's shooting."

But no one was shooting. George began to sing. "We shall overcome." His voice was soothing, deep. Enough people started singing with him, almost as if by command, that the movement stopped. The verse kept going. George kept singing. And in a few minutes the crowd was back to its previous self. "We will always have those who try to scare us and drag us down," George said in benediction. "But we are strong. And our cause is just."

The "amens" came like the end of a service.

I tried to orient myself. The gunfire came from the left of the stage, which put the shooter back in the large parking lot area.

I moved in that direction, taking care to make sure I wasn't left exposed, just in case the shooter was still hanging there. I doubted it. Too big a crowd. Too much exposure of his own. He likely took his one shot, then went to ground.

By the time I had navigated into the parking area, Vanderbilt and Metro police had it cordoned. Don Mercer was there. He put his fingers in his mouth and whistled loudly to get my attention.

I had already seen him.

"Get over here." He motioned with his arm. "Now."

"See anybody?"

"There's all kinds of people in the area. I think some were watching the protest from their cars. You know. Too wet and cold."

"They're just spectators."

"Or too smart to get soaked. Anyway, we're making the rounds, got everybody rounded up and waiting to be interviewed."

"Everybody behaving? Anybody see anything?"

"Nobody's seen anything. And mostly behaving. A drunk Kappa Sig wandering through. Another undergrad objecting to waiting."

"What's his beef?"

"Says he just pulled into the lot and has to get to the library."

"Typical undergraduate."

"Not that typical. He looked familiar to me. Turns out he's the puppy dog that follows the history professor around."

"Willa Winter's lap moose? Really? His name's Alex."

"That's it. Well, he's sitting over there in that Dodge Polaris cooling his heels. Metro told him he could just wait until they got to him. If you want to know the truth, he'll be last."

"Fair enough." I turned away from Mercer and began to walk toward the Dodge in the back of the lot.

"Hey, where are you going?"

"I think I'll go keep Alex company."

"Don't screw around, Jackson.

"Not at all. Just helping a brother out."

Alex squirmed in his seat, fussing with the steering wheel, moving it left and right in small jerks. Next to him on the bench seat was a notebook and a small paperback on the French Revolution. He didn't see me until I rapped on the passenger side window. He jumped. Then scowled. "What?"

I opened the door and slid onto the seat. "Hey, Alex. What's going on, man?"

He turned away, looking toward fraternity row. "I don't have anything to say to you."

"That was some dramatic entrance a few nights ago. What was all that about?"

He continued to look away. "I was worried about Willa. Dr. Winter."

"You could have stayed, you know. That was on offer."

"I was worried about her. I didn't know what was going on."

I motioned toward the stage. "Just planning for a safe protest. Then," I made a pistol with my hands, "Boom."

"Yeah. I heard."

"You weren't here, then? Didn't see anything?"

"As I told the officer, I just got here. I am studying for a mid-term."

"Yeah? You drove from the library to park here? Why not walk? Ten minutes, tops."

He put his elbow on the ledge of the window. "It's a music theory class. I went over to The Blair School's library."

Blair was the music school on the edge of campus, unaffiliated but with cross-registered classes. "Classical? Baroque?"

"Huh?" He turned finally to look at me. "Oh. Sure."

"Any focus on the course? You know, I always thought sym-phonies were the thing until I learned about string quartets."

"What do you want, for God's sake?"

I held my hands up, palms facing him. "Easy now. I just thought I was passing the time."

"I don't want to pass the time with you. Get out of my car."

"That's cool." I pulled the handle to open the door. "Just a word of advice, Alex."

"Yeah?"

"Don't go showing up unannounced. It's just the sort of thing that surprises people. And some people don't react well to surprises."

"Thanks. I'll keep it in mind."

"No charge for the tip." Especially since the most interesting thing he'd told me was that he hadn't been studying at all. Music theory and the French Revolution don't co-exist, not when one is the thing you're studying and the other is not. And it stood to reason if he was lying about the obvious, there was a less obvious reason for the lie.

VU's Emergency Room serves all of Nashville, but not much of Nashville seemed to have need of its service that day. I found Stump pacing in an examination area just off the main lobby. He was dressed and ready to leave, but his face told a different story. "You look like hell, Stump."

"I look like hell because I been through hell. What hap-pened out there? Did they get that guy who shot at me?"

"Nobody found anybody yet. And I don't know whether they will or not. That shot came from across the parking lot."

"Are you telling me that nobody can find somebody who was that close? What the hell? What kind of police is this?"

"It's the kind of police that's got a lot at stake in getting this right, Stump. I don't think you can question their motives. It looks bad for them. If they don't find out who did this. Besides, this was just a lucky shot. Shooter was at least eighty, hundred yards away. Unless he's an expert marksman, a handgun at that distance is just a 'take a chance' shot."

Art nodded. "It's true. Metro's got every reason to try to find out who shot at you. And the Vanderbilt police has absolutely have every reason to try to find out. It looks bad on them if this goes unsolved. Or worse, if something happens tomorrow."

"You mean to tell me that what I got to do is just cool my jets? I just need to be copasetic about somebody taking a pot shot at me? Does that sound right?"

I tried to look cooler than I felt. "That's not it at all, Stump. All it means is that you've got to be careful tomorrow."

"I'll tell you how careful I'm going to be. I will be bringing my gun. Somebody shoots at me? I'm gonna shoot back."

"Not a good idea, my man. This is the sort of thing that can get you in trouble."

"I'm already in trouble. My man." He snorted. "Don't 'my man' me."

"What you are is a man who's got a target on him. I don't think you need to be in the position where you are also taking target practice at somebody else. A black man with a big gun? That is not going to fly in Metro Nashville." I sat half an ass cheek on the bed. "Not when you're supposed to be leading a peaceful protest."

"What am I supposed to do? Just stand up there and take it? Get my face blown off?"

"I don't think that's exactly the idea. But I do have a plan."

"Yeah. My man with the plan. That strikes me as the sort of thing that can get me in major trouble."

Art drew closer. "What have you got in mind, Jackson? You know something we don't know?"

I wasn't about to speculate in front of Stump. Or Art for that matter. "Here's what I know. I know that somebody took a shot at Stump. I know that whoever did it knows they did not accomplish their goal. Unless their goal was just to scare him."

"Well, I got a feeling their goal was not to scare me. I think they had other things in mind."

"I think they probably did too. And that's why I'm saying this. Let me have your gun tomorrow."

"Oh, no. Nunh uh. Ain't no way I'm giving up my gun."

"Give me a chance, Stump. I need for you to trust me, to give me that gun. And then we'll do something that will get you off the hook and get me on to it."

"Whoa, now. I don't like the sound of that, Jackson." Art gave me the look, the one where he twitches the handlebar mustache.

"Don't worry. Art. This is the sort of thing that we can pull off. But we're going to have to be smart about it. And we sure enough can't make a mistake."

"I don't know, Jackson. The idea of you, some harebrained plan, and there not being a mistake somewhere? Well, let's just say the odds are not good."

I don't usually cop an attitude with Art. But I did. And it got his attention. "The odds are going to be really good if we mind what we're doing. And I think it's the only way we can get Stump out of this jam."

Stump chewed his lower lip. "I don't like it."

I grinned. "Freddy's ready. Best let him be."

Chapter Thirty-Six

THE PHONE WAS RINGING when I got back to my apartment. There was something in its range, a kind of insistent jangle, that made me rush to it for no particular reason other than the fact that my nerves were a little shot. Hearing a gunshot will do that if you've got a little PTSD going on.

"Jackson?" I recognized the voice. It was Irma.

"Irma? I didn't expect to hear from you again."

"I was there today. I saw what happened. Is your friend okay?"

"He's fine. He'll be back tomorrow. Nothing to see there." I lied.

"You need to be careful." Irma's voice was strained, quiet.

"Tell me about it. Some damn redneck, I bet. He didn't want protesters and he takes a gun out. Probably fired it into the air, trying to cause a riot." I didn't say what I suspected was true. That it wasn't a redneck at all.

Irma's voice was thin, tight. "Do the police have anything?"

"Not the last I checked. They were questioning everyone in the area, especially anyone who looked like they didn't have a good excuse for being where they were. Problem is, there's plenty of people running around that don't look like they'd be game for a protest, but they are. Like you, Irma."

"People like me have all kinds of surprising political orientations, Jackson. Just because you don't approve of me doesn't mean that I don't believe in something. It doesn't mean I can't have a passion."

I left that opening alone. I knew all about Irma's passions. "I'm not pointing fingers, Irma. I'm just saying that it's hard to find the shooter in a crowd as spread out as that one."

"Well, I can tell you that I happened to be looking away from the stage when the shot happened. It didn't come from near the stage. It came from near the SAE house. And it wasn't shot up in the air, either."

"Come on, Irma. I don't believe for a minute that some SAE shot at the stage. Those guys, whatever they are, aren't killers. A little too oriented toward the country club set, maybe. But not killers."

"I didn't say it came from the house. I said it came from the parking lot near the house. I saw a muzzle flash, isn't that what you call it? I was looking right at it."

"And you told the police this?"

"The police didn't come near me, so no."

"You should tell the police what you know, Irma. They're investigating this."

"I saw the police at work today. They're worried, but they're mostly worried about something getting out of hand. To tell the truth, I'm not sure anything I say wouldn't get buried in a pile of paperwork. Everybody who was there probably thinks they saw something."

"Just like you?"

"Yes, just like me. But I did see something. I'm not making this up."

"So, you saw the muzzle flash. Did you see the shooter too?" I wasn't too sure Irma had seen anything. Or that she'd seen something and constructed a story to fit it. Muzzle flash? And not at night? In low light on a rainy day, maybe you could see something like that. But probably not.

Irma paused." I don't want to say this as if I know. But it's an undergraduate. Someone I've seen before, for sure. I can't place him."

"What's he look like?"

"He's sort of tall but not so much that he's huge. Kind of a baby face, I think. At least that's the impression I have. I just can't place it. It was pretty far away."

I could place it. I'd seen him over and over. Just a boy. Except he was a boy with a problem. In his case, the problem was Willa Winter. Or rather, anyone who came close to her.

"That actually helps, Irma. It confirms something."

"I did the right thing? Not going to the police? Telling you?"

"We'll know by this time tomorrow, I expect." I was to put the phone down. Then I stopped." Did you see anything else? Anyone else?"

"Just this young man. I saw the shot. I got a glimpse of him, and then he disappeared."

"Hard to believe no one else heard that, or saw that, him being as close to others as he was."

"Could be," she said. "Or it could be that, when an area is that crowded, everything is close and far away all at once."

That was true enough. I've been close all along. And I'd never seen it.

Chapter
Thirty-Seven

IT WAS GOING TO be an interesting day. Nashville was on edge. The protest was bigger. People from out of town were there, lots of civil rights celebrities. The moment was slightly bigger than we expected. The gunshot, even something denied as a gunshot, had made it so. We had managed to keep the papers away from Stump's scrape. Metro didn't want it in the media that he had been winged. Stump didn't want it out either. It ran against his legend, against his mythology. He was Stump Collins. No one took a shot at him and got away with it.

That's what he was telling me. "My shoulder better be wrapped up tight so nobody can tell. I'm not wanting anybody thinking that I'm weak."

Willa was standing next to him. "No one thinks you're weak, Stump. No one even knows."

"That's right," I said. "The best thing we've done in this whole business is to keep the news about you locked down. But that doesn't mean you're going to be on the stage much, my friend. We've got a different plan going."

"What different plan are you talking about? I'm going to introduce everybody. This is our show."

"It's not your show, Stump. It's everyone's show now. And with the big boys here there taking the lead, you are playing a secondary role now."

His eyes knitted together. If he could have managed it, steam would have come out his ears and maybe out his nose. As it was, he exhaled forcefully. "I started this shit. I'm going to see it through."

"Remember what we said last night, back in the hospital. You and I are working together. We're going to nail this son of a bitch. And were going to do it cleanly."

"What I would like to do is get this guy in a room and work him over. We'll see how tough he is when he doesn't have a gun."

"That would be all right as a plan, Stump, in a hypothetical world. But he does have a gun. And you can hand me yours." I held out my hand, waiting.

The moment was tense. Whatever he agreed to last night while he was in pain, he clearly had more time to think about it. "I don't think it's a good idea for me to give up my weapon. I might need it."

"No, I will need your weapon. Like I said last night, a black man this weekend in Nashville does not need to be carrying. It is a recipe for trouble."

"That's right, Mr. Collins". I heard the booming voice of Art Blake behind me and soon enough saw his shadow fall across us both. "Metro has you covered, Mr. Collins. And Jackson, well, Jackson is just smart enough to manage things that don't make sense. When things do make sense, he's not so good. But in a pinch, in a bind, when things look pretty awful, well, I just say I'd put my trust in him."

I thought to myself that Art had changed his tune. But I said nothing. No need to poke the bear.

Art sat down between us, looked from one of us to the other. "He's right about the gun too. You don't need to be carrying today, not up on stage, not with all these important folks. You don't want the one whose stray round hit somebody."

Stump grumbled. He waffled. He whined a little. But in the end, he handed his 44 Magnum to me. "Be careful," he said. "The recoil on this mother is fierce."

I stood up and poked the 44 into my beltline in the back, glad it was a short barrel and not one of the Dirty Harry types. I pulled my coat around it. "Don't worry. I know how to use it. I hope I won't have to."

Day one of the protest had been cold and wet. It had been a bit of a festival except near the gym, where protesters got into it with attendees, both going in and going out. There had been some unpleasantness. A couple of people had spit on well-heeled Nashvillians going to watch tennis. At least one young man had grown impatient with Metro and had to be restrained. But until the shot, or the loud backfire as Metro had it, there had been little to note. It was a protest, to be sure. It was a huge one by Nashville standards. And it had been focused. But in the end, it'd been just a larger version of what had gone on around Kirkland Hall for several months. Signs. Chants. And more than a little of a feeling of solidarity. Us against the University. Us against South Africa. The stakes weren't so high as to be uncomfortable.

Something that sounded like a gunshot had changed that.

No one knew that Stump had been hit. There were people around him, but Art and I and a few of the students had managed to obstruct views until Metro could mount a curtain. The Tennessean had said that it could have been a car backfiring. The Banner had opined that with tensions so high any sound could be taken as gunfire. Both had bought the official line that it wasn't gunfire and, besides, nothing had come of it.

North Nashville suspected different. North Nashville knew that if a black man was on stage yelling things about white people, then gunfire was not out of the realm of possibility. North Nashville knew what gunfire sounded like. And north

Nashville was pretty sure that the media were lying. Most of the time.

The protest began again, this time on the Capitol grounds and this time led by the national organization people, the celebrities, the big names. They walked eight abreast down Broadway and West End with a long banner proclaiming that apartheid was evil. Behind them ranged some 3000 people, many of them new to Nashville and there to make their voices heard. I walked again along the side toward the back. Today, more people had come out to line the streets. Some, like yesterday's crowd, were hostile to the whole event, but there were enough people interspersed who were in sympathy, and so the sidewalks and the sides of streets were tense with people alternately raising a fist in support or raising a fist in anger. Where yesterday had been lighter fare and more like a stroll, today was more like a march. More, indeed, like a march into the unknown.

By the time we got to campus all the associated dignitaries stood on the platform for a round of photos. This had become a national event. All three networks had camera crews there. There was evidence of both the AP and UPI, with reporters in the crowd and photographers taking pictures. There was a buzz in the air. It was electric but, at the same time, it felt staged. Yesterday had been organic, something run by the north side and directed at Nashville, at Vanderbilt. This one, today, had been co-opted by the protest machine. It had its good works to do. It was bringing notice in a way that the north side could not. But it was no longer organic. It was national. It was about apartheid. And it had Movement stamped all over it.

Stump and I stood at the back of the platform. "This shit done got big, didn't it?" Stump looked at the back of my coat, checking for his gun.

"Does that bother you? It seems that the more notice this attracts, the better."

"We worked pretty hard. We got the businesses and churches to march with us. This belonged to us. Now? I don't know. Seems like it's a whole different deal now."

"You don't think it's making the point? You don't think that this is what you wanted?"

"Not a question of what I want, Jackson. It's a question of who owns this. We wanted to make our point. We wanted to make our point about Vanderbilt and about Nashville. I guess that point will get made, but I guarantee when John Chancellor starts the news on NBC tonight, he'll be talking about South Africa. He's not going to talk about Nashville. We're not the reason anymore. We're just the location."

The day warmed slightly, though the chill remained in the air. The speeches were long, and they were endless. At one point, a couple of Vanderbilt faculty got up to say a few words, but their time was brief before more speakers, who were not from Nashville, got up to say their piece.

I wouldn't say that anything they had to say was wrong. Everything they said was exactly right. But as the day wore on, the protest really did start to feel like a warmed-over version of 1968 and 1969, times when the statements in the street were real and the possibilities of change seemed imminent. A time when proximity to radical change seemed right there.

Today though? The air was chilly and the proximity to radical change was, well, let's just say it was not in evidence. There were people who had passion, no doubt. But their passion was largely performance. Having failed to achieve radical change, they had settled for discomfort. Both their own and that of those they protested.

As the day went on, Stump grew silent. He watched the platform less and less and scanned the crowd.

I offered him a cigarette. He refused. "Even if you see him, you wouldn't know him."

"I might know him if he had a gun pointed at me."

"Give it a minute. Our plan goes into effect in just a few." I looked at my watch. "Fifteen minutes and it's go-time."

Go-time came. Stump and I walked toward Memorial Gym's basement entrance. It was easy to see us if you were looking for us. Two men about the same size. One wearing a camo jacket and a sock cap. That was Stump. The other wearing a cowboy hat, long hair flowing out from under it and a leather jacket. Both in jeans, both wearing white Chuck Taylor's, both with leather gloves. Both moving hurriedly toward the building. Once inside, we went into action.

We exchanged coats and head coverings, and I stuffed my hair up inside the sock cap. We kept our leather gloves on.

"You know where you're going, right?" I had explained it to him. We hadn't had time for me to show him.

"I know," Stump said. "Just up the steps. Then around the upper deck and hang out in section 3C. Where we hope that the sonofabitch won't go because he is not fooled by any of this."

"He'll be fooled, Stump. Trust me. He just ain't that smart."

"You sound like you know who it is."

"I know what he is. And I know somebody who fits the description. But we'll have to see."

"Either way, save a piece for me."

Stump disappeared and I was left alone in the bowels of Memorial Gym. My job was to make it easy to find me and hard to kill me. Most of my life, seems like the job has been to be hard to find. This was a whole new type of life plan.

Whether it's the bottom of the church basement or the bottom of a large multipurpose event venue, the humidity is about the same. I slipped through the dank, wet cool of Memorial's underground. I kept my ears open. It helped that my Chuck Taylor's could be quiet. On the gym floor, they would squeak, but placed just right on concrete they did not. Before too long, though, I heard the deliberate click of someone's heels. Heels with taps on. The kind some of the cool kids had, ostensibly to keep the wear to a minimum. But mostly just because they were cool. And loud.

What an idiot. But how appropriate.

I waited until he should be rounding into view, and I took off. I made a little more noise than was entirely necessary. The Chuck Taylor's squeaked. Just in case he missed hearing me.

But he heard me all right. As I turned the corner, I heard the shot and it ricocheted off the tile behind me.

Great. He seemed willing to shoot it out here.

I got to the end of the hallway where the men's room was. I ducked inside. Here was the showdown. Here was the OK corral. And here was where I wanted him.

Chapter Thirty-Eight

THERE WERE TWELVE STALLS. I went into the one furthest from the entry, locked the door, and stood on the toilet seat. If I crouched down enough, there was no way to see me. And you couldn't see my legs under the door. Maybe it wasn't the most elegant plan, but I had the 44. And I had the advantage of knowing he was coming.

And boy, he did come.

He must have kicked the door open, or put considerable weight into it, because I heard it bounce off the wall.

"Collins." He screamed it, the anger cutting through the rank air. "You're here. I'm here. Let's get it on."

I knew whose voice it should be, but I couldn't definitively place it in the screaming. Southern accent. Not quite preppy but distinctive.

"You can't hide in these stalls, pal. You might as well come out." He dropped his voice an octave. "I have a present for you," he crooned.

It was the voice on the phone, the one threatening me. The one who'd warned me off. But how could that be? How did shooting Stump square with Tippy? It made no sense.

"All right. We'll play it your way. But when I find you, I won't play around. I've got my buddy here. Mr. Colt. You almost met him yesterday. He's eager to see you."

I heard him kick the first stall door open.

"Here we go. I bet you think you can talk me out of this when the time comes. Bet you think you're just that persuasive."

The second door flew open and banged against the side of the stall.

"I bet you think you're so cool your shit don't stink. Like you can talk your way out of anything."

Bang, went the third stall door.

"That the way you get on with the ladies? Talk, talk, talk?"

That sounded familiar. The fourth door flew open.

"But do you think that Dr. Winter is fooled by that street patter? A woman like her? Why would she waste her time on you?"

It was Alexander. The undergrad. The hanger on.

"You think I won't do this, Collins?" He kicked another door in. "You think I won't deal with you the same way I dealt with Tippy Taylor?"

And like the tumbler on a combination lock, the last turn caused everything to open up. Willa Winter had a friendship with Tippy, and that threatened Alexander. Tippy died. Stump had flirted with Willa. Another threat. Now Alexander was taking care of that business too. He'd taken a shot at me too. Because he thought I was getting close. Because I was a threat.

And Alex was getting closer, too. I waited. He worked his way down the lines of stalls, kicking them open one by one.

Finally, he stood in front of my stall. "All right, Mr. Big. I know you're in this one because there's only this one left. You chicken shit."

He gave a mighty kick and the frame bent. As he regrouped, I reached over and flicked the flange. As he slammed his foot into the door again, it gave way. Of course, he misjudged the force he needed. His plant foot slipped, and he landed on his backside.

When he looked up, he saw me standing on the toilet seat. And he saw the 44. I had my finger on the outside of the trigger guard. It wouldn't take much for me to get a shot off, but his Colt was single action. He could certainly get a shot off more quickly than I could. Even with a round already in the chamber.

I felt my heart pounding. I had to hope that most of what he knew about firearms he'd learned on television and not in a weapons class. He was splayed out on his back, and the Colt was not in position to do any shooting. Not yet anyway.

"Slide Mr. Colt over there under the sinks, Alexander."

"What if I don't?"

"Then we'll see just how big a hole this magnum will make." I gestured with the barrel. "You know what Dirty Harry says. The most powerful handgun in the world."

You could still see the undergraduate in him. He would someday grow into his nose and someday he would be a big strapping fellow instead of the sinewy kid he was now. But he would grow that way in prison. As long as he did what I said.

"Slide it, Alexander. Right over there."

He did as he was told.

I breathed. "Now sit up and slide your backside in the other direction.

"What the hell, man?"

"I want you where I can see you."

"Where's Collins?" He stopped sliding. You could see the wheels turning, trying to figure his way out of his situation.

"Never mind that. Collins is not your problem. I'm your problem right now." I climbed down, keeping the barrel pointed toward him.

He smirked. The way snotty undergrads do when they think, no matter what has happened, that they are superior to you.

"How'd you do it, Alexander? How'd you kill Tippy Taylor?" I stood just out of reach of his legs. But I was watching. Closely.

"Ha." He almost snorted. "Taylor was easy. He was a user. An addict. He was higher than a kite."

"And he just happened to invite you in?"

"I was waiting for him. Easy as pie."

"And you got out with no one seeing you? White boy like you, in that part of town?"

"If you wrap your head in a hooded sweatshirt that says Fisk on the front. Keep your gloves on. Takes a sharp eye to see past that in the dark. Especially if the bicycle is moving fast." He puffed his chest a little. "You'd be surprised how easy it is."

"And you just took him out back and threw him in the dumpster."

"Yeah. That's where he belonged. With the rest of the trash."

He had worked himself into a crouch and he sprang in the direction of his gun, twenty feet away. I pointed the magnum at the mirrors above the sink, pulled the trigger. Glass splattered everywhere, including where Alexander's hands slid on the floor. He grimaced as the shards opened tiny holes. Small streaks of blood appeared. I kicked the gun across the tile floor.

"Don't get cute, sonny boy."

Looking at his hands, he fell back and landed on more broken mirror. He shouted a profanity and jumped, and his leather soled shoes slipped again. He reached out involuntarily with his hand, and skidded again, gathering more glass into his palm.

"All you have to do is sit your butt down, Alex. This is over."

I heard movement to my right. Keeping the magnum trained on Alexander, I turned to see Flood come into view, his service revolver coming down into firing position. Seeing me, he raised it but kept an eye on Alexander. "My, what a big revolver you have, Grandma."

I turned back toward Alex. He was picking glass out of his hand as best he could. "The better to call for help with, little piggie."

He laughed a little. "That's not funny."

"You're the one who made me the big bad wolf. You must be one of the three pigs. I'm willing to grant that you're the one with the brick house."

He stepped over Alex's legs and retrieved the Colt. "This is his?"

"Yeah. Odds are it'll match the slug they pulled out of the platform yesterday."

Flood gave the boy the once over. "And Taylor?"

"He told me he did it. I bet he'll tell you."

He shook his head and motioned toward Stump's gun. "You can put that down now. I assume you have a permit for it. Or someone does."

"I would assume." Like hell. If Stump Collins had a registered firearm, I was his uncle.

A couple of Metro uniforms arrived, and Flood pointed a finger toward Alexander. "On your feet, baby cakes. Go with the nice men in blue."

He watched as Alexander rose, trying hard not to put his hands on the floor again, and left in handcuffs. "I don't get how a dweeb like this is in the killing business."

I put Stump's magnum in the oversized pocket of the camo jacket. "Love, baby. It's always about love."

After a rigamarole at Metro, followed by exchanging clothing with Stump, I accepted a ride back to my place from Flood.

"You always end up on the right side of a scrape, Trade. How is that?"

"Luck, I guess. Certainly not skill."

"You sure about that?" He was chewing on a toothpick. It was pointing at me from the side of his mouth.

"Even a blind squirrel finds an acorn once in a while."

The toothpick shifted, pointed out the windshield. "For a blind squirrel you end up with a lot of nuts." He managed somehow to flip the toothpick so that the end he was chewing faced outward and the pointy end was between his teeth. "At a certain point, it looks like skill more than luck."

"At a certain point, if you hang around enough, the odds even out. That's all."

He dropped me off and I turned in. I didn't even look at the bottle of Beam on my counter. I was too tired. And I wasn't all that thirsty. I brushed my teeth, peeled off my clothes, and climbed under the covers.

I slept until noon the next day.

Chapter Thirty-Nine

THE BIRDS WERE ESPECIALLY loud. The sky was particularly blue. The pavement was warm for the first time all year. Spring had arrived and accelerated into the middle of June, even though it was just March. That's the way Nashville is sometimes. Or maybe that's just the way it is after you get your bones soaked and frozen two days straight. Or after people have been shot at.

Or after you confront a killer.

It didn't matter to me. I had a clear head and nothing on my mind but a heaping plate of food. The sleep had done wonders for my attitude and my appetite.

Hannigan's was just revving into gear and the Sunday lunch bunch was straggling in. It wasn't the sort of place that attracted the church-going crowd, and the folks it did attract were the sort who wouldn't be up until later in the afternoon.

Today, though, seemed a little different. Katie swung past me at the door, carrying a platter with three chicken dinners, and motioned with her head. "People looking for you in the back. Bring you a bourbon? Beer?"

"Coffee." She stopped almost imperceptibly. "Please."

The parties she referred to were sitting in the back corner, furthest from the kitchen. Stump Collins. Wardell Robinson. Wardell looked up and saw me. He motioned me over.

"The man of the hour." Wardell smiled. Or at least what passed for a smile with him.

Stump stood and clasped my hand. "Jackson, my brother." He motioned where Wardell had scooted over. "Sit with us, Freddy."

Katie brought a coffee cup, and refilled Wardell's and Stump's before filling mine. "You guys want to order?"

Wardell shook his head and Stump looked at me. "Go ahead if you want. We're just waiting on you."

"I'll wait." The coffee felt hot and dark on my tongue. "Last time I saw Wardell in here, he was putting me on Tippy's case. Y'all come to give me more business?"

Wardell gave me the quasi-smile again, and then it disappeared. "I remember what we said. Brother needs his friends more than ever now. And you came through, Jackson."

"No. I failed Tippy. Until Stump got a target on his back." I didn't tell them I'd put the strong arm on LaSalle. No need now. Water under the bridge.

Stump nodded. "And you put the target on yours."

"You'd have done it for me."

"Maybe." His hands circled the cup, but he didn't drink. "Maybe not." He leaned forward, held out his hand. "When the time came, you were ready, Freddy. That's what matters"

There wasn't much to say to that. It felt good to come through. It felt better to have been trusted. "No problem, man."

Wardell leaned forward now too. The three of us sat like conspirators. "You remember what you told me? First time I was here? When I was asking you to find Tippy's killer?"

I didn't. I said no.

"You said that Dean Blake was trying to resurrect you, but you'd failed to rise."

"Fair enough." It was the truth.

"And I said that maybe this would do the trick. You remember what you said?"

I didn't have to remember. "I probably said there was no way it would happen."

"Indeed, you did. But look here. You found Tippy's killer. You saved Stump. You helped the biggest protest in Nashville history go down."

I looked down at my coffee. "That's not a resurrection, Wardell."

"I don't know what you'd call it. Stump says you were ready when the time came. What I'd say is that you got your mojo back. Whatever you lost. Whatever it was that was keeping you from being what you needed to be. You got it back."

Stump agreed and bumped fists with Wardell. "Yeah. Mojo. That's the way to think about it."

"Mojo means magic. I don't see that I've got any magic. Or that I ever had any."

"What's magic? You say the word or do the thing. Abracadabra. Things change." Wardell's skin absorbed the light and shone. "When you got your own mojo, you can call yourself into being. Change things. Put your fingerprints on the world and make them stick." He smiled, this time for real. "And resurrect yourself. Bring yourself back from the walking dead."

"Put a brother on the right path, too." Stump was grinning now as well. "See, being mayor on the north side is one thing, but it isn't a real thing."

"What path are you on, Stump?" I took my hands off the coffee cup. I wasn't drinking any. No need to hold it as if I was.

"Those national cats that were on the platform yesterday?"

"NAACP? CORE? Those guys?"

"That's it. They want me to come work in Atlanta, at the southern regional headquarters. They said they could use someone with my skills. My vision." He grabbed my forearm. "What do you think about that?"

I had to admit it seemed right. And it seemed well-deserved. Stump had made the march happen. He had provided the spark at the beginning. And the fire at the end. "Congratulations."

"That's your mojo too, Jackson." He squeezed my forearm. "None of that happens without you."

It was a nice thought. But it was irrelevant. "Right place. Right time. That's all."

"You don't give yourself enough credit, brother. But that's all right." He motioned to himself and Wardell. "We do. And Jackson?" He put his other hand on my forearm. "Thank you."

I looked from one to the other. Wardell put a hand on my hand. "Tippy thanks you." Then the other hand. "And I thank you."

"If y'all were preachers, I'd say the laying on of hands is followed by a prayer."

"Prayer's done been answered, brother." Stump let go and slapped my shoulder. "You get down Atlanta way, you call."

"Just like I called you when I went Northside?"

"Yeah, just like that." He laughed. "Except next time, do call."

We got out of the booth and shook hands. Wardell leaned into his handshake. "Stay in touch, okay?"

"You bet, Wardell. Call me anytime."

I watched as they left. Two men. Good at what they did. One of them with a professional practice. The other with a future, though who could say where it would lead.

I heard my name called from the front of Hannigan's. It was Katie. Yelling. Half the heads in booths turned to see what the commotion was.

I went to the front of the restaurant to see.

There stood Betty, her head slightly dropped. "I told her I could find you."

Katie was grinning. "Jackson is the center of attention today. I wouldn't be surprised if half these people came just to see his shining face today."

Betty looked like she had her traveling clothes on. It was her favorite coat, a trench coat, and jeans, simple T-shirt, and tennis shoes. Even in an outfit that simple, she looked good.

We slid into a booth. "It was all over the news," she said. "You're some kind of hero."

"I'm not a hero. I'm a guy who got chased by a bad guy with a gun. The rest took care of itself."

"People are saying that's the definition of a hero. I'd take it."

"Hero. Fool. The only difference is the ending. Could just as easily gone the other way."

"It never does, though, does it, Jackson? Eventually it goes your way."

I could've told her that it had gone wrong any number of times in my life. Nearly every week in combat. Nearly once a month, it seems, since I've been back there's always something. And I can't tell you the differences, the real difference, between me and Tippy Taylor. Except I didn't end up in a dumpster.

"That looks like your traveling case," I said.

"I got a call from Stax Records. In Memphis. One of the executives wants me to come and listen to a couple of artists work my songs."

"I always thought you had more of a Memphis vibe than a Nashville one."

"Must be all that Al Green I play in my apartment." She smiled. "They want me there Monday." She looked away again. "Tomorrow."

"If it's what pays the bills, then that's what you got to do," I said.

"Seems like we're always just getting started. And then, something happens."

"Things are what they are," I said. "Things will be what they will be. I sound like some old Doris Day movie, don't I?"

"You could never sound like her, Jackson. She would be appalled."

"True enough." Katie came by, poured more coffee in my cup and without speaking put a cup on the table in front of

Betty. Betty covered it with her hand. "Nothing for me. I'm just here to say goodbye."

"Not goodbye," I said. "You're just going your way for a while."

"I may not be back."

"Que sera, sera."

"That's the way the cookie crumbles?"

"To everything there is a season. You know. Turn, turn, turn."

"What if it doesn't turn back, Jackson?"

I remembered enough from my undergraduate course in philosophy to recognize a little fatalism when I heard it, so I reversed course. "Look," I said, "Nobody knows what's coming." I took her hand "You'll do great in Memphis. You get around all those famous guys, like Booker T and the MGs, and Al Green, and you'll forget all about Nashville. You'll be in your element."

"Will you be okay, Jackson?"

Whether I'm going to be okay is a question that's always on the table. "I'll be fine."

"You do seem to be doing okay. Hero and all, you know."

"Everything's fine. I've been paid."

I had finally sat down to a Western omelet and my fourth cup of coffee when I looked up to see Willa Winter. She slid into the booth without ceremony.

Her eyes were red and so were her cheeks. She refused the cup that Katie offered her.

Katie sighed and gave me a frown. "I can't give these away today. Except for you."

After Katie withdrew, Willa sat for a moment, then finally looked at me from under heavy eyelids.

"I feel like it's my fault."

I pushed the plate to the side and reached for her hands. "It's Alex's fault."

"No. I was the adult. The professional. I should have seen the signs."

"There weren't signs to see. How do you recognize the difference between simple hero-worship and flat-out homicidal maniac behavior? Did he ever plonk Irma Beddington on the head when she contradicted you?"

She allowed herself a smile. "He probably thought I'd smack Irma myself." She looked down again, away from me.

"Irma needs to be smacked. But even if he had, who would guess he killed Tippy? Or tried to kill Stump?" I left out that he'd taken a shot at me too. "And even if you suspected, how would you have proceeded? Where was your evidence going to come from?"

"You think I'm being silly."

"I think you're feeling guilty. But you're only guilty of thinking you had an admirer. One you probably deserve."

She flushed redder. "What's that supposed to mean?"

"You're an up and comer. Undergraduates are supposed to attach to you. Graduate students will come just to study with you, in time. You're a rising star."

"I doubt it. At least not at Vanderbilt." She looked up, then down again. "I've given my notice."

"You quit? Just like that?"

"The department is happy for me to go. For that matter, I suspect the School of Arts and Sciences is just as happy not to have me around."

"What will you do? Where will you go?"

"I'm heading back to Chicago. I can latch on to something. I have some savings." She wouldn't meet my eyes. "I'll be fine."

I didn't know what to say but I understood. You could call it running from your problems. Or you could just say that you were starting over. Either way, she had a right.

"Seems like I'm saying this a lot today. Stay in touch. That is, if you feel like it."

Finally, she looked at me. "You're a strange one, Jackson. I thought you were awful. Now? I think you're remarkable, but not in the usual way."

"Nothing remarkable here."

"No. You're wrong." She started to slide over to leave. "You'll see."

Someone blocked her from exiting the booth. Bobby Flood. "Detective," she said. Now she wasn't looking at either of us.

Flood gave an abbreviated bow. "Professor. Good to see you." If he'd had a hat, he would have tipped it. A falsely friendly greeting.

Willa understood it. Brushing past him, she got up, and I did too. She gave me a brief hug. "I'll give you an address when I have one," she whispered.

And then she was gone.

Flood raised his eyebrows at the pantomime. "Mind if I sit down?"

I sat back down and held my hand out. "Confessional's empty. Come and confess your sins."

"How's she taking it?"

"Pretty well, I guess. Shocked as hell. Leaving town for good. Sounds about right."

"Sounds about right," echoed Flood. "I would get out of town. For no other reason than the papers will be after her for months. Bad enough as it is."

He was right. I'd seen the papers. VANDERBILT LOVE NEST? In big type. Never mind that there wasn't a love nest. Or that the real Vanderbilt love nest was somewhere else.

"What about you, Trade? What's next for you? You're not leaving town, are you?"

"I got nowhere to go, Flood. Besides, why would I leave all this?" I gestured around Hannigan's. "Got all I want here."

"Yeah, but you're not here as much. Sure, you used to be." He grinned when I raised my eyebrows. "Yeah, I've noticed.

A couple other people noticed too. You clean up your act, or what?"

I held up my empty coffee cup for Katie to see. She nodded, came over and refilled it. "Let me know when you're switching to bourbon," she said. "You're getting a little caffeinated."

I just nodded.

"You know, I've gone from thinking you were an asshole to thinking you were a cocky son of a bitch to thinking that you probably just attract trouble. And maybe you do."

"Maybe I do." Katie was right. I could feel the coffee. It was making my foot jiggle my leg all the way to my hip. I put the cup down.

"Maybe. But maybe you've got a nose for stuff. Like I've got a nose for stuff."

"I don't think there's that much we have in common, detective."

"Don't sell yourself short, Trade. You and me, we've got a lot in common."

"Name one thing."

"Neither of us likes loose ends. I like my business tied up neatly with a big bow on top. Until it gets that way? I'm not real happy. You're the same way."

"I could argue that point. Name something else."

"All right, here's another. You really, really want the right thing to happen. But you're patient. You are not going to force things."

I forced LaSalle, with disastrous results, but I let it alone. "Seems like I forced things pretty good yesterday with Alex."

"No, that's not forcing things. You let him come to you and then you lowered the boom. That takes patience. For guys like us, it wraps things up. Neat, with a bow on top. Patience is really hard to come by."

"Okay. I'll give you that one. Maybe you got something."

"You bet, I got something. I got something else too. How would you like a job?"

"Why you think I need a job? I'm doing fine."

"You take jobs as they come. How would you like a career?"

My hackles stood up. It wasn't the coffee. "What kind of career?"

"You are dense when you want to be. A career with Metro, dumb shit. You could, you know. Be a cop. Be a detective, eventually."

I knew a few guys who got out of the military and became cops. To tell the truth, I didn't think much about it myself. I spent a long year in Vietnam, with things exploding in my face. AK-47s. MD-82s. Toe poppers. "I don't know, Flood. I like my life as drama-free as possible these days."

"That's why you're perfect. Lots of guys go into this work because they like to pull a trigger. There's not enough like you and me. The ones who won't pull the trigger until it has to be pulled, the ones who know that time almost never comes."

"I don't know, Flood."

"You don't have to know right now. The Academy isn't going anywhere. But I've asked around. A guy like you, with an honorable discharge and a college education, you can probably bank on Metro paying your tuition to the Academy. After that, you pay it off with a five-year commitment. Get yourself assigned to a detective unit. After that first five years, take the sergeant's exam when you're ready. Then, the lieutenant's exam after that."

"I don't know if that's what I want. I never even thought of it like that."

"Just another thing in your favor, Trade. You never thought about it. You just do the things that make us think you'd be good at it. You got the right instincts. You just need the training, certification, the blessing of the city. You'll be great."

"It's a lot to think about."

"Of course, it is. Take your time. And get back to me next week, tell me what you're thinking. Any questions you got." He leaned forward. "Look, Jackson. You're made for this. You're absolutely a guy who can excel. And if you're the guy we think you are, Metro needs you."

Bobby Flood got up and left. But he left behind a whole string of questions behind the opportunity he offered. I wasn't sure they were questions I wanted to even ask.

Later that night, Mercer and I sat on bar stools, looking into the mirror behind the bar, minutes between sentences. The beer cup I had was half-full and warm. I had been sitting behind it the better part of an hour. Mercer had just ordered his second and took a sip.

"Is it that you don't think you're cut out to be a cop? Because I can tell you, you either are or you aren't."

"When did you know, Don?"

He waited almost a minute. "I knew the first time I broke up a fight on campus. It wasn't much of a fight, but they were drunk enough that it could've gotten bad real fast, what with all their friends around them egging them on. It was the sort of thing where the voice of reason needed to be coming from a place of power. It's when I knew I could actually make a difference."

"What the hell, Don? Voices of reason from a place of power? That's not been my experience. With MPs. With cops in general. With a few in particular."

He waited another minute, then another. "I agree. Plenty of people hide behind the shield. They got the power and that's the only reason they need. But unless there's more of us, those other shitasses can cause real problems."

"But that's you, Don. What about me?"

This time he drank the whole beer before he answered. "I don't know about you, Jackson. You had a good run, then you had a real rough go these last few years. Lately, you always came out on top, but I don't know whether that's because you deserve to or because luck just broke your way. It might be you're just the luckiest stiff ever."

"If you're a cop, luck can't break your way? Is that some kind of disqualification?"

"Cops have to have luck break their way every damn time. It's not enough to be good. You got to be lucky too. Every damn time. Good. And lucky."

"I think you're trying to talk me out of going to the Academy, Don."

He spun on the stool to face me. "The question you have to ask yourself is this. Is it who I am? Is it who I absolutely, one hundred per cent, have to be?" He poked a finger into my chest. "Because it doesn't matter if it's a cop, or an administrator, or a businessman. If it's not who you are supposed to be, you're wasting time." Don's dark brown eyes bore into me. "You're wasting everyone's time."

He spun back to face the mirror behind the bar and waved to the barkeeper for another beer. "Be who you are, Jackson. At long last, and for God's sake, just be who you are." He closed his eyes. "Don't you think it's about time?"

I looked at the half-drunk, piss-warm beer.

Yes. It was probably time.

Also By TJ Arant

Thanks for enjoying *Even Trade*. If this is your first Jackson Trade novel, click on books one and two below. They are exclusive to Amazon and you can also enjoy them as a subscriber to the Kindle Unlimited program.

Nashville Trade http://getbook.at/NashvilleTrade
One Trade Too Many http://getbook.at/OneTradeTooMany

If you would like to keep up with publication news and other information, plus receive a free novella about Jackson's first case, just head over to https://BookHip.com/CNFHFKfor a copy of TRADER. All you have to do is tell me where to send it.